This book belongs to:

_____

The Complete
TALES &
POEMS
of
Winnie-the-Pooh

A. A. MILNE

The Complete
TALES &
POEMS
of
Winnie-the-Pooh

With Decorations by
Ernest H. Shepard

BOOK-OF-THE-MONTH CLUB • NEW YORK

Designed by the Antler & Baldwin Design Group

Printed in the United States of America

ABOUT A. A. MILNE

Alan Alexander Milne was born in London on January 18, 1882. He was the third and youngest son of London schoolteachers, and to the surprise of no one in the family, he could read when he was two. As a schoolboy he began to write verses, parodies, and short humorous pieces for his school's paper. He went on to Cambridge, where he edited the undergraduate paper.

In 1903 he left school and went to London to write. At the end of a year he had spent all of his money and earned almost nothing. He continued writing. During the second year he earned considerably more and supported himself on his earnings. In 1906 he was offered a position at *Punch* magazine. He was an editor at *Punch* for the next eight years, during which time he wrote his first book; three collections of his contributions to the magazine were also published.

In 1913 he married Dorothy, known as Daphne, de Selincourt. In 1915, during World War I, he enlisted in the Royal Warwickshire Regiment and served in France. During his military service he wrote three plays, all of which were produced on the London stage.

After the war he declined to return to *Punch*, choosing instead to write when and where he pleased. In 1919 his play *Mr. Pim Passes By* was a huge success, affording the Milnes financial independence.

Christopher Robin Milne, the author's only child, was born in 1920. He soon became an inspiration to his father, who later wrote:

> If a writer, why not write
> On whatever comes in sight?
> So—the Children's Books; a short
> Intermezzo of a sort:
> When I wrote them, little thinking
> All my years of pen-and-inking
> Would be almost lost among
> Those four trifles for the young.

When Christopher Robin was a year old, he was given a stuffed bear from Harrods, and later a tiger, pig, and donkey. The idea of bringing these toys to life in a children's book is credited to Daphne Milne. In 1924 A. A. Milne had published *When We Were Very Young*, a collection of verses, which had met with great success on both sides of the Atlantic. In 1926 *Winnie-the-Pooh* was released, promptly establishing Milne as a major author of children's books. *Now We Are Six*, a second collection of verses, followed in 1927. In 1928 came *The House At Pooh Corner*. All four were illustrated by Ernest H. Shepard, who visited the Milnes at Cotchford Farm and based his drawings on Christopher Robin and his toys.

The Pooh books have reached a worldwide audience. While A. A. Milne is remembered primarily for his children's books, he did go on to write more plays, a detective novel, political nonfiction, and his autobiography.

Alan Alexander Milne died on January 31, 1956.

ABOUT E. H. SHEPARD

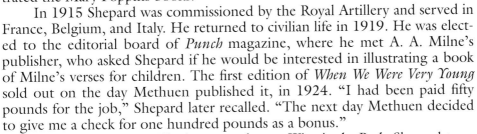

ERNEST HOWARD SHEPARD was born on December 10, 1879, in London. His father was an architect, and his mother—who died when Ernest was ten years old—was the daughter of a watercolorist. It was she who encouraged young Ernest to paint and draw. Shepard attended St. Paul's School, Heatherley's Art School, and the Royal Academy Schools. There was never any doubt that he would be an artist. His first picture was exhibited in the Royal Academy in 1901. Later, he supported himself by producing book illustrations, oil paintings, and black-and-white drawings for illustrated papers.

In 1903 Shepard married Florence Chaplin, a mural painter and fellow student at the Academy. They had two children: Graham, who was killed in World War II, and Mary, who later illustrated the Mary Poppins books.

In 1915 Shepard was commissioned by the Royal Artillery and served in France, Belgium, and Italy. He returned to civilian life in 1919. He was elected to the editorial board of *Punch* magazine, where he met A. A. Milne's publisher, who asked Shepard if he would be interested in illustrating a book of Milne's verses for children. The first edition of *When We Were Very Young* sold out on the day Methuen published it, in 1924. "I had been paid fifty pounds for the job," Shepard later recalled. "The next day Methuen decided to give me a check for one hundred pounds as a bonus."

Before illustrating Milne's next volume, *Winnie-the-Pooh*, Shepard traveled to Sussex, where the Milne family lived. He visited the pine trees, the stream, the bridge, and Christopher Robin and his stuffed animals, on which the illustrations for the later three Pooh books were based.

The success of the Pooh books made Shepard famous and widely sought after. For nearly thirty years he illustrated books, for both adults and children. Among them is Kenneth Grahame's classic, *The Wind in the Willows*.

Florence died in 1927. Shepard remarried in 1944, and in 1955 he closed his London studio and retired to the Sussex village of Lodsworth. In 1969, on the occasion of his ninetieth birthday, the Victoria and Albert Museum honored the artist with an exhibition of the three hundred sketches from the Pooh books that Shepard had donated to the museum. In 1973 he colored his drawings for *Winnie-the-Pooh* for a special edition of that book.

Ernest Shepard died in 1976. His work has been loved by children and adults for generations. When *Winnie-the-Pooh* was first published in the United States, by E. P. Dutton, Milne wrote this tribute to his collaborator:

> When I am gone
> Let Shepard decorate my tomb,
> And put (if there is room)
> Two pictures on the stone;
> Piglet from page a hundred and eleven
> And Pooh and Piglet walking (157) . . .
> And Peter, thinking that they are my own,
> Will welcome me to heaven.

CONTENTS

Winnie-the-Pooh

The House At Pooh Corner

When We Were Very Young

*This poem, being in the Library of the Queen's Dolls' House, is printed here by special permission.

Now We Are Six

To Her

Hand in hand we come
    Christopher Robin and I
To lay this book in your lap.
        Say you're surprised?
        Say you like it?
        Say it's just what you wanted?
            Because it's yours—
            Because we love you.

WINNIE-THE-POOH

Introduction

IF YOU HAPPEN to have read another book about Christopher Robin, you may remember that he once had a swan (or the swan had Christopher Robin, I don't know which) and that he used to call this swan Pooh. That was a long time ago, and when we said good-bye, we took the name with us, as we didn't think the swan would want it any more. Well, when Edward Bear said that he would like an exciting name all to himself, Christopher Robin said at once, without stopping to think, that he was Winnie-the-Pooh. And he was. So, as I have explained the Pooh part, I will now explain the rest of it.

You can't be in London for long without going to the Zoo. There are some people who begin the Zoo at the beginning, called WAYIN, and walk as quickly as they can past every cage until they get to the one called WAYOUT, but the nicest people go straight to the animal they love the most, and stay there. So when Christopher Robin goes to the Zoo, he goes to where the Polar Bears are, and he whispers something to the third keeper from the left, and doors are unlocked, and we wander through dark passages and up steep stairs, until at last we come to the special cage, and the cage is opened, and out trots something brown and furry, and with a happy cry of "Oh, Bear!" Christopher Robin rushes into its arms. Now this bear's name is Winnie, which shows what a good name for bears it is, but the funny thing is that we can't remember whether Winnie is called after Pooh, or Pooh after Winnie. We did know once, but we have forgotten....

I had written as far as this when Piglet looked up and said in his squeaky voice, "What about *Me?*" "My dear Piglet," I said, "the whole book is about you." "So it is about Pooh," he squeaked. You see what it is. He is jealous because he thinks Pooh is having a Grand Introduction all to himself. Pooh is the favourite, of course, there's no denying it, but Piglet comes in for a good many things which Pooh misses; because you can't take Pooh to school without everybody knowing it, but Piglet is so small that he slips into a pocket, where it is very comfortable to feel him when you are not quite sure whether twice seven is twelve or twenty-two. Sometimes he slips out and has a good look in the ink-pot, and in this way he has got more education than Pooh, but Pooh doesn't mind. Some have brains, and some haven't, he says, and there it is.

And now all the others are saying, "What about *Us?*" So perhaps the best thing to do is to stop writing Introductions and get on with the book.

A.A.M.

CHAPTER ONE

In Which

We Are Introduced to Winnie-the-Pooh and Some Bees, and the Stories Begin

HERE IS Edward Bear, coming downstairs now, bump, bump, bump, on the back of his head, behind Christopher Robin. It is, as far as he knows, the only way of coming downstairs, but sometimes he feels that there really is another way, if only he could stop bumping for a moment and think of it. And then he feels that perhaps there isn't. Anyhow, here he is at the bottom, and ready to be introduced to you. Winnie-the-Pooh.

When I first heard his name, I said, just as you are going to say, "But I thought he was a boy?"

"So did I," said Christopher Robin.

"Then you can't call him Winnie?"

"I don't."

"But you said——"

"He's Winnie-ther-Pooh. Don't you know what *'ther'* means?"

"Ah, yes, now I do," I said quickly; and I hope you do too, because it is all the explanation you are going to get.

Sometimes Winnie-the-Pooh likes a game of some sort when he comes downstairs, and sometimes he likes to sit quietly in front of the fire and listen to a story. This evening——

"What about a story?" said Christopher Robin.

"*What* about a story?" I said.

"Could you very sweetly tell Winnie-the-Pooh one?"

"I suppose I could," I said. "What sort of stories does he like?"

"About himself. Because he's *that* sort of Bear."

"Oh, I see."

"So could you very sweetly?"

"I'll try," I said.

So I tried.

– Once upon a time, a very long time ago now, about last Friday, Winnie-the-Pooh lived in a forest all by himself under the name of Sanders.

("What does 'under the name' mean?" asked Christopher Robin.

"It means he had the name over the door in gold letters, and lived under it."

"Winnie-the-Pooh wasn't quite sure," said Christopher Robin.

"Now I am," said a growly voice.
"Then I will go on," said I.)

One day when he was out walking, he came to an open place in the middle of the forest, and in the middle of this place was a large oak-tree, and, from the top of the tree, there came a loud buzzing-noise.

Winnie-the-Pooh sat down at the foot of the tree, put his head between his paws and began to think.

First of all he said to himself: "That buzzing-noise means something. You don't get a buzzing-noise like that, just buzzing and buzzing, without its meaning something. If there's a buzzing-noise, somebody's making a buzzing-noise, and the only reason for making a buzzing-noise that *I* know of is because you're a bee."

Then he thought another long time, and said: "And the only reason for being a bee that I know of is making honey."

And then he got up, and said: "And the only reason for making honey is so as *I* can eat it." So he began to climb the tree.

He
climbed
and
he
climbed
and
he
climbed,
and
as
he
climbed
he
sang
a
little
song
to
himself.
It
went
like
this:

Isn't it funny
How a bear likes honey?
Buzz! Buzz! Buzz!
I wonder why he does?

Then he climbed a little further . . . and a little further . . . and then just a little further. By that time he had thought of another song.

> It's a very funny thought that, if Bears were Bees,
> They'd build their nests at the *bottom* of trees.
> And that being so (if the Bees were Bears),
> We shouldn't have to climb up all these stairs.

He was getting rather tired by this time, so that is why he sang a Complaining Song. He was nearly there now, and if he just stood on that branch . . .
Crack!

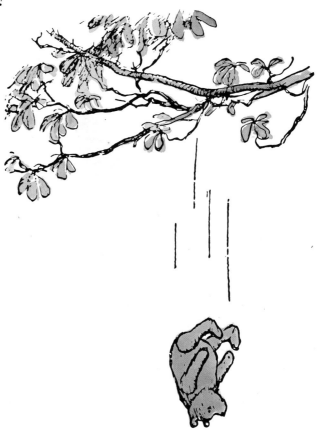

6

"Oh, help!" said Pooh, as he dropped ten feet on the branch below him.

"If only I hadn't——" he said, as he bounced twenty feet on to the next branch.

"You see, what I *meant* to do," he explained, as he turned head-over-heels, and crashed on to another branch thirty feet below, "what I *meant* to do——"

"Of course, it *was* rather——" he admitted, as he slithered very quickly through the next six branches.

"It all comes, I suppose," he decided, as he said good-bye to the last branch, spun round three times, and flew gracefully into a gorse-bush, "it all comes of *liking* honey so much. Oh, help!"

He crawled out of the gorse-bush, brushed the prickles from his nose, and began to think again. And the first person he thought of was Christopher Robin.

("Was that me?" said Christopher Robin in an awed voice, hardly daring to believe it.

"That was you."

Christopher Robin said nothing, but his eyes got larger and larger, and his face got pinker and pinker.)

So Winnie-the-Pooh went round to his friend Christopher Robin, who lived behind a green door in another part of the forest.

"Good morning, Christopher Robin," he said.

"Good morning, Winnie-*ther*-Pooh," said you.

"I wonder if you've got such a thing as a balloon about you?"

"A balloon?"

"Yes, I just said to myself coming along: 'I wonder if Christopher Robin has such a thing as a balloon about him?' I just said it to myself, thinking of balloons, and wondering."

"What do you want a balloon for?" you said.

Winnie-the-Pooh looked round to see that nobody was listening, put his paw to his mouth, and said in a deep whisper: *"Honey!"*

"But you don't get honey with balloons!"

"*I* do," said Pooh.

Well, it just happened that you had been to a party the day before at the house of your friend Piglet, and you had balloons at the party. You had had a big green balloon; and one of Rabbit's relations had had a big blue one, and had left it behind, being really too young to go to a party at all; and so you had brought the green one *and* the blue one home with you.

"Which one would you like?" you asked Pooh.

He put his head between his paws and thought very carefully.

"It's like this," he said. "When you go after honey with a balloon, the great thing is not to let the bees know you're coming. Now, if you have a green balloon, they might think you were only part of the tree, and not notice you, and if you have a blue balloon, they might think you were only part of the sky, and not notice you, and the question is: Which is most likely?"

"Wouldn't they notice *you* underneath the balloon?" you asked.

"They might or they might not," said Winnie-the-Pooh. "You never can tell with bees." He thought for a moment and said: "I shall try to look like a small black cloud. That will deceive them."

"Then you had better have the blue balloon," you said; and so it was decided.

Well, you both went out with the blue balloon, and you took your gun with you, just in case, as you always did, and Winnie-the-Pooh went to a very muddy place that he knew of, and rolled and rolled until he was black all over; and then, when the balloon was

blown up as big as big, and you and Pooh were both holding on to the string, you let go suddenly, and Pooh Bear floated gracefully up into the sky, and stayed there—level with the top of the tree and about twenty feet away from it.

"Hooray!" you shouted.

"Isn't that fine?" shouted Winnie-the-Pooh down to you. "What do I look like?"

"You look like a Bear holding on to a balloon," you said.

"Not—" said Pooh anxiously, "—not like a small black cloud in a blue sky?"

"Not very much."

"Ah, well, perhaps from up here it looks different. And, as I say, you never can tell with bees."

There was no wind to blow him nearer to the tree,

so there he stayed. He could see the honey, he could smell the honey, but he couldn't quite reach the honey.

After a little while he called down to you.

"Christopher Robin!" he said in a loud whisper.

"Hallo!"

"I think the bees *suspect* something!"

"What sort of thing?"

"I don't know. But something tells me that they're *suspicious*!"

"Perhaps they think that you're after their honey."

"It may be that. You never can tell with bees."

There was another little silence, and then he called down to you again.

"Christopher Robin!"

"Yes?"

"Have you an umbrella in your house?"

"I think so."

"I wish you would bring it out here, and walk up and down with it, and look up at me every now and then, and say 'Tut-tut, it looks like rain.' I think, if you did that, it would help the deception which we are practising on these bees."

Well, you laughed to yourself, "Silly old Bear!" but you didn't say it aloud because you were so fond of him, and you went home for your umbrella.

"Oh, there you are!" called down Winnie-the-Pooh, as soon as you got back to the tree. "I was beginning to get anxious. I have discovered that the bees are now definitely Suspicious."

"Shall I put my umbrella up?" you said.

"Yes, but wait a moment. We must be practical. The important bee to deceive is the Queen Bee. Can you see which is the Queen Bee from down there?"

"No."

"A pity. Well, now, if you walk up and down with your umbrella, saying, 'Tut-tut, it looks like rain,' I shall do what I can by singing a little Cloud Song, such as a cloud might sing. . . . Go!"

So, while you walked up and down and wondered
if it would rain, Winnie-the-Pooh sang this song:

> How sweet to be a Cloud
>   Floating in the Blue!
> Every little cloud
> *Always* sings aloud.

> "How sweet to be a Cloud
>   Floating in the Blue!"
> It makes him very proud
> To be a little cloud.

The bees were still buzzing as suspiciously as ever.
Some of them, indeed, left their nest and flew all
round the cloud as it began the second verse of this

song, and one bee sat down on the nose of the cloud for a moment, and then got up again.

"Christopher—*ow!*—Robin," called out the cloud.

"Yes?"

"I have just been thinking, and I have come to a very important decision. *These are the wrong sort of bees.*"

"Are they?"

"Quite the wrong sort. So I should think they would make the wrong sort of honey, shouldn't you?"

"Would they?"

"Yes. So I think I shall come down."

"How?" asked you.

Winnie-the-Pooh hadn't thought about this. If he let go of the string, he would fall—*bump*—and he didn't like the idea of that. So he thought for a long time, and then he said:

"Christopher Robin, you must shoot the balloon with your gun. Have you got your gun?"

"Of course I have," you said. "But if I do that, it will spoil the balloon," you said.

"But if you *don't,*" said Pooh, "I shall have to let go, and that would spoil *me.*"

When you put it like this, you saw how it was, and you aimed very carefully at the balloon, and fired.

"*Ow!*" said Pooh.

"Did I miss?" you asked.

"You didn't exactly *miss,*" said Pooh, "but you missed the *balloon.*"

"I'm so sorry," you said, and you fired again, and this time you hit the balloon, and the air came slowly out, and Winnie-the-Pooh floated down to the ground.

But his arms were so stiff from holding on to the string of the balloon all that time that they stayed up straight in the air for more than a week, and whenever a fly came and settled on his nose he had to blow it off. And I think—but I am not sure—that *that* is why he was always called Pooh.

"Is that the end of the story?" asked Christopher Robin.

"That's the end of that one. There are others."

"About Pooh and Me?"

"And Piglet and Rabbit and all of you. Don't you remember?"

"I do remember, and then when I try to remember, I forget."

"That day when Pooh and Piglet tried to catch the Heffalump——"

"They didn't catch it, did they?"

"No."

"Pooh couldn't, because he hasn't any brain. Did *I* catch it?"

"Well, that comes into the story."

Christopher Robin nodded.

"I do remember," he said, "only Pooh doesn't very well, so that's why he likes having it told to him again. Because then it's a real story and not just a remembering."

"That's just how *I* feel," I said.

Christopher Robin gave a deep sigh, picked his Bear up by the leg, and walked off to the door, trailing Pooh behind him. At the door he turned and said, "Coming to see me have my bath?"

"I might," I said.

"I didn't hurt him when I shot him, did I?"

"Not a bit."

He nodded and went out, and in a moment I heard Winnie-the-Pooh—*bump, bump, bump*—going up the stairs behind him.

CHAPTER TWO

In Which

Pooh Goes Visiting and Gets Into a Tight Place

EDWARD BEAR, known to his friends as Winnie-the-Pooh, or Pooh for short, was walking through the forest one day, humming proudly to himself. He had made up a little hum that very morning, as he was doing his Stoutness Exercises in front of the glass: *Tra-la-la, tra-la-la,* as he stretched up as high as he could go, and then *Tra-la-la, tra-la—oh, help!—la,* as he tried to reach his toes. After breakfast he had said it over and over to himself until he had learnt it off by heart, and now he was humming it right through, properly. It went like this:

Tra-la-la, tra-la-la,
Tra-la-la, tra-la-la,
Rum-tum-tiddle-um-tum.
Tiddle-iddle, tiddle-iddle,
Tiddle-iddle, tiddle-iddle,
Rum-tum-tum-tiddle-um.

Well, he was humming this hum to himself, and walking along gaily, wondering what everybody else was doing, and what it felt like, being somebody else, when suddenly he came to a sandy bank, and in the bank was a large hole.

"Aha!" said Pooh. (*Rum-tum-tiddle-um-tum.*) "If I know anything about anything, that hole means Rabbit," he said, "and Rabbit means Company," he said, "and Company means Food and Listening-to-Me-Humming and such like. *Rum-tum-tum-tiddle-um.*"

So he bent down, put his head into the hole, and called out:

"Is anybody at home?"

There was a sudden scuffling noise from inside the hole, and then silence.

"What I said was, 'Is anybody at home?'" called out Pooh very loudly.

"No!" said a voice; and then added, "you needn't shout so loud. I heard you quite well the first time."

"Bother!" said Pooh. "Isn't there anybody here at all?"

"Nobody."

Winnie-the-Pooh took his head out of the hole, and thought for a little, and he thought to himself, "There must be somebody there, because somebody must have *said* 'Nobody.'" So he put his head back in the hole, and said:

"Hallo, Rabbit, isn't that you?"

"No," said Rabbit, in a different sort of voice this time.

"But isn't that Rabbit's voice?"

"I don't *think* so," said Rabbit. "It isn't *meant* to be."

"Oh!" said Pooh.

He took his head out of the hole, and had another think, and then he put it back, and said:

"Well, could you very kindly tell me where Rabbit is?"

"He has gone to see his friend Pooh Bear, who is a great friend of his."

"But this *is* Me!" said Bear, very much surprised.

"What sort of Me?"

"Pooh Bear."

"Are you sure?" said Rabbit, still more surprised.

"Quite, quite sure," said Pooh.

"Oh, well, then, come in."

So Pooh pushed and pushed and pushed his way through the hole, and at last he got in.

"You were quite right," said Rabbit, looking at him all over. "It *is* you. Glad to see you."

"Who did you think it was?"

"Well, I wasn't sure. You know how it is in the Forest. One can't have *anybody* coming into one's house. One has to be *careful*. What about a mouthful of something?"

Pooh always liked a little something at eleven o'-clock in the morning, and he was very glad to see Rabbit getting out the plates and mugs; and when Rabbit said, "Honey or condensed milk with your bread?" he was so excited that he said, "Both," and then, so as not to seem greedy, he added, "but don't bother about the bread, please." And for a long time after that he said nothing . . . until at last, humming to himself in a rather sticky voice, he got up, shook Rabbit lovingly by the paw, and said that he must be going on.

"Must you?" said Rabbit politely.

"Well," said Pooh, "I could stay a little longer if it—if you——" and he tried very hard to look in the direction of the larder.

"As a matter of fact," said Rabbit, "I was going out myself directly."

"Oh, well, then, I'll be going on. Good-bye."

"Well, good-bye, if you're sure you won't have any more."

"*Is* there any more?" asked Pooh quickly.

Rabbit took the covers off the dishes, and said no, there wasn't.

"I thought not," said Pooh, nodding to himself. "Well, good-bye. I must be going on."

So he started to climb out of the hole. He pulled with his front paws, and pushed with his back paws, and in a little while his nose was out in the open again . . . and then his ears . . . and then his front paws . . . and then his shoulders . . . and then——

"Oh, help!" said Pooh. "I'd better go back."

"Oh, bother!" said Pooh. "I shall have to go on."

"I can't do either!" said Pooh. "Oh, help *and* bother!"

Now by this time Rabbit wanted to go for a walk too, and finding the front door full, he went out by the back door, and came round to Pooh, and looked at him.

"Hallo, are you stuck?" he asked.

"N-no," said Pooh carelessly. "Just resting and thinking and humming to myself."

"Here, give us a paw."

Pooh Bear stretched out a paw, and Rabbit pulled and pulled and pulled. . . .

"*Ow!*" cried Pooh. "You're hurting!"

"The fact is," said Rabbit, "you're stuck."

"It all comes," said Pooh crossly, "of not having front doors big enough."

"It all comes," said Rabbit sternly, "of eating too much. I thought at the time," said Rabbit, "only I didn't like to say anything," said Rabbit, "that one of us was eating too much," said Rabbit, "and I knew it wasn't *me*," he said. "Well, well, I shall go and fetch Christopher Robin."

Christopher Robin lived at the other end of the Forest, and when he came back with Rabbit, and saw the front half of Pooh, he said, "Silly old Bear," in such a loving voice that everybody felt quite hopeful again.

"I was just beginning to think," said Bear, sniffing slightly, "that Rabbit might never be able to use his front door again. And I should *hate* that," he said.

"So should I," said Rabbit.

"Use his front door again?" said Christopher Robin. "Of course he'll use his front door again."

"Good," said Rabbit.

"If we can't pull you out, Pooh, we might push you back."

Rabbit scratched his whiskers thoughtfully, and pointed out that, when once Pooh was pushed back, he was back, and of course nobody was more glad to see Pooh than *he* was, still there it was, some lived in trees and some lived underground, and——

"You mean I'd *never* get out?" said Pooh.

"I mean," said Rabbit, "that having got *so* far, it seems a pity to waste it."

Christopher Robin nodded.

"Then there's only one thing to be done," he said. "We shall have to wait for you to get thin again."

"How long does getting thin take?" asked Pooh anxiously.

"About a week, I should think."

"But I can't stay here for a *week*!"

"You can *stay* here all right, silly old Bear. It's getting you out which is so difficult."

"We'll read to you," said Rabbit cheerfully. "And I hope it won't snow," he added. "And I say, old fellow, you're taking up a good deal of room in my house—*do* you mind if I use your back legs as a towel-horse? Because, I mean, there they are—doing nothing—and it would be very convenient just to hang the towels on them."

"A week!" said Pooh gloomily. *"What about meals?"*

"I'm afraid no meals," said Christopher Robin, "because of getting thin quicker. But we *will* read to you."

Bear began to sigh, and then found he couldn't because he was so tightly stuck; and a tear rolled down his eye, as he said:

"Then would you read a Sustaining Book, such as would help and comfort a Wedged Bear in Great Tightness?"

So for a week Christopher Robin read that sort of book at the North end of Pooh,

and Rabbit hung his washing on the South end . . .

and in between Bear felt himself getting slenderer and slenderer. And at the end of the week Christopher Robin said, *"Now!"*

So he took hold of Pooh's front paws and Rabbit took hold of Christopher Robin, and all Rabbit's friends and relations took hold of Rabbit, and they all pulled together. . . .

And for a long time Pooh only said *"Ow!"* . . .

And *"Oh!"* . . .

And then, all of a sudden, he said *"Pop!"* just as if a cork were coming out of a bottle.

And Christopher Robin and Rabbit and all Rabbit's friends and relations went head-over-heels backwards . . . and on the top of them came Winnie-the-Pooh—free!

So, with a nod of thanks to his friends, he went on with his walk through the forest, humming proudly to himself. But, Christopher Robin looked after him lovingly, and said to himself, "Silly old Bear!"

CHAPTER THREE

In Which

Pooh and Piglet Go Hunting and Nearly Catch a Woozle

THE PIGLET lived in a very grand house in the middle of a beech-tree, and the beech-tree was in the middle of the forest, and the Piglet lived in the middle of the house. Next to his house was a piece of broken board which had: "TRESPASSERS W" on it. When Christopher Robin asked the Piglet what it meant, he said it was his grandfather's name, and had been in the family for a long time. Christopher Robin said you *couldn't* be called Trespassers W, and Piglet said yes, you could, because his grandfather was, and it was short for Trespassers Will, which was short for Trespassers William. And his grandfather had had two names in case he lost one—Trespassers after an uncle, and William after Trespassers.

"I've got two names," said Christopher Robin carelessly.

"Well, there you are, that proves it," said Piglet.

One fine winter's day when Piglet was brushing away the snow in front of his house, he happened to look up, and there was Winnie-the-Pooh. Pooh was walking round and round in a circle, thinking of something else, and when Piglet called to him, he just went on walking.

"Hallo!" said Piglet, "what are *you* doing?"

"Hunting," said Pooh.

"Hunting what?"

"Tracking something," said Winnie-the-Pooh very mysteriously.

"Tracking what?" said Piglet, coming closer.

"That's just what I ask myself. I ask myself, What?"

"What do you think you'll answer?"

"I shall have to wait until I catch up with it," said Winnie-the-Pooh. "Now, look there." He pointed to the ground in front of him. "What do you see there?"

"Tracks," said Piglet. "Paw-marks." He gave a little squeak of excitement. "Oh, Pooh! Do you think it's a—a—a Woozle?"

"It may be," said Pooh. "Sometimes it is, and sometimes it isn't. You never can tell with paw-marks."

With these few words he went on tracking, and Piglet, after watching him for a minute or two, ran after him. Winnie-the-Pooh had come to a sudden stop, and was bending over the tracks in a puzzled sort of way.

"What's the matter?" asked Piglet.

"It's a very funny thing," said Bear, "but there seem to be *two* animals now. This—whatever-it-was—has been joined by another—whatever-it-is—and the two of them are now proceeding in company. Would you mind coming with me, Piglet, in case they turn out to be Hostile Animals?"

Piglet scratched his ear in a nice sort of way, and said that he had nothing to do until Friday, and would be delighted to come, in case it really *was* a Woozle.

"You mean, in case it really is two Woozles," said Winnie-the-Pooh, and Piglet said that anyhow he had nothing to do until Friday. So off they went together.

There was a small spinney of larch trees just here, and it seemed as if the two Woozles, if that is what they were, had been going round this spinney; so round this spinney went Pooh and Piglet after them, Piglet passing the time by telling Pooh what his Grandfather Trespassers W had done to Remove Stiffness after Tracking, and how his Grandfather Trespassers W had suffered in his later years from Shortness of Breath, and other matters of interest, and Pooh wondering what a Grandfather was like, and if perhaps this was Two Grandfathers they were after now, and, if so, whether he would be allowed to take one home and keep it, and what Christopher Robin would say. And still the tracks went on in front of them. . . .

Suddenly Winnie-the-Pooh stopped and pointed excitedly in front of him. *"Look!"*

"What?" said Piglet, with a jump. And then, to show that he hadn't been frightened, he jumped up and down once or twice in an exercising sort of way.

"The tracks!" said Pooh. *"A third animal has joined the other two!"*

"Pooh!" cried Piglet. "Do you think it is another Woozle?"

"No," said Pooh, "because it makes different marks. It is either Two Woozles and one, as it might be, Wizzle, or Two, as it might be, Wizzles and one, if so it is, Woozle. Let us continue to follow them."

So they went on, feeling just a little anxious now, in case the three animals in front of them were of Hostile Intent. And Piglet wished very much that his Grandfather T. W. were there, instead of elsewhere, and Pooh thought how nice it would be if they met Christopher Robin suddenly but quite accidentally, and only because he liked Christopher Robin so much. And then, all of a sudden, Winnie-the-Pooh stopped again, and licked the tip of his nose in a cooling manner, for he was feeling more hot and anxious than ever in his life before. *There were four animals in front of them!*

"Do you see, Piglet? Look at their tracks! Three, as it were, Woozles, and one, as it was, Wizzle. *Another Woozle has joined them!*"

And so it seemed to be. There were the tracks; crossing over each other here, getting muddled up with each other there; but, quite plainly every now and then, the tracks of four sets of paws.

"I *think*," said Piglet, when he had licked the tip of his nose too, and found that it brought very little comfort, "I *think* that I have just remembered something. I have just remembered something that I forgot to do yesterday and shan't be able to do tomorrow. So I suppose I really ought to go back and do it now."

"We'll do it this afternoon, and I'll come with you," said Pooh.

"It isn't the sort of thing you can do in the afternoon," said Piglet quickly. "It's a very particular morning thing, that has to be done in the morning, and, if possible, between the hours of—— What would you say the time was?"

"About twelve," said Winnie-the-Pooh, looking at the sun.

"Between, as I was saying, the hours of twelve and twelve five. So, really, dear old Pooh, if you'll excuse me—— *What's that?*"

Pooh looked up at the sky, and then, as he heard

the whistle again, he looked up into the branches of a big oak-tree, and then he saw a friend of his.

"It's Christopher Robin," he said.

"Ah, then you'll be all right," said Piglet. "You'll be quite safe with *him*. Good-bye," and he trotted off home as quickly as he could, very glad to be Out of All Danger again.

Christopher Robin came slowly down his tree.

"Silly old Bear," he said, "what *were* you doing? First you went round the spinney twice by yourself, and then Piglet ran after you and you went round again together, and then you were just going round a fourth time——"

"Wait a moment," said Winnie-the-Pooh, holding up his paw.

He sat down and thought, in the most thoughtful way he could think. Then he fitted his paw into one of the Tracks . . . and then he scratched his nose twice, and stood up.

"Yes," said Winnie-the-Pooh.

"I see now," said Winnie-the-Pooh.

"I have been Foolish and Deluded," said he, "and I am a Bear of No Brain at All."

"You're the Best Bear in All the World," said Christopher Robin soothingly.

"Am I?" said Pooh hopefully. And then he brightened up suddenly.

"Anyhow," he said, "it is nearly Luncheon Time."

So he went home for it.

CHAPTER FOUR

In Which

Eeyore Loses a Tail and Pooh Finds One

THE OLD GREY DONKEY, Eeyore, stood by him-self in a thistly corner of the forest, his front feet well apart, his head on one side, and thought about things. Sometimes he thought sadly to himself,

"Why?" and sometimes he thought, "Wherefore?" and sometimes he thought, "Inasmuch as which?"— and sometimes he didn't quite know what he *was* thinking about. So when Winnie-the-Pooh came stumping along, Eeyore was very glad to be able to stop thinking for a little, in order to say "How do you do?" in a gloomy manner to him.

"And how are you?" said Winnie-the-Pooh.

Eeyore shook his head from side to side.

"Not very how," he said. "I don't seem to have felt at all how for a long time."

"Dear, dear," said Pooh, "I'm sorry about that. Let's have a look at you."

So Eeyore stood there, gazing sadly at the ground, and Winnie-the-Pooh walked all round him once.

"Why, what's happened to your tail?" he said in surprise.

"What *has* happened to it?" said Eeyore.

"It isn't there!"

"Are you sure?"

"Well, either a tail *is* there or it isn't there. You can't make a mistake about it. And yours *isn't* there!"

"Then what is?"

"Nothing."

"Let's have a look," said Eeyore, and he turned slowly round to the place where his tail had been a little while ago, and then, finding that he couldn't catch it up, he turned round the other way, until he came back to where he was at first, and then he put his head down and looked between his front legs, and at last he said, with a long, sad sigh, "I believe you're right."

"Of course I'm right," said Pooh.

"That Accounts for a Good Deal," said Eeyore gloomily. "It Explains Everything. No Wonder."

"You must have left it somewhere," said Winnie-the-Pooh.

"Somebody must have taken it," said Eeyore. "How Like Them," he added, after a long silence.

Pooh felt that he ought to say something helpful about it, but didn't quite know what. So he decided to do something helpful instead.

"Eeyore," he said solemnly, "I, Winnie-the-Pooh, will find your tail for you."

"Thank you, Pooh," answered Eeyore. "You're a real friend," said he. "Not like Some," he said.

So Winnie-the-Pooh went off to find Eeyore's tail.

It was a fine spring morning in the forest as he started out. Little soft clouds played happily in a blue sky, skipping from time to time in front of the sun as if they had come to put it out, and then sliding away suddenly so that the next might have his turn. Through them and between them the sun shone bravely; and a copse which had worn its firs all the year round seemed old and dowdy now beside the new green lace which the beeches had put on so prettily. Through copse and spinney marched Bear; down open slopes of gorse and heather, over rocky beds of streams, up steep banks of sandstone into the heather again; and so at last, tired and hungry, to the Hundred Acre Wood. For it was in the Hundred Acre Wood that Owl lived.

"And if anyone knows anything about anything," said Bear to himself, "it's Owl who knows something about something," he said, "or my name's not Winnie-the-Pooh," he said. "Which it is," he added. "So there you are."

Owl lived at The Chestnuts, an old-world residence of great charm, which was grander than anybody else's, or seemed so to Bear, because it had both a knocker *and* a bell-pull. Underneath the knocker there was a notice which said:

PLES RING IF AN RNSER IS REQIRD.

Underneath the bell-pull there was a notice which said:

PLEZ CNOKE IF AN RNSR IS NOT REQID.

These notices had been written by Christopher Robin, who was the only one in the forest who could spell; for Owl, wise though he was in many ways, able to read and write and spell his own name WOL, yet somehow went all to pieces over delicate words like MEASLES and BUTTERED TOAST.

Winnie-the-Pooh read the two notices very carefully, first from left to right, and afterwards, in case he had missed some of it, from right to left. Then, to make quite sure, he knocked and pulled the knocker, and he pulled and knocked the bell-rope, and he called out in a very loud voice, "Owl! I require an answer! It's Bear speaking." And the door opened, and Owl looked out.

"Hallo, Pooh," he said. "How's things?"

"Terrible and Sad," said Pooh, "because Eeyore, who is a friend of mine, has lost his tail. And he's Moping about it. So could you very kindly tell me how to find it for him?"

"Well," said Owl, "the customary procedure in such cases is as follows."

"What does Crustimoney Proseedcake mean?" said Pooh. "For I am a Bear of Very Little Brain, and long words Bother me."

"It means the Thing to Do."

"As long as it means that, I don't mind," said Pooh humbly.

"The thing to do is as follows. First, Issue a Reward. Then——"

"Just a moment," said Pooh, holding up his paw. "*What* do we do to this—what you were saying? You sneezed just as you were going to tell me."

"I *didn't* sneeze."

"Yes, you did, Owl."

"Excuse me, Pooh, I didn't. You can't sneeze without knowing it."

"Well, you can't know it without something having been sneezed."

"What I *said* was, 'First *Issue* a Reward.'"

"You're doing it again," said Pooh sadly.

"A Reward!" said Owl very loudly. "We write a notice to say that we will give a large something to anybody who finds Eeyore's tail."

"I see, I see," said Pooh, nodding his head. "Talking about large somethings," he went on dreamily, "I generally have a small something about now—about this time in the morning," and he looked wistfully at the cupboard in the corner of Owl's parlour; "just a mouthful of condensed milk or what not, with perhaps a lick of honey——"

"Well, then," said Owl, "we write out this notice, and we put it up all over the forest."

"A lick of honey," murmured Bear to himself, "or—or not, as the case may be." And he gave a deep sigh, and tried very hard to listen to what Owl was saying.

But Owl went on and on, using longer and longer words, until at last he came back to where he started, and he explained that the person to write out this notice was Christopher Robin.

"It was he who wrote the ones on my front door for me. Did you see them, Pooh?"

For some time now Pooh had been saying "Yes" and "No" in turn, with his eyes shut, to all that Owl was saying, and having said, "Yes, yes," last time, he said "No, not at all," now, without really knowing what Owl was talking about.

"Didn't you see them?" said Owl, a little surprised. "Come and look at them now."

So they went outside. And Pooh looked at the knocker and the notice below it, and he looked at the bell-rope and the notice below it, and the more he looked at the bell-rope, the more he felt that he had seen something like it, somewhere else, sometime before.

"Handsome bell-rope, isn't it?" said Owl.

Pooh nodded.

"It reminds me of something," he said, "but I can't think what. Where did you get it?"

"I just came across it in the Forest. It was hanging over a bush, and I thought at first somebody lived there, so I rang it, and nothing happened, and then I rang it again very loudly, and it came off in my hand,

and as nobody seemed to want it, I took it home, and——"

"Owl," said Pooh solemnly, "you made a mistake. Somebody did want it."

"Who?"

"Eeyore. My dear friend Eeyore. He was—he was fond of it."

"Fond of it?"

"Attached to it," said Winnie-the-Pooh sadly.

So with these words he unhooked it, and carried it back to Eeyore; and when Christopher Robin had nailed it on in its right place again, Eeyore frisked

about the forest, waving his tail so happily that Winnie-the-Pooh came over all funny, and had to hurry home for a little snack of something to sustain him. And, wiping his mouth half an hour afterwards, he sang to himself proudly:

Who found the Tail?
  "I," said Pooh,
"At a quarter to two
  (Only it was quarter to eleven really),
I found the Tail!"

CHAPTER FIVE

In Which

Piglet Meets a Heffalump

ONE DAY, when Christopher Robin and Winnie-the-Pooh and Piglet were all talking together, Christopher Robin finished the mouthful he was eating and said carelessly: "I saw a Heffalump to-day, Piglet."

"What was it doing?" asked Piglet.

"Just lumping along," said Christopher Robin. "I don't think it saw *me*."

"I saw one once," said Piglet. "At least, I think I did," he said. "Only perhaps it wasn't."

"So did I," said Pooh, wondering what a Heffalump was like.

"You don't often see them," said Christopher Robin carelessly.

"Not now," said Piglet.

"Not at this time of year," said Pooh.

Then they all talked about something else, until it was time for Pooh and Piglet to go home together. At first as they stumped along the path which edged the Hundred Acre Wood, they didn't say much to each other; but when they came to the stream and had helped each other across the stepping stones, and were able to walk side by side again over the heather, they began to talk in a friendly way about this and that, and Piglet said, "If you see what I mean, Pooh," and Pooh said, "It's just what I think myself, Piglet," and Piglet said, "But, on the other hand, Pooh, we must remember," and Pooh said, "Quite true, Piglet, although I had forgotten it for the moment." And then, just as they came to the Six Pine Trees, Pooh looked round to see that nobody else was listening, and said in a very solemn voice:

"Piglet, I have decided something."

"What have you decided, Pooh?"

"I have decided to catch a Heffalump."

Pooh nodded his head several times as he said this, and waited for Piglet to say "How?" or "Pooh, you couldn't!" or something helpful of that sort, but Piglet said nothing. The fact was Piglet was wishing that *he* had thought about it first.

"I shall do it," said Pooh, after waiting a little longer, "by means of a trap. And it must be a Cunning Trap, so you will have to help me, Piglet."

"Pooh," said Piglet, feeling quite happy again now, "I will." And then he said, "How shall we do it?" and Pooh said, "That's just it. How?" And then they sat down together to think it out.

Pooh's first idea was that they should dig a Very Deep Pit, and then the Heffalump would come along and fall into the Pit, and——

"Why?" said Piglet.

"Why what?" said Pooh.

"Why would he fall in?"

Pooh rubbed his nose with his paw, and said that the Heffalump might be walking along, humming a little song, and looking up at the sky, wondering if it would rain, and so he wouldn't see the Very Deep Pit until he was half-way down, when it would be too late.

Piglet said that this was a very good Trap, but supposing it were raining already?

Pooh rubbed his nose again, and said that he hadn't thought of that. And then he brightened up, and said that, if it were raining already, the Heffalump would be looking at the sky wondering if it would *clear up,* and so he wouldn't see the Very Deep Pit until he was half-way down. . . . When it would be too late.

Piglet said that, now that this point had been explained, he thought it was a Cunning Trap.

Pooh was very proud when he heard this, and he felt that the Heffalump was as good as caught already, but there was just one other thing which had to be thought about, and it was this. *Where should they dig the Very Deep Pit?*

Piglet said that the best place would be somewhere where a Heffalump was, just before he fell into it, only about a foot farther on.

"But then he would see us digging it," said Pooh.

"Not if he was looking at the sky."

"He would Suspect," said Pooh, "if he happened to look down." He thought for a long time and then added sadly, "It isn't as easy as I thought. I suppose that's why Heffalumps hardly *ever* get caught."

"That must be it," said Piglet.

They sighed and got up; and when they had taken

a few gorse prickles out of themselves they sat down again; and all the time Pooh was saying to himself, "If only I could *think* of something!" For he felt sure that a Very Clever Brain could catch a Heffalump if only he knew the right way to go about it.

"Suppose," he said to Piglet, "*you* wanted to catch *me*, how would you do it?"

"Well," said Piglet, "I should do it like this. I should make a Trap, and I should put a Jar of Honey in the Trap, and you would smell it, and you would go in after it, and——"

"And I would go in after it," said Pooh excitedly, "only very carefully so as not to hurt myself, and I would get to the Jar of Honey, and I should lick round the edges first of all, pretending that there wasn't any more, you know, and then I should walk away and think about it a little, and then I should come back and start licking in the middle of the jar, and then——"

"Yes, well never mind about that. There you would be, and there I should catch you. Now the first thing to think of is, What do Heffalumps like? I should think acorns, shouldn't you? We'll get a lot of ——I say, wake up, Pooh!"

Pooh, who had gone into a happy dream, woke up with a start, and said that Honey was a much more trappy thing than Haycorns. Piglet didn't think so; and they were just going to argue about it, when Piglet remembered that, if they put acorns in the Trap, *he* would have to find the acorns, but if they put honey, then Pooh would have to give up some of his own honey, so he said, "All right, honey then," just as Pooh remembered it too, and was going to say, "All right, haycorns."

"Honey," said Piglet to himself in a thoughtful way, as if it were now settled. "*I'll* dig the pit, while *you* go and get the honey."

"Very well," said Pooh, and he stumped off.

As soon as he got home, he went to the larder; and he stood on a chair, and took down a very large jar of honey from the top shelf. It had HUNNY written on it, but, just to make sure, he took off the paper cover and looked at it, and it *looked* just like honey. "But you never can tell," said Pooh. "I remember my uncle saying once that he had seen cheese just this colour." So he put his tongue in, and took a large lick. "Yes," he said, "it is. No doubt about that. And honey, I should say, right down to the bottom of the jar. Unless, of course," he said, "somebody put cheese in at the bottom just for a joke. Perhaps I had better go a *little* further . . . just in case . . . in case Heffalumps *don't* like cheese . . . same as me. . . . Ah!" And he gave a deep sigh. "I *was* right. It *is* honey, right the way down."

Having made certain of this, he took the jar back to Piglet, and Piglet looked up from the bottom of his Very Deep Pit, and said "Got it?" and Pooh said,

"Yes, but it isn't quite a full jar," and he threw it down to Piglet, and Piglet said, "No, it isn't! Is that all you've got left?" and Pooh said "Yes." Because it was. So Piglet put the jar at the bottom of the Pit, and climbed out, and they went off home together.

"Well, good night, Pooh," said Piglet, when they had got to Pooh's house. "And we meet at six o'clock tomorrow morning by the Pine Trees, and see how many Heffalumps we've got in our Trap."

"Six o'clock, Piglet. And have you got any string?"

"No. Why do you want string?"

"To lead them home with."

"Oh! . . . I *think* Heffalumps come if you whistle."

"Some do and some don't. You never can tell with Heffalumps. Well, good night!"

"Good night!"

And off Piglet trotted to his house, TRESPASSERS W, while Pooh made his preparations for bed.

Some hours later, just as the night was beginning to steal away, Pooh woke up suddenly with a sinking feeling. He had had that sinking feeling before, and he knew what it meant. *He was hungry.* So he went to the larder, and he stood on a chair and reached up to the top shelf, and found—nothing.

"That's funny," he thought. "I know I had a jar of honey there. A full jar, full of honey right up to the top, and it had HUNNY written on it, so that I should know it was honey. That's very funny." And then he began to wander up and down, wondering where it was and murmuring a murmur to himself. Like this:

It's very, very funny,
'Cos I *know* I had some honey;
'Cos it had a label on,
    Saying HUNNY.

A goloptious full-up pot too,
And I don't know where it's got to,
No, I don't know where it's gone—
    Well, it's funny.

He had murmured this to himself three times in a singing sort of way, when suddenly he remembered. He had put it into the Cunning Trap to catch the Heffalump.

"Bother!" said Pooh. "It all comes of trying to be kind to Heffalumps." And he got back into bed.

But he couldn't sleep. The more he tried to sleep, the more he couldn't. He tried Counting Sheep, which is sometimes a good way of getting to sleep, and, as that was no good, he tried counting Heffalumps. And that was worse. Because every Heffalump that he counted was making straight for a pot of Pooh's honey, *and eating it all*. For some minutes

he lay there miserably, but when the five hundred and eighty-seventh Heffalump was licking its jaws, and saying to itself, "Very good honey this, I don't know when I've tasted better," Pooh could bear it no longer. He jumped out of bed, he ran out of the house, and he ran straight to the Six Pine Trees.

The Sun was still in bed, but there was a lightness in the sky over the Hundred Acre Wood which seemed to show that it was waking up and would soon be kicking off the clothes. In the half-light the Pine Trees looked cold and lonely, and the Very Deep Pit seemed deeper than it was, and Pooh's jar of honey at the bottom was something mysterious, a

shape and no more. But as he got nearer to it his nose told him that it was indeed honey, and his tongue came out and began to polish up his mouth, ready for it.

"Bother!" said Pooh, as he got his nose inside the jar. "A Heffalump has been eating it!" And then he thought a little and said, "Oh, no, *I* did. I forgot."

Indeed, he had eaten most of it. But there was a little left at the very bottom of the jar, and he pushed his head right in, and began to lick. . . .

By and by Piglet woke up. As soon as he woke he said to himself, "Oh!" Then he said bravely, "Yes," and then, still more bravely, "Quite so." But he didn't feel very brave, for the word which was really jiggeting about in his brain was "Heffalumps."

What was a Heffalump like?

Was it Fierce?

Did it come when you whistled? And *how* did it come?

Was it Fond of Pigs at all?

If it was Fond of Pigs, did it make any difference *what sort of Pig*?

Supposing it was Fierce with Pigs, would it make any difference *if the Pig had a grandfather called TRESPASSERS WILLIAM*?

He didn't know the answer to any of these questions . . . and he was going to see his first Heffalump in about an hour from now!

Of course Pooh would be with him, and it was much more Friendly with two. But suppose Heffalumps were Very Fierce with Pigs *and* Bears? Wouldn't it be better to pretend that he had a headache, and couldn't go up to the Six Pine Trees this morning? But then suppose that it was a very fine day, and there was no Heffalump in the trap, here he would be, in bed all the morning, simply wasting his time for nothing. What should he do?

And then he had a Clever Idea. He would go up very quietly to the Six Pine Trees now, peep very cautiously into the Trap, and see if there *was* a Heffalump there. And if there was, he would go back to bed, and if there wasn't, he wouldn't.

So off he went. At first he thought that there wouldn't be a Heffalump in the Trap, and then he thought that there would, and as he got nearer he was *sure* that there would, because he could hear it heffalumping about it like anything.

"Oh, dear, oh, dear, oh, dear!" said Piglet to himself. And he wanted to run away. But somehow, having got so near, he felt that he must just see what a Heffalump was like. So he crept to the side of the Trap and looked in. . . .

And all the time Winnie-the-Pooh had been trying

to get the honey-jar off his head. The more he shook it, the more tightly it stuck. *"Bother!"* he said, inside the jar, and *"Oh, help!"* and, mostly *"Ow!"* And he tried bumping it against things, but as he couldn't see what he was bumping it against, it didn't help him; and he tried to climb out of the Trap, but as he could see nothing but jar, and not much of that, he couldn't find his way. So at last he lifted up his head, jar and all, and made a loud, roaring noise of Sadness and Despair . . . and it was at that moment that Piglet looked down.

"Help, help!" cried Piglet, "a Heffalump, a Horrible Heffalump!" and he scampered off as hard as he could, still crying out, "Help, help, a Herrible Hof-

falump! Hoff, Hoff, a Hellible Horralump! Holl, Holl, a Hoffable Hellerump!" And he didn't stop crying and scampering until he got to Christopher Robin's house.

"Whatever's the matter, Piglet?" said Christopher Robin, who was just getting up.

"Heff," said Piglet, breathing so hard that he could hardly speak, "a Hell—a Heff—a Heffalump."

"Where?"

"Up there," said Piglet, waving his paw.

"What did it look like?"

"Like—like——It had the biggest head you ever saw, Christopher Robin. A great enormous thing, like —like nothing. A huge big—well, like a—I don't know—like an enormous big nothing. Like a jar."

"Well," said Christopher Robin, putting on his shoes, "I shall go and look at it. Come on."

Piglet wasn't afraid if he had Christopher Robin with him, so off they went. . . .

"I can hear it, can't you?" said Piglet anxiously, as they got near.

"I can hear *something*," said Christopher Robin.

It was Pooh bumping his head against a tree-root he had found.

"There!" said Piglet. "Isn't it *awful*?" And he held on tight to Christopher Robin's hand.

Suddenly Christopher Robin began to laugh . . . and he laughed . . . and he laughed . . . and he laughed. And while he was still laughing—*Crash* went the Heffalump's head against the tree-root, Smash went the jar, and out came Pooh's head again. . . .

Then Piglet saw what a Foolish Piglet he had been, and he was so ashamed of himself that he ran straight off home and went to bed with a headache. But Christopher Robin and Pooh went home to breakfast together.

"Oh, Bear!" said Christopher Robin. "How I do love you!"

"So do I," said Pooh.

CHAPTER SIX

In Which

Eeyore Has a Birthday and Gets Two Presents

EYORE, the old grey Donkey, stood by the side of the stream, and looked at himself in the water.

"Pathetic," he said. "That's what it is. Pathetic."

He turned and walked slowly down the stream for twenty yards, splashed across it, and walked slowly back on the other side. Then he looked at himself in the water again.

"As I thought," he said. "No better from *this* side. But nobody minds. Nobody cares. Pathetic, that's what it is."

There was a crackling noise in the bracken behind him, and out came Pooh.

"Good morning, Eeyore," said Pooh.

"Good morning, Pooh Bear," said Eeyore gloomily. "If it *is* a good morning," he said. "Which I doubt," said he.

"Why, what's the matter?"

"Nothing, Pooh Bear, nothing. We can't all, and some of us don't. That's all there is to it."

"Can't all *what*?" said Pooh, rubbing his nose.

"Gaiety. Song-and-dance. Here we go round the mulberry bush."

"Oh!" said Pooh. He thought for a long time, and then asked, "What mulberry bush is that?"

"Bon-hommy," went on Eeyore gloomily. "French word meaning bonhommy," he explained. "I'm not complaining, but There It Is."

Pooh sat down on a large stone, and tried to think this out. It sounded to him like a riddle, and he was never much good at riddles, being a Bear of Very Little Brain. So he sang *Cottleston Pie* instead:

Cottleston, Cottleston, Cottleston Pie,
A fly can't bird, but a bird can fly.
Ask me a riddle and I reply:
"Cottleston, Cottleston, Cottleston Pie."

That was the first verse. When he had finished it, Eeyore didn't actually say that he didn't like it, so Pooh very kindly sang the second verse to him:

> Cottleston, Cottleston, Cottleston Pie,
> A fish can't whistle and neither can I.
> Ask me a riddle and I reply:
> *"Cottleston, Cottleston, Cottleston Pie."*

Eeyore still said nothing at all, so Pooh hummed the third verse quietly to himself:

> Cottleston, Cottleston, Cottleston Pie,
> Why does a chicken, I don't know why.
> Ask me a riddle and I reply:
> *"Cottleston, Cottleston, Cottleston Pie."*

"That's right," said Eeyore. "Sing. Umty-tiddly, umty-too. Here we go gathering Nuts and May. Enjoy yourself."

"I am," said Pooh.

"Some can," said Eeyore.

"Why, what's the matter?"

"*Is* anything the matter?"

"You seem so sad, Eeyore."

"Sad? Why should I be sad? It's my birthday. The happiest day of the year."

"Your birthday?" said Pooh in great surprise.

"Of course it is. Can't you see? Look at all the presents I have had." He waved a foot from side to side. "Look at the birthday cake. Candles and pink sugar."

Pooh looked—first to the right and then to the left.

"Presents?" said Pooh. "Birthday cake?" said Pooh. "*Where?*"

"Can't you see them?"

"No," said Pooh.

"Neither can I," said Eeyore. "Joke," he explained. "Ha ha!"

Pooh scratched his head, being a little puzzled by all this.

"But is it really your birthday?" he asked.

"It is."

"Oh! Well, Many happy returns of the day, Eeyore."

"And many happy returns to you, Pooh Bear."

"But it isn't *my* birthday."

"No, it's mine."

"But you said 'Many happy returns'——"

"Well, why not? You don't always want to be miserable on my birthday, do you?"

"Oh, I see," said Pooh.

"It's bad enough," said Eeyore, almost breaking down, "being miserable myself, what with no presents and no cake and no candles, and no proper notice taken of me at all, but if everybody else is going to be miserable too——"

This was too much for Pooh. "Stay there!" he called to Eeyore, as he turned and hurried back home as quick as he could; for he felt that he must get poor Eeyore a present of *some* sort at once, and he could always think of a proper one afterwards.

Outside his house he found Piglet, jumping up and down trying to reach the knocker.

"Hallo, Piglet," he said.

"Hallo, Pooh," said Piglet.

"What are *you* trying to do?"

"I was trying to reach the knocker," said Piglet. "I just came round——"

"Let me do it for you," said Pooh kindly. So he reached up and knocked at the door. "I have just seen Eeyore," he began, "and poor Eeyore is in a Very Sad Condition, because it's his birthday, and nobody has taken any notice of it, and he's very Gloomy—you know what Eeyore is—and there he was, and ——What a long time whoever lives here is answering this door." And he knocked again.

"But Pooh," said Piglet, "it's your own house!"

"Oh!" said Pooh. "So it is," he said. "Well, let's go in."

So in they went. The first thing Pooh did was to go to the cupboard to see if he had quite a small jar of honey left; and he had, so he took it down.

"I'm giving this to Eeyore," he explained, "as a present. What are *you* going to give?"

"Couldn't I give it too?" said Piglet. "From both of us?"

"No," said Pooh. "That would *not* be a good plan."

"All right, then, I'll give him a balloon. I've got one left from my party. I'll go and get it now, shall I?"

"That, Piglet, is a *very* good idea. It is just what Eeyore wants to cheer him up. Nobody can be un-cheered with a balloon."

So off Piglet trotted; and in the other direction went Pooh, with his jar of honey.

It was a warm day, and he had a long way to go. He hadn't gone more than half-way when a sort of funny feeling began to creep all over him. It began

at the tip of his nose and trickled all through him and out at the soles of his feet. It was just as if some-body inside him were saying, "Now then, Pooh, time for a little something."

"Dear, dear," said Pooh, "I didn't know it was as

late as that." So he sat down and took the top off his jar of honey. "Lucky I brought this with me," he thought. "Many a bear going out on a warm day like this would never have thought of bringing a little something with him." And he began to eat.

"Now let me see," he thought, as he took his last lick of the inside of the jar, "where was I going? Ah, yes, Eeyore." He got up slowly.

And then, suddenly, he remembered. He had eaten Eeyore's birthday present!

"*Bother!*" said Pooh. "What *shall* I do? I *must* give him *something*."

For a little while he couldn't think of anything. Then he thought: "Well, it's a very nice pot, even if there's no honey in it, and if I washed it clean, and got somebody to write '*A Happy Birthday*' on it,

Eeyore could keep things in it, which might be Useful." So, as he was just passing the Hundred Acre Wood, he went inside to call on Owl, who lived there.

"Good morning, Owl," he said.

"Good morning, Pooh," said Owl.

"Many happy returns of Eeyore's birthday," said Pooh.

"Oh, is that what it is?"

"What are you giving him, Owl?"

"What are *you* giving him, Pooh?"

"I'm giving him a Useful Pot to Keep Things In, and I wanted to ask you——"

"Is this it?" said Owl, taking it out of Pooh's paw.

"Yes, and I wanted to ask you——"

"Somebody has been keeping honey in it," said Owl.

"You can keep *anything* in it," said Pooh earnestly. "It's Very Useful like that. And I wanted to ask you——"

"You ought to write 'A Happy Birthday' on it."

"*That* was what I wanted to ask you," said Pooh. "Because my spelling is Wobbly. It's good spelling but it Wobbles, and the letters get in the wrong places. Would *you* write 'A Happy Birthday' on it for me?"

"It's a nice pot," said Owl, looking at it all round.

"Couldn't I give it too? From both of us?"

"No," said Pooh. "That would *not* be a good plan. Now I'll just wash it first, and then you can write on it."

Well, he washed the pot out, and dried it, while Owl licked the end of his pencil, and wondered how to spell "birthday."

"Can you read, Pooh?" he asked, a little anxiously. "There's a notice about knocking and ringing outside my door, which Christopher Robin wrote. Could you read it?"

"Christopher Robin told me what it said, and *then* I could."

"Well, I'll tell you what *this* says, and then you'll be able to."

So Owl wrote . . . and this is what he wrote:

HIPY PAPY BTHUTHDTH THUTHDA
BTHUTHDY.

Pooh looked on admiringly.

"I'm just saying 'A Happy Birthday,'" said Owl carelessly.

"It's a nice long one," said Pooh, very much impressed by it.

"Well, *actually*, of course, I'm saying 'A Very Happy Birthday with love from Pooh.' Naturally it takes a good deal of pencil to say a long thing like that."

"Oh, I see," said Pooh.

While all this was happening, Piglet had gone back to his own house to get Eeyore's balloon. He held it very tightly against himself, so that it shouldn't blow away, and he ran as fast as he could so as to get to Eeyore before Pooh did; for he thought that he would like to be the first one to give a present, just as if he had thought of it without being told by anybody. And running along, and thinking how pleased Eeyore would be, he didn't look where he was going . . . and suddenly he put his foot in a rabbit hole, and fell down flat on his face.

BANG!!!???***!!!

Piglet lay there, wondering what had happened. At first he thought that the whole world had blown up; and then he thought that perhaps only the Forest part of it had; and then he thought that perhaps only *he* had, and he was now alone in the moon or somewhere, and would never see Christopher Robin or Pooh or Eeyore again. And then he thought, "Well, even if I'm in the moon, I needn't be face downwards all the time," so he got cautiously up and looked about him.

He was still in the Forest!

"Well, that's funny," he thought. "I wonder what that bang was. I couldn't have made such a noise just falling down. And where's my balloon? And what's that small piece of damp rag doing?"

It was the balloon!

"Oh, dear!" said Piglet. "Oh, dear, oh, dearie, dearie, dear! Well, it's too late now. I can't go back, and I haven't another balloon, and perhaps Eeyore doesn't *like* balloons so *very* much."

So he trotted on, rather sadly now, and down he came to the side of the stream where Eeyore was, and called out to him.

"Good morning, Eeyore," shouted Piglet.

"Good morning, Little Piglet," said Eeyore. "If it *is* a good morning," he said. "Which I doubt," said he. "Not that it matters," he said.

"Many happy returns of the day," said Piglet, having now got closer.

Eeyore stopped looking at himself in the stream, and turned to stare at Piglet.

"Just say that again," he said.

"Many hap——"

"Wait a moment."

Balancing on three legs, he began to bring his fourth leg very cautiously up to his ear. "I did this yesterday," he explained, as he fell down for the third time. "It's quite easy. It's so as I can hear better. . . . There, that's done it! Now then, what were you saying?" He pushed his ear forward with his hoof.

"Many happy returns of the day," said Piglet again.

"Meaning me?"

"Of course, Eeyore."

"My birthday?"

"Yes."

"Me having a real birthday?"

"Yes, Eeyore, and I've brought you a present."

Eeyore took down his right hoof from his right ear, turned round, and with great difficulty put up his left hoof.

"I must have that in the other ear," he said. "Now then."

"A present," said Piglet very loudly.

"Meaning me again?"

"Yes."

"My birthday still?"

"Of course, Eeyore."

"Me going on having a real birthday?"

"Yes, Eeyore, and I brought you a balloon."

"Balloon?" said Eeyore. "You did say balloon? One of those big coloured things you blow up? Gaiety, song-and-dance, here we are and there we are?"

"Yes, but I'm afraid—I'm very sorry, Eeyore—but when I was running along to bring it you, I fell down."

"Dear, dear, how unlucky! You ran too fast, I expect. You didn't hurt yourself, Little Piglet?"

"No, but I—I—oh, Eeyore, I burst the balloon!"

There was a very long silence.

"My balloon?" said Eeyore at last.

Piglet nodded.

"My birthday balloon?"

"Yes, Eeyore," said Piglet sniffing a little. "Here it is. With—with many happy returns of the day." And he gave Eeyore the small piece of damp rag.

"Is this it?" said Eeyore, a little surprised.

Piglet nodded.

"My present?"

Piglet nodded again.

"The balloon?"

"Yes."

"Thank you, Piglet," said Eeyore. "You don't mind my asking," he went on, "but what colour was this balloon when it—when it *was* a balloon?"

"Red."

"I just wondered. . . . Red," he murmured to himself. "My favourite colour. . . . How big was it?"

"About as big as me."

"I just wondered. . . . About as big as Piglet," he said to himself sadly. "My favourite size. Well, well."

Piglet felt very miserable, and didn't know what to say. He was still opening his mouth to begin something, and then deciding that it wasn't any good saying *that*, when he heard a shout from the other side of the river, and there was Pooh.

"Many happy returns of the day," called out Pooh, forgetting that he had said it already.

"Thank you, Pooh, I'm having them," said Eeyore gloomily.

"I've brought you a little present," said Pooh excitedly.

"I've had it," said Eeyore.

Pooh had now splashed across the stream to Eeyore, and Piglet was sitting a little way off, his head in his paws, snuffling to himself.

"It's a Useful Pot," said Pooh. "Here it is. And it's got 'A Very Happy Birthday with love from Pooh' written on it. That's what all that writing is. And it's for putting things in. There!"

When Eeyore saw the pot, he became quite excited.

"Why!" he said. "I believe my Balloon will just go into that Pot!"

"Oh, no, Eeyore," said Pooh. "Balloons are much too big to go into Pots. What you do with a balloon is, you hold the balloon——"

"Not mine," said Eeyore proudly. "Look, Piglet!" And as Piglet looked sorrowfully round, Eeyore picked the balloon up with his teeth, and placed it carefully in the pot; picked it out and put it on the ground; and then picked it up again and put it carefully back.

"So it does!" said Pooh. "It goes in!"

"So it does!" said Piglet. "And it comes out!"

"Doesn't it?" said Eeyore. "It goes in and out like anything."

"I'm very glad," said Pooh happily, "that I thought of giving you a Useful Pot to put things in."

"I'm very glad," said Piglet happily, "that I thought of giving you Something to put in a Useful Pot."

But Eeyore wasn't listening. He was taking the balloon out, and putting it back again, as happy as could be. . . .

"And didn't *I* give him anything?" asked Christopher Robin sadly.

"Of course you did," I said. "You gave him— don't you remember—a little—a little——"

"I gave him a box of paints to paint things with."

"That was it."

"Why didn't I give it to him in the morning?"

"You were so busy getting his party ready for him. He had a cake with icing on the top, and three candles, and his name in pink sugar, and——"

"Yes, *I* remember," said Christopher Robin.

CHAPTER SEVEN

In Which

Kanga and Baby Roo
Come to the Forest,
and Piglet Has a Bath

NOBODY seemed to know where they came from, but there they were in the Forest: Kanga and Baby Roo. When Pooh asked Christopher Robin, "How did they come here?" Christopher Robin said, "In the Usual Way, if you know what I mean, Pooh," and Pooh, who didn't, said "Oh!" Then he nodded his head twice and said, "In the Usual Way. Ah!" Then he went to call upon his friend Piglet to see what *he* thought about it. And at Piglet's house he found Rabbit. So they all talked about it together.

"What I don't like about it is this," said Rabbit. "Here are we—you, Pooh, and you, Piglet, and Me —and suddenly——"

"And Eeyore," said Pooh.

"And Eeyore—and then suddenly——"

"And Owl," said Pooh.

"And Owl—and then all of a sudden——"

"Oh, and Eeyore," said Pooh. "I was forgetting *him*."

"Here—we—are," said Rabbit very slowly and carefully, "all—of—us, and then, suddenly, we wake up one morning and, what do we find? We find a Strange Animal among us. An animal of whom we have never even heard before! An animal who carries her family about with her in her pocket! Suppose *I* carried *my* family about with me in *my* pocket, how many pockets should I want?"

"Sixteen," said Piglet.

"Seventeen, isn't it?" said Rabbit. "And one more for a handkerchief—that's eighteen. Eighteen pockets in one suit! I haven't time."

There was a long and thoughtful silence . . . and then Pooh, who had been frowning very hard for some minutes, said: "*I* make it fifteen."

"What?" said Rabbit.

"Fifteen."

"Fifteen what?"

"Your family."

"What about them?"

Pooh rubbed his nose and said that he thought Rabbit had been talking about his family.

"Did I?" said Rabbit carelessly.

"Yes, you said——"

"Never mind, Pooh," said Piglet impatiently.

"The question is, What are we to do about Kanga?"

"Oh, I see," said Pooh.

"The best way," said Rabbit, "would be this. The best way would be to steal Baby Roo and hide him, and then when Kanga says, 'Where's Baby Roo?' we say, *'Aha!'*"

"Aha!" said Pooh, practising. *"Aha! Aha! . . .* Of course," he went on, "we could say 'Aha!' even if we hadn't stolen Baby Roo."

"Pooh," said Rabbit kindly, "you haven't any brain."

"I know," said Pooh humbly.

"We say *'Aha!'* so that Kanga knows that *we* know where Baby Roo is. *'Aha!'* means 'We'll tell you where Baby Roo is, if you promise to go away from the Forest and never come back.' Now don't talk while I think."

Pooh went into a corner and tried saying "Aha!" in that sort of voice. Sometimes it seemed to him that it did mean what Rabbit said, and sometimes it seemed to him that it didn't. "I suppose it's just practice," he thought. "I wonder if Kanga will have to practise too so as to understand it."

"There's just one thing," said Piglet, fidgeting a bit. "I was talking to Christopher Robin, and he said that a Kanga was Generally Regarded as One of the Fiercer Animals. I am not frightened of Fierce Animals in the ordinary way, but it is well known that, if One of the Fiercer Animals is Deprived of Its Young, it becomes as fierce as Two of the Fiercer Animals. In which case *'Aha!'* is perhaps a *foolish* thing to say."

"Piglet," said Rabbit, taking out a pencil, and licking the end of it, "you haven't any pluck."

"It is hard to be brave," said Piglet, sniffing slightly, "when you're only a Very Small Animal."

Rabbit, who had begun to write very busily, looked up and said:

"It is because you are a very small animal that you will be Useful in the adventure before us."

Piglet was so excited at the idea of being Useful that he forgot to be frightened any more, and when Rabbit went on to say that Kangas were only Fierce during the winter months, being at other times of an Affectionate Disposition, he could hardly sit still, he was so eager to begin being useful at once.

"What about me?" said Pooh sadly. "I suppose *I* shan't be useful?"

"Never mind, Pooh," said Piglet comfortingly. "Another time perhaps."

"Without Pooh," said Rabbit solemnly as he sharpened his pencil, "the adventure would be impossible."

"Oh!" said Piglet, and tried not to look disappointed. But Pooh went into a corner of the room and said proudly to himself, "Impossible without Me! *That* sort of Bear."

"Now listen all of you," said Rabbit when he had finished writing, and Pooh and Piglet sat listening very eagerly with their mouths open. This was what Rabbit read out:

PLAN TO CAPTURE BABY ROO

1. *General Remarks.* Kanga runs faster than any of Us, even Me.

2. *More General Remarks.* Kanga never takes her eye off Baby Roo, except when he's safely buttoned up in her pocket.

3. *Therefore.* If we are to capture Baby Roo, we must get a Long Start, because Kanga runs faster than any of Us, even Me. (*See* 1.)

4. *A Thought.* If Roo had jumped out of Kanga's pocket and Piglet had jumped in, Kanga wouldn't know the difference, because Piglet is a Very Small Animal.

5. Like Roo.

6. But Kanga would have to be looking the other way first, so as not to see Piglet jumping in.

7. See 2.

8. *Another Thought*. But if Pooh was talking to her very excitedly, she *might* look the other way for a moment.

9. And then I could run away with Roo.

10. Quickly.

11. *And Kanga wouldn't discover the difference until Afterwards.*

Well, Rabbit read this out proudly, and for a little while after he had read it nobody said anything. And then Piglet, who had been opening and shutting his mouth without making any noise, managed to say very huskily:

"And—Afterwards?"

"How do you mean?"

"When Kanga *does* Discover the Difference?"

"Then we all say '*Aha!*'"

"All three of us?"

"Yes."

"Oh!"

"Why, what's the trouble, Piglet?"

"Nothing," said Piglet, "as long as *we all three* say it. As long as we all three say it," said Piglet, "I don't mind," he said, "but I shouldn't care to say *'Aha!'* by myself. It wouldn't sound *nearly* so well. By the way," he said, "you *are* quite sure about what you said about the winter months?"

"The winter months?"

"Yes, only being Fierce in the Winter Months."

"Oh, yes, yes, that's all right. Well, Pooh? You see what you have to do?"

"No," said Pooh Bear. "Not yet," he said. "What *do* I do?"

"Well, you just have to talk very hard to Kanga so as she doesn't notice anything."

"Oh! What about?"

"Anything you like."

"You mean like telling her a little bit of poetry or something?"

"That's it," said Rabbit. "Splendid. Now come along."

So they all went out to look for Kanga.

Kanga and Roo were spending a quiet afternoon in a sandy part of the Forest. Baby Roo was practising very small jumps in the sand, and falling down mouse-holes and climbing out of them, and Kanga was fidgeting about and saying "Just one more jump, dear, and then we must go home." And at that moment who should come stumping up the hill but Pooh.

"Good afternoon, Kanga."

"Good afternoon, Pooh."

"Look at me jumping," squeaked Roo, and fell into another mouse-hole.

"Hallo, Roo, my little fellow!"

"We were just going home," said Kanga. "Good afternoon, Rabbit. Good afternoon, Piglet."

Rabbit and Piglet, who had now come up from the other side of the hill, said, "Good afternoon," and "Hallo, Roo," and Roo asked them to look at him jumping, so they stayed and looked.

And Kanga looked too. . . .

"Oh, Kanga," said Pooh, after Rabbit had winked at him twice, "I don't know if you are interested in Poetry at all?"

"Hardly at all," said Kanga.

"Oh!" said Pooh.

"Roo, dear, just one more jump and then we must go home."

There was a short silence while Roo fell down another mouse-hole.

"Go on," said Rabbit in a loud whisper behind his paw.

"Talking of Poetry," said Pooh, "I made up a little piece as I was coming along. It went like this. Er— now let me see——"

"Fancy!" said Kanga. "Now Roo, dear——"

"You'll like this piece of poetry," said Rabbit.

"You'll love it," said Piglet.

"You must listen very carefully," said Rabbit.

"So as not to miss any of it," said Piglet.

"Oh, yes," said Kanga, but she still looked at Baby Roo.

"*How* did it go, Pooh?" said Rabbit.

Pooh gave a little cough and began.

LINES WRITTEN BY A BEAR
OF VERY LITTLE BRAIN

On Monday, when the sun is hot
I wonder to myself a lot:
"Now is it true, or is it not,
"That what is which and which is what?"

On Tuesday, when it hails and snows,
The feeling on me grows and grows
That hardly anybody knows
If those are these or these are those.

On Wednesday, when the sky is blue,
And I have nothing else to do,
I sometimes wonder if it's true
That who is what and what is who.

On Thursday, when it starts to freeze
And hoar-frost twinkles on the trees,
How very readily one sees
That these are whose—but whose are these?

On Friday——

"Yes, it is, isn't it?" said Kanga, not waiting to hear
what happened on Friday. "Just one more jump, Roo,
dear, and then we really *must* be going."

Rabbit gave Pooh a hurrying-up sort of nudge.

"Talking of Poetry," said Pooh quickly, "have you
ever noticed that tree right over there?"

"Where?" said Kanga. "Now, Roo——"

"Right over there," said Pooh, pointing behind Kanga's back.

"No," said Kanga. "Now jump in, Roo, dear, and we'll go home."

"You ought to look at that tree right over there," said Rabbit. "Shall I lift you in, Roo?" And he picked up Roo in his paws.

"I can see a bird in it from here," said Pooh. "Or is it a fish?"

"You ought to see that bird from here," said Rabbit. "Unless it's a fish."

"It isn't a fish, it's a bird," said Piglet.

"So it is," said Rabbit.

"Is it a starling or a blackbird?" said Pooh.

"That's the whole question," said Rabbit. "Is it a blackbird or a starling?"

And then at last Kanga did turn her head to look. And the moment that her head was turned, Rabbit said in a loud voice "In you go, Roo!" and in jumped Piglet into Kanga's pocket, and off scampered Rabbit, with Roo in his paws, as fast as he could.

"Why, where's Rabbit?" said Kanga, turning round again. "Are you all right, Roo, dear?"

Piglet made a squeaky Roo-noise from the bottom of Kanga's pocket.

"Rabbit had to go away," said Pooh. "I think he thought of something he had to go and see about suddenly."

"And Piglet?"

"I think Piglet thought of something at the same time. Suddenly."

"Well, we must be getting home," said Kanga. "Good-bye, Pooh." And in three large jumps she was gone.

Pooh looked after her as she went.

"I wish I could jump like that," he thought. "Some can and some can't. That's how it is."

But there were moments when Piglet wished that Kanga couldn't. Often, when he had had a long walk home through the Forest, he had wished that he were a bird; but now he thought jerkily to himself at the bottom of Kanga's pocket,

this   take

"If   is   shall   really   to

flying I   never   it."

And as he went up in the air, he said, *"Ooooooo!"*

and as he came down he said, *"Ow!"* And he was saying, *"Ooooooo-ow, Ooooooo-ow, Ooooooo-ow"* all the way to Kanga's house.

Of course as soon as Kanga unbuttoned her pocket, she saw what had happened. Just for a moment, she thought she was frightened, and then she knew she wasn't; for she felt quite sure that Christopher Robin would never let any harm happen to Roo. So she said to herself, "If they are having a joke with me, I will have a joke with them."

"Now then, Roo, dear," she said, as she took Piglet out of her pocket. "Bed-time."

"*Aha!*" said Piglet, as well as he could after his Terrifying Journey. But it wasn't a very good "*Aha!*" and Kanga didn't seem to understand what it meant.

"Bath first," said Kanga in a cheerful voice.

"*Aha!*" said Piglet again, looking round anxiously for the others. But the others weren't there. Rabbit was playing with Baby Roo in his own house, and feeling more fond of him every minute, and Pooh, who had decided to be a Kanga, was still at the sandy place on the top of the Forest, practising jumps.

"I am not at all sure," said Kanga in a thoughtful voice, "that it wouldn't be a good idea to have a *cold* bath this evening. Would you like that, Roo, dear?"

Piglet, who had never been really fond of baths,

shuddered a long indignant shudder, and said in as brave a voice as he could:

"Kanga, I see the time has come to spleak painly."

"Funny little Roo," said Kanga, as she got the bath-water ready.

"I am *not* Roo," said Piglet loudly. "I am Piglet!"

"Yes, dear, yes," said Kanga soothingly. "And imitating Piglet's voice too! So clever of him," she went on, as she took a large bar of yellow soap out of the cupboard. "What *will* he be doing next?"

"Can't you *see*?" shouted Piglet. "Haven't you got *eyes*? Look at me!"

"I *am* looking, Roo, dear," said Kanga rather severely. "And you know what I told you yesterday about making faces. If you go on making faces like Piglet's, you will grow up to *look* like Piglet—and *then* think how sorry you will be. Now then, into the bath, and don't let me have to speak to you about it again."

Before he knew where he was, Piglet was in the bath, and Kanga was scrubbing him firmly with a large lathery flannel.

"Ow!" cried Piglet. "Let me out! I'm Piglet!"

"Don't open the mouth, dear, or the soap goes in," said Kanga. "There! What did I tell you?"

"You—you—you did it on purpose," spluttered Piglet, as soon as he could speak again . . . and then accidentally had another mouthful of lathery flannel.

"That's right, dear, don't say anything," said Kanga, and in another minute Piglet was out of the bath, and being rubbed dry with a towel.

"Now," said Kanga, "there's your medicine, and then bed."

"W-w-what medicine?" said Piglet.

"To make you grow big and strong, dear. You don't want to grow up small and weak like Piglet, do you? Well, then!"

At that moment there was a knock at the door.

"Come in," said Kanga, and in came Christopher Robin.

"Christopher Robin, Christopher Robin!" cried Piglet. "Tell Kanga who I am! She keeps saying I'm Roo. I'm *not* Roo, am I?"

Christopher Robin looked at him very carefully, and shook his head.

"You can't be Roo," he said, "because I've just seen Roo playing in Rabbit's house."

"Well!" said Kanga. "Fancy that! Fancy my making a mistake like that."

"There you are!" said Piglet. "I told you so. I'm Piglet."

Christopher Robin shook his head again.

"Oh, you're not Piglet," he said. "I know Piglet well, and he's *quite* a different colour."

Piglet began to say that this was because he had just had a bath, and then he thought that perhaps he wouldn't say that, and as he opened his mouth to say something else, Kanga slipped the medicine spoon in, and then patted him on the back and told him that it was really quite a nice taste when you got used to it.

"I knew it wasn't Piglet," said Kanga. "I wonder who it can be."

"Perhaps it's some relation of Pooh's," said Christopher Robin. "What about a nephew or an uncle or something?"

Kanga agreed that this was probably what it was, and said that they would have to call it by some name.

"I shall call it Pootel," said Christopher Robin. "Henry Pootel for short."

And just when it was decided, Henry Pootel wriggled out of Kanga's arms and jumped to the ground. To his great joy Christopher Robin had left the door open. Never had Henry Pootel Piglet run so fast as he ran then, and he didn't stop running until he had got quite close to his house. But when he was a hundred yards away he stopped running, and rolled the rest of the way home, so as to get his own nice comfortable colour again. . . .

So Kanga and Roo stayed in the Forest. And every Tuesday Roo spent the day with his great friend Rabbit, and every Tuesday Kanga spent the day with her great friend Pooh, teaching him to jump, and every Tuesday Piglet spent the day with his great friend Christopher Robin. So they were all happy again.

CHAPTER EIGHT

In Which

Christopher Robin Leads an Expotition to the North Pole

ONE FINE DAY Pooh had stumped up to the top of the Forest to see if his friend Christopher Robin was interested in Bears at all. At breakfast that morning (a simple meal of marmalade spread lightly over a honeycomb or two) he had suddenly thought of a new song. It began like this:

"Sing Ho! for the life of a Bear!"

When he had got as far as this, he stretched his head, and thought to himself "That's a very good start for a song, but what about the second line?" He tried singing "Ho," two or three times, but it didn't seem to help. "Perhaps it would be better," he thought, "if I sang Hi for the life of a Bear." So he sang it . . . but it wasn't. "Very well, then," he said, "I shall sing that first line twice, and perhaps if I sing it very quickly, I shall find myself singing the third and fourth lines before I have time to think of them, and that will be a Good Song. Now then:"

> Sing Ho! for the life of a Bear!
> Sing Ho! for the life of a Bear!
> I don't much mind if it rains or snows,
> 'Cos I've got a lot of honey on my nice
> new nose,
> I don't much care if it snows or thaws,
> 'Cos I've got a lot of honey on my nice
> clean paws!
> Sing Ho! for a Bear!
> Sing Ho! for a Pooh!
> And I'll have a little something in an hour
> or two!

He was so pleased with this song that he sang it all the way to the top of the Forest, "and if I go on singing it much longer," he thought, "it will be time for the little something, and then the last line won't be true." So he turned it into a hum instead.

Christopher Robin was sitting outside his door, putting on his Big Boots. As soon as he saw the Big Boots, Pooh knew that an Adventure was going to happen, and he brushed the honey off his nose with the back of his paw, and spruced himself up as well as he could, so as to look Ready for Anything.

"Good-morning, Christopher Robin," he called out.

"Hallo, Pooh Bear. I can't get this boot on."

"That's bad," said Pooh.

"Do you think you could very kindly lean against me, 'cos I keep pulling so hard that I fall over backwards."

Pooh sat down, dug his feet into the ground, and pushed hard against Christopher Robin's back, and Christopher Robin pushed hard against his, and pulled and pulled at his boot until he had got it on.

"And that's that," said Pooh. "What do we do next?"

"We are all going on an Expedition," said Christopher Robin, as he got up and brushed himself. "Thank you, Pooh."

"Going on an Expotition?" said Pooh eagerly. "I don't think I've ever been on one of those. Where are we going to on this Expotition?"

"Expedition, silly old Bear. It's got an 'x' in it."

"Oh!" said Pooh. "I know." But he didn't really.

"We're going to discover the North Pole."

"Oh!" said Pooh again. "What *is* the North Pole?" he asked.

"It's just a thing you discover," said Christopher Robin carelessly, not being quite sure himself.

"Oh! I see," said Pooh. "Are bears any good at discovering it?"

"Of course they are. And Rabbit and Kanga and all of you. It's an Expedition. That's what an Expedition means. A long line of everybody. You'd better tell the others to get ready, while I see if my gun's all right. And we must all bring Provisions."

"Bring what?"

"Things to eat."

"Oh!" said Pooh happily. "I thought you said Provisions. I'll go and tell them." And he stumped off.

The first person he met was Rabbit.

"Hallo, Rabbit," he said, "is that you?"

"Let's pretend it isn't," said Rabbit, "and see what happens."

"I've got a message for you."

"I'll give it to him."

"We're all going on an Expotition with Christopher Robin!"

"What is it when we're on it?"

"A sort of boat, I think," said Pooh.

"Oh! that sort."

"Yes. And we're going to discover a Pole or something. Or was it a Mole? Anyhow we're going to discover it."

"We are, are we?" said Rabbit.

"Yes. And we've got to bring Po—things to eat with us. In case we want to eat them. Now I'm going down to Piglet's. Tell Kanga, will you?"

He left Rabbit and hurried down to Piglet's house. The Piglet was sitting on the ground at the door of his house blowing happily at a dandelion, and wondering whether it would be this year, next year, sometime or never. He had just discovered that it would be never, and was trying to remember what *"it"* was, and hoping it wasn't anything nice, when Pooh came up.

"Oh! Piglet," said Pooh excitedly, "we're going on an Expotition, all of us, with things to eat. To discover something."

"To discover what?" said Piglet anxiously.

"Oh! just something."

"Nothing fierce?"

"Christopher Robin didn't say anything about fierce. He just said it had an 'x'."

"It isn't their necks I mind," said Piglet earnestly. "It's their teeth. But if Christopher Robin is coming I don't mind anything."

In a little while they were all ready at the top of the Forest, and the Expotition started. First came Christopher Robin and Rabbit, then Piglet and Pooh; then Kanga, with Roo in her pocket, and Owl; then Eeyore; and, at the end, in a long line, all Rabbit's friends-and-relations.

"I didn't ask them," explained Rabbit carelessly. "They just came. They always do. They can march at the end, after Eeyore."

"What I say," said Eeyore, "is that it's unsettling. I didn't want to come on this Expo—what Pooh said. I only came to oblige. But here I am; and if I am the end of the Expo—what we're talking about—then let me *be* the end. But if, every time I want to sit down for a little rest, I have to brush away half a dozen of Rabbit's smaller friends-and-relations first, then this isn't an Expo—whatever it is—at all, it's simply a Confused Noise. That's what *I* say."

"I see what Eeyore means," said Owl. "If you ask me——"

"I'm not asking anybody," said Eeyore. "I'm just telling everybody. We can look for the North Pole, or we can play 'Here we go gathering Nuts and May' with the end part of an ant's nest. It's all the same to me."

There was a shout from the top of the line.

"Come on!" called Christopher Robin.

"Come on!" called Pooh and Piglet.

"Come on!" called Owl.

"We're starting," said Rabbit. "I must go." And he hurried off to the front of the Expotition with Christopher Robin.

"All right," said Eeyore. "We're going. Only Don't Blame Me."

So off they all went to discover the Pole. And as they walked, they chattered to each other of this and that, all except Pooh, who was making up a song.

"This is the first verse," he said to Piglet, when he was ready with it.

"First verse of what?"

"My song."

"What song?"

"This one."

"Which one?"

"Well, if you listen, Piglet, you'll hear it."

"How do you know I'm not listening?"

Pooh couldn't answer that one, so he began to sing.

> They all went off to discover the Pole,
>> Owl and Piglet and Rabbit and all;
> It's a Thing you Discover, as I've been tole
>> By Owl and Piglet and Rabbit and all.
> Eeyore, Christopher Robin and Pooh
> And Rabbit's relations all went too——
> And where the Pole was none of them knew. . . .
>> Sing Hey! for Owl and Rabbit and all!

"Hush!" said Christopher Robin turning round to Pooh, "we're just coming to a Dangerous Place."

"Hush!" said Pooh turning round quickly to Piglet.

"Hush!" said Piglet to Kanga.

"Hush!" said Kanga to Owl, while Roo said "Hush!" several times to himself very quietly.

"Hush!" said Owl to Eeyore.

"Hush!" said Eeyore in a terrible voice to all Rabbit's friends-and-relations, and "Hush!" they said hastily to each other all down the line, until it got to the last one of all. And the last and smallest friend-and-relation was so upset to find that the whole Expotition was saying "Hush!" to *him,* that he buried himself head downwards in a crack in the ground,

and stayed there for two days until the danger was over, and then went home in a great hurry, and lived quietly with his Aunt ever-afterwards. His name was Alexander Beetle.

They had come to a stream which twisted and tumbled between high rocky banks, and Christopher Robin saw at once how dangerous it was.

"It's just the place," he explained, "for an Ambush."

"What sort of bush?" whispered Pooh to Piglet. "A gorse-bush?"

"My dear Pooh," said Owl in his superior way, "don't you know what an Ambush is?"

"Owl," said Piglet, looking round at him severely,

"Pooh's whisper was a perfectly private whisper, and there was no need——"

"An Ambush," said Owl, "is a sort of Surprise."

"So is a gorse-bush sometimes," said Pooh.

"An Ambush, as I was about to explain to Pooh," said Piglet, "is a sort of Surprise."

"If people jump out at you suddenly, that's an Ambush," said Owl.

"It's an Ambush, Pooh, when people jump at you suddenly," explained Piglet.

Pooh, who now knew what an Ambush was, said that a gorse-bush had sprung at him suddenly one day when he fell off a tree, and he had taken six days to get all the prickles out of himself.

"We are not *talking* about gorse-bushes," said Owl a little crossly.

"I am," said Pooh.

They were climbing very cautiously up the stream now, going from rock to rock, and after they had gone a little way they came to a place where the banks widened out at each side, so that on each side of the water there was a level strip of grass on which they could sit down and rest. As soon as he saw this, Christopher Robin called "Halt!" and they all sat down and rested.

"I think," said Christopher Robin, "that we ought to eat all our Provisions now, so that we shan't have so much to carry."

"Eat all our what?" said Pooh.

"All that we've brought," said Piglet, getting to work.

"That's a good idea," said Pooh, and he got to work too.

"Have you all got something?" asked Christopher Robin with his mouth full.

"All except me," said Eeyore. "As Usual." He looked round at them in his melancholy way. "I suppose none of you are sitting on a thistle by any chance?"

"I believe I am," said Pooh. "Ow!" He got up, and looked behind him. "Yes, I was. I thought so."

"Thank you, Pooh. If you've quite finished with it." He moved across to Pooh's place, and began to eat.

"It don't do them any Good, you know, sitting on them," he went on, as he looked up munching. "Takes all the Life out of them. Remember that another time, all of you. A little Consideration, a little Thought for Others, makes all the difference."

As soon as he had finished his lunch Christopher Robin whispered to Rabbit, and Rabbit said, "Yes, yes, of course," and they walked a little way up the stream together.

"I didn't want the others to hear," said Christopher Robin.

"Quite so," said Rabbit, looking important.

"It's—I wondered—It's only—Rabbit, I suppose *you* don't know, What does the North Pole *look* like."

"Well," said Rabbit, stroking his whiskers. "Now you're asking me."

"I did know once, only I've sort of forgotten," said Christopher Robin carelessly.

"It's a funny thing," said Rabbit, "but I've sort of forgotten too, although I did know *once*."

"I suppose it's just a pole stuck in the ground?"

"Sure to be a pole," said Rabbit, "because of calling a pole, and if it's a pole, well, I should think it would be sticking in the ground, shouldn't you, because there'd be nowhere else to stick it."

"Yes, that's what I thought."

"The only thing," said Rabbit, "is, *where is it sticking?*"

"That's what we're looking for," said Christopher Robin.

They went back to the others. Piglet was lying on his back, sleeping peacefully. Roo was washing his face and paws in the stream, while Kanga explained to everybody proudly that this was the first time he had ever washed his face himself, and Owl was telling Kanga an Interesting Anecdote full of long words like Encyclopædia and Rhododendron to which Kanga wasn't listening.

"I don't hold with all this washing," grumbled Eeyore. "This modern Behind-the-ears nonsense. What do *you* think, Pooh?"

"Well," said Pooh, "*I* think——"

But we shall never know what Pooh thought, for there came a sudden squeak from Roo, a splash, and a loud cry of alarm from Kanga.

"So much for *washing*," said Eeyore.

"Roo's fallen in!" cried Rabbit, and he and Christopher Robin came rushing down to the rescue.

"Look at me swimming!" squeaked Roo from the middle of his pool, and was hurried down a waterfall into the next pool.

"Are you all right, Roo dear?" called Kanga anxiously.

"Yes!" said Roo. "Look at me sw——" and down he went over the next waterfall into another pool.

Everybody was doing something to help. Piglet, wide awake suddenly, was jumping up and down and making "Oo, I say" noises; Owl was explaining that in a case of Sudden and Temporary Immersion the Important Thing was to keep the Head Above Water; Kanga was jumping along the bank, saying "Are you *sure* you're all right, Roo dear?" to which Roo, from whatever pool he was in at the moment, was answering "Look at me swimming!" Eeyore had turned round and hung his tail over the first pool into which Roo fell, and with his back to the accident was grumbling quietly to himself, and saying, "All this washing; but catch on to my tail, little Roo, and you'll be all right"; and, Christopher Robin and Rabbit came hurrying past Eeyore, and were calling out to the others in front of them.

"All right, Roo, I'm coming," called Christopher Robin.

"Get something across the stream lower down, some of you fellows," called Rabbit.

But Pooh was getting something. Two pools below Roo he was standing with a long pole in his paws, and Kanga came up and took one end of it, and between them they held it across the lower

part of the pool; and Roo, still bubbling proudly, "Look at me swimming," drifted up against it, and climbed out.

"Did you see me swimming?" squeaked Roo excitedly, while Kanga scolded him and rubbed him down. "Pooh, did you see me swimming? That's called swimming, what I was doing. Rabbit, did you see what I was doing? Swimming. Hallo, Piglet! I say, Piglet! What do you think I was doing! Swimming! Christopher Robin, did you see me——"

But Christopher Robin wasn't listening. He was looking at Pooh.

"Pooh," he said, "where did you find that pole?"

Pooh looked at the pole in his hands.

"I just found it," he said. "I thought it ought to be useful. I just picked it up."

"Pooh," said Christopher Robin solemnly, "the Expedition is over. You have found the North Pole!"

"Oh!" said Pooh.

Eeyore was sitting with his tail in the water when they all got back to him.

"Tell Roo to be quick, somebody," he said. "My tail's getting cold. I don't want to mention it, but I just mention it. I don't want to complain but there it is. My tail's cold."

"Here I am!" squeaked Roo.

"Oh, there you are."

"Did you see me swimming?"

Eeyore took his tail out of the water, and swished it from side to side.

"As I expected," he said. "Lost all feeling. Numbed it. That's what it's done. Numbed it. Well, as long as nobody minds, I suppose it's all right."

"Poor old Eeyore. I'll dry it for you," said Christopher Robin, and he took out his handkerchief and rubbed it up.

"Thank you, Christopher Robin. You're the only one who seems to understand about tails. They don't think—that's what's the matter with some of these others. They've no imagination. A tail isn't a tail to *them*, it's just a Little Bit Extra at the back."

"Never mind, Eeyore," said Christopher Robin, rubbing his hardest. "Is *that* better?"

"It's feeling more like a tail perhaps. It Belongs again, if you know what I mean."

"Hullo, Eeyore," said Pooh, coming up to them with his pole.

"Hullo, Pooh. Thank you for asking, but I shall be able to use it again in a day or two."

"Use what?" said Pooh.

"What we are talking about."

"I wasn't talking about anything," said Pooh, looking puzzled.

"My mistake again. I thought you were saying how sorry you were about my tail, being all numb, and could you do anything to help?"

"No," said Pooh. "That wasn't me," he said. He thought for a little and then suggested helpfully, "Perhaps it was somebody else."

"Well, thank him for me when you see him."

Pooh looked anxiously at Christopher Robin.

"Pooh's found the North Pole," said Christopher Robin. "Isn't that lovely?"

Pooh looked modestly down.

"Is that it?" said Eeyore.

"Yes," said Christopher Robin.

"Is that what we were looking for?"

"Yes," said Pooh.

"Oh!" said Eeyore. "Well, anyhow—it didn't rain," he said.

They stuck the pole in the ground, and Christopher Robin tied a message on to it.

NORTH POLE
DISCOVERED BY POOH
POOH FOUND IT.

Then they all went home again. And I think, but I am not quite sure, that Roo had a hot bath and went straight to bed. But Pooh went back to his own house, and feeling very proud of what he had done, had a little something to revive himself.

CHAPTER NINE

In Which

Piglet Is Entirely Surrounded by Water

I T RAINED and it rained and it rained. Piglet told himself that never in all his life, and *he* was goodness knows *how* old—three, was it, or four?— never had he seen so much rain. Days and days and days.

"If only," he thought, as he looked out of the window, "I had been in Pooh's house, or Christopher Robin's house, or Rabbit's house when it began to rain, then I should have had Company all this time, instead of being here all alone, with nothing to do except wonder when it will stop." And he imagined himself with Pooh, saying, "Did you ever see such rain, Pooh?" and Pooh saying, "Isn't it *awful*, Piglet?" and Piglet saying, "I wonder how it is over Christopher Robin's way" and Pooh saying, "I should think poor old Rabbit is about flooded out by this time." It would have been jolly to talk like this, and really, it wasn't much good having anything exciting like floods, if you couldn't share them with somebody.

For it was rather exciting. The little dry ditches in which Piglet had nosed about so often had become streams, the little streams across which he had splashed were rivers, and the river, between whose steep banks they had played so happily, had sprawled out of its own bed and was taking up so much room everywhere, that Piglet was beginning to wonder whether it would be coming into *his* bed soon.

"It's a little Anxious," he said to himself, "to be a Very Small Animal Entirely Surrounded by Water. Christopher Robin and Pooh could escape by Climbing Trees, and Kanga could escape by Jumping, and Rabbit could escape by Burrowing, and Owl could escape by Flying, and Eeyore could escape by—by Making a Loud Noise Until Rescued, and here am I, surrounded by water and I can't do *anything*."

It went on raining, and every day the water got a little higher, until now it was nearly up to Piglet's window . . . and still he hadn't done anything.

"There's Pooh," he thought to himself. "Pooh hasn't much Brain, but he never comes to any harm. He does silly things and they turn out right. There's Owl. Owl hasn't exactly got Brain, but he Knows Things. He would know the Right Thing to Do when

Surrounded by Water. There's Rabbit. He hasn't Learnt in Books, but he can always Think of a Clever Plan. There's Kanga. She isn't Clever, Kanga isn't,

but she would be so anxious about Roo that she would do a Good Thing to Do without thinking about it. And then there's Eeyore. And Eeyore is so miserable anyhow that he wouldn't mind about this. But I wonder what Christopher Robin would do?"

Then suddenly he remembered a story which Christopher Robin had told him about a man on a desert island who had written something in a bottle and thrown it in the sea; and Piglet thought that if he wrote something in a bottle and threw it in the water, perhaps somebody would come and rescue *him*!

He left the window and began to search his house, all of it that wasn't under water, and at last he found a pencil and a small piece of dry paper, and a bottle with a cork to it. And he wrote on one side of the paper:

HELP!

PIGLET (ME)

and on the other side:

IT'S ME PIGLET, HELP HELP.

Then he put the paper in the bottle, and he corked the bottle up as tightly as he could, and he leant out of his window as far as he could lean without falling in, and he threw the bottle as far as he could throw—*splash!*—and in a little while it bobbed up again on the water; and he watched it floating slowly away in the distance, until his eyes ached with looking, and sometimes he thought it was the bottle, and sometimes he thought it was just a ripple on the water which he was following, and then suddenly he knew that he would never see it again and that he had done all that he could do to save himself.

"So now," he thought, "somebody else will have to do something, and I hope they will do it soon, because if they don't I shall have to swim, which I can't, so I hope they do it soon." And then he gave a very long sigh and said, "I wish Pooh were here. It's so much more friendly with two."

When the rain began Pooh was asleep. It rained, and it rained, and it rained, and he slept and he slept and he slept. He had had a tiring day. You remember how he discovered the North Pole; well, he was so proud of this that he asked Christopher Robin if there were any other Poles such as a Bear of Little Brain might discover.

"There's a South Pole," said Christopher Robin, "and I expect there's an East Pole and a West Pole, though people don't like talking about them."

Pooh was very excited when he heard this, and suggested that they should have an Expotition to discover the East Pole, but Christopher Robin had thought of something else to do with Kanga; so Pooh went out to discover the East Pole by himself. Whether he discovered it or not, I forget; but he was so tired when he got home that, in the very middle of his supper, after he had been eating for little more than half-an-hour, he fell fast asleep in his chair, and slept and slept and slept.

Then suddenly he was dreaming. He was at the East Pole, and it was a very cold pole with the coldest sort of snow and ice all over it. He had found a bee-hive to sleep in, but there wasn't room for his legs, so he had left them outside. And Wild Woozles, such as inhabit the East Pole, came and nibbled all the fur off his legs to make nests for their Young. And the more they nibbled, the colder his legs got, until suddenly he woke up with an *Ow!*—and there he was, sitting in his chair with his feet in the water, and water all round him!

He splashed to his door and looked out. . . .

"This is Serious," said Pooh. "I must have an Escape."

So he took his largest pot of honey and escaped with it to a broad branch of his tree, well above the water, and then he climbed down again and escaped with another pot . . . and when the whole Escape was finished, there was Pooh sitting on his branch, dangling his legs, and there, beside him, were ten pots of honey. . . .

Two days later, there was Pooh, sitting on his branch, dangling his legs, and there, beside him, were four pots of honey. . . .

Three days later, there was Pooh, sitting on his

branch, dangling his legs, and there, beside him, was one pot of honey.

Four days later, there was Pooh . . .

And it was on the morning of the fourth day that Piglet's bottle came floating past him, and with one loud cry of "Honey!" Pooh plunged into the water, seized the bottle, and struggled back to his tree again.

"Bother!" said Pooh, as he opened it. "All that wet for nothing. What's that bit of paper doing?"

He took it out and looked at it.

"It's a Missage," he said to himself, "that's what it is. And that letter is a 'P,' and so is that, and so is that, and 'P' means 'Pooh,' so it's a very important Missage to me, and I can't read it. I must find Christopher Robin or Owl or Piglet, one of those Clever Readers who can read things, and they will tell me what this missage means. Only I can't swim. Bother!"

Then he had an idea, and I think that for a Bear of

Very Little Brain, it was a good idea. He said to himself:

"If a bottle can float, then a jar can float, and if a jar floats, I can sit on the top of it, if it's a very big jar."

So he took his biggest jar, and corked it up. "All boats have to have a name," he said, "so I shall call mine *The Floating Bear*." And with these words he dropped his boat into the water and jumped in after it.

For a little while Pooh and *The Floating Bear* were uncertain as to which of them was meant to be on the top, but after trying one or two different positions, they settled down with *The Floating Bear* underneath and Pooh triumphantly astride it, paddling vigorously with his feet.

Christopher Robin lived at the very top of the Forest. It rained, and it rained, and it rained, but the water couldn't come up to *his* house. It was rather

jolly to look down into the valleys and see the water all round him, but it rained so hard that he stayed indoors most of the time, and thought about things. Every morning he went out with his umbrella and put a stick in the place where the water came up to, and every next morning he went out and couldn't see his stick any more, so he put another stick in the place where the water came up to, and then he walked home again, and each morning he had a shorter way to walk than he had had the morning before. On the morning of the fifth day he saw the water all round him, and knew that for the first time in his life he was on a real island. Which was very exciting.

It was on this morning that Owl came flying over the water to say "How do you do," to his friend Christopher Robin.

"I say, Owl," said Christopher Robin, "isn't this fun? I'm on an island!"

"The atmospheric conditions have been very un-favourable lately," said Owl.

"The what?"

"It has been raining," explained Owl.

"Yes," said Christopher Robin. "It has."

"The flood-level has reached an unprecedented height."

"The who?"

"There's a lot of water about," explained Owl.

"Yes," said Christopher Robin, "there is."

"However, the prospects are rapidly becoming more favourable. At any moment—"

"Have you seen Pooh?"

"No. At any moment—"

"I hope he's all right," said Christopher Robin. "I've been wondering about him. I expect Piglet's with him. Do you think they're all right, Owl?"

"I expect so. You see, at any moment—"

"Do go and see, Owl. Because Pooh hasn't got very much brain, and he might do something silly, and I do love him so, Owl. Do you see, Owl?"

"That's all right," said Owl. "I'll go. Back directly." And he flew off.

In a little while he was back again.

"Pooh isn't there," he said.

"Not there?"

"Has *been* there. He's been sitting on a branch of his tree outside his house with nine pots of honey. But he isn't there now."

"Oh, Pooh!" cried Christopher Robin. "Where *are* you?"

"Here I am," said a growly voice behind him.

"Pooh!"

They rushed into each other's arms.

"How did you get here, Pooh?" asked Christopher Robin, when he was ready to talk again.

"On my boat," said Pooh proudly. "I had a Very Important Missage sent me in a bottle, and owing to having got some water in my eyes, I couldn't read it, so I brought it to you. On my boat."

With these proud words he gave Christopher Robin the missage.

"But it's from Piglet!" cried Christopher Robin when he had read it.

"Isn't there anything about Pooh in it?" asked Bear, looking over his shoulder.

Christopher Robin read the message aloud.

"Oh, are those 'P's' Piglets? I thought they were Poohs."

"We must rescue him at once! I thought he was with *you*, Pooh. Owl, could you rescue him on your back?"

"I don't think so," said Owl, after grave thought. "It is doubtful if the necessary dorsal muscles——"

"Then would you fly to him at *once* and say that Rescue is Coming? And Pooh and I will think of a Rescue and come as quick as ever we can. Oh, don't *talk*, Owl, go on quick!" And, still thinking of something to say, Owl flew off.

"Now then, Pooh," said Christopher Robin, "where's your boat?"

"I ought to say," explained Pooh as they walked down to the shore of the island, "that it isn't just an ordinary sort of boat. Sometimes it's a Boat, and sometimes it's more of an Accident. It all depends."

"Depends on what?"

"On whether I'm on the top of it or underneath it."

"Oh! Well, where is it?"

"There!" said Pooh, pointing proudly to *The Floating Bear.*

It wasn't what Christopher Robin expected, and the more he looked at it, the more he thought what a Brave and Clever Bear Pooh was, and the more Christopher Robin thought this, the more Pooh looked modestly down his nose and tried to pretend he wasn't.

"But it's too small for two of us," said Christopher Robin sadly.

"Three of us with Piglet."

"That makes it smaller still. Oh, Pooh Bear, what shall we do?"

And then this Bear, Pooh Bear, Winnie-the-Pooh, F.O.P. (Friend of Piglet's), R.C. (Rabbit's Companion), P.D. (Pole Discoverer), E.C. and T.F. (Eeyore's Comforter and Tail-finder)—in fact, Pooh himself—said something so clever that Christopher Robin could only look at him with mouth open and eyes staring, wondering if this was really the Bear of Very Little Brain whom he had known and loved so long.

"We might go in your umbrella," said Pooh.

"?"

"We might go in your umbrella," said Pooh.

"? ?"

"We might go in your umbrella," said Pooh.

"! ! ! ! ! !"

For suddenly Christopher Robin saw that they might. He opened his umbrella and put it point downwards in the water. It floated but wobbled. Pooh got in. He was just beginning to say that it was all right now, when he found that it wasn't, so after a short drink which he didn't really want he waded back to Christopher Robin. Then they both got in together, and it wobbled no longer.

"I shall call this boat *The Brain of Pooh*," said Christopher Robin, and *The Brain of Pooh* set sail forthwith in a south-westerly direction, revolving gracefully.

You can imagine Piglet's joy when at last the ship came in sight of him. In after-years he liked to think that he had been in Very Great Danger during the Terrible Flood, but the only danger he had really been in was in the last half-hour of his imprisonment, when Owl, who had just flown up, sat on a branch of his tree to comfort him, and told him a very long story about an aunt who had once laid a seagull's egg by mistake, and the story went on and on, rather like this sentence, until Piglet who was listening out of his window without much hope, went to sleep quietly and naturally, slipping slowly out of the window towards the water until he was only hanging on by his toes, at which moment luckily, a sudden loud squawk from Owl, which was really part of the story, being what his aunt said, woke the Piglet up and just gave him time to jerk himself back into safety and say,

"How interesting, and did she?" when—well, you can imagine his joy when at last he saw the good ship, *The Brain of Pooh* (*Captain*, C. Robin; *1st Mate*, P. Bear) coming over the sea to rescue him.

And that is really the end of the story, and as I am very tired after that last sentence, I think I shall stop there.

CHAPTER TEN

In Which

Christopher Robin Gives Pooh a Party, and We Say Good-bye

ONE DAY when the sun had come back over the Forest, bringing with it the scent of May, and all the streams of the Forest were tinkling happily to find themselves their own pretty shape again, and the little pools lay dreaming of the life they had seen and the big things they had done, and in the warmth and quiet of the Forest the cuckoo was trying over his voice carefully and listening to see if he liked it, and wood-pigeons were complaining gently to themselves in their lazy comfortable way that it was the other fellow's fault, but it didn't matter very much; on such a day as this Christopher Robin whistled in a special way he had, and Owl came flying out of the Hundred Acre Wood to see what was wanted.

"Owl," said Christopher Robin, "I am going to give a party."

"You are, are you?" said Owl.

"And it's to be a special sort of party, because it's because of what Pooh did when he did what he did to save Piglet from the flood."

"Oh, that's what it's for, is it?" said Owl.

"Yes, so will you tell Pooh as quickly as you can, and all the others, because it will be tomorrow."

"Oh, it will, will it?" said Owl, still being as helpful as possible.

"So will you go and tell them, Owl?"

Owl tried to think of something very wise to say, but couldn't, so he flew off to tell the others. And the first person he told was Pooh.

"Pooh," he said, "Christopher Robin is giving a party."

"Oh!" said Pooh. And then seeing that Owl expected him to say something else, he said, "Will there be those little cake things with pink sugar icing?"

Owl felt that it was rather beneath him to talk about little cake things with pink sugar icing, so he told Pooh exactly what Christopher Robin had said, and flew off to Eeyore.

"A party for Me?" thought Pooh to himself. "How grand!" And he began to wonder if all the other animals would know that it was a special Pooh Party, and if Christopher Robin had told them about *The Floating Bear* and *The Brain of Pooh* and all the wonderful ships he had invented and sailed on, and he began to think how awful it would be if everybody had forgotten about it, and nobody quite knew what the party was for; and the more he thought like this, the more the party got muddled in his mind, like a dream when

nothing goes right. And the dream began to sing itself over in his head until it became a sort of song. It was an

ANXIOUS POOH SONG.

3 Cheers for Pooh!
(*For Who?*)
For Pooh—
(*Why what did he do?*)
I thought you knew;
He saved his friend from a wetting!
3 Cheers for Bear!
(*For where?*)
For Bear—
He couldn't swim,
But he rescued him!

(He rescued who?)
Oh, listen, do!
I am talking of Pooh—
(Of who?)
Of Pooh!
(I'm sorry I keep forgetting.)
Well, Pooh was a Bear of Enormous Brain
(Just say it again!)
Of enormous brain—
(Of enormous what?)
Well, he ate a lot,
And I don't know if he could swim or not,
But he managed to float
On a sort of boat
(On a sort of what?)
Well, a sort of pot—
So now let's give him three hearty cheers
(So now let's give him three hearty whiches?)
And hope he'll be with us for years and years,
And grow in health and wisdom and riches!
3 Cheers for Pooh!
(For who?)
For Pooh—
3 Cheers for Bear!
(For where?)
For Bear—
3 Cheers for the wonderful Winnie-the-Pooh!
(Just tell me, Somebody—WHAT DID HE DO?)

While this was going on inside him, Owl was talking to Eeyore.

"Eeyore," said Owl, "Christopher Robin is giving a party."

"Very interesting," said Eeyore. "I suppose they will be sending me down the odd bits which got trodden on. Kind and Thoughtful. Not at all, don't mention it."

"There is an Invitation for you."
"What's that like?"
"An Invitation!"

"Yes, I heard you. Who dropped it?"

"This isn't anything to eat, it's asking you to the party. Tomorrow."

Eeyore shook his head slowly.

"You mean Piglet. The little fellow with the excited ears. That's Piglet. I'll tell him."

"No, no!" said Owl, getting quite fussy. "It's you!"

"Are you sure?"

"Of course I'm sure. Christopher Robin said 'All of them! Tell all of them.'"

"All of them, except Eeyore?"

"All of them," said Owl sulkily.

"Ah!" said Eeyore. "A mistake, no doubt, but still, I shall come. Only don't blame *me* if it rains."

But it didn't rain. Christopher Robin had made a long table out of some long pieces of wood, and they all sat around it. Christopher Robin sat at one end, and Pooh sat at the other, and between them on one side were Owl and Eeyore and Piglet, and between them on the other side were Rabbit, and Roo and Kanga. And all Rabbit's friends-and-relations spread themselves about on the grass, and waited hopefully in case anybody spoke to them, or dropped anything, or asked them the time.

It was the first party to which Roo had ever been, and he was very excited. As soon as ever they had sat down he began to talk.

"Hallo, Pooh!" he squeaked.

"Hallo, Roo!" said Pooh.

Roo jumped up and down in his seat for a little while and then began again.

"Hallo, Piglet!" he squeaked.

Piglet waved a paw at him, being too busy to say anything.

"Hallo, Eeyore!" said Roo.

Eeyore nodded gloomily at him. "It will rain soon, you see if it doesn't," he said.

Roo looked to see if it didn't, and it didn't, so he said "Hallo, Owl!"—and Owl said "Hallo, my little fellow," in a kindly way, and went on telling Christopher Robin about an accident which had nearly happened to a friend of his whom Christopher Robin didn't know, and Kanga said to Roo, "Drink up your milk first, dear, and talk afterwards." So Roo, who

was drinking his milk, tried to say that he could do both at once . . . and had to be patted on the back and dried for quite a long time afterwards.

When they had all nearly eaten enough, Christopher Robin banged on the table with his spoon, and everybody stopped talking and was very silent, except Roo who was just finishing a loud attack of hiccups and trying to look as if it was one of Rabbit's relations.

"This party," said Christopher Robin, "is a party because of what someone did, and we all know who it was, and it's his party, because of what he did, and I've got a present for him and here it is." Then he felt about a little and whispered, "Where is it?"

While he was looking, Eeyore coughed in an impressive way and began to speak.

"Friends," he said, "including oddments, it is a great pleasure, or perhaps I had better say it has been a pleasure so far, to see you at my party. What I did was nothing. Any of you—except Rabbit and Owl and Kanga—would have done the same. Oh, and Pooh. My remarks do not, of course, apply to Piglet and Roo, because they are too small. Any of you would have done the same. But it just happened to be Me. It was not, I need hardly say, with an idea of getting what Christopher Robin is looking for now" —and he put his front leg to his mouth and said in a loud whisper, "Try under the table"—"that I did what I did—but because I feel that we should all do what we can to help. I feel that we should all——"

"H—hup!" said Roo accidentally.

"Roo, dear!" said Kanga reproachfully.

"Was it me?" asked Roo, a little surprised.

"What's Eeyore talking about?" Piglet whispered to Pooh.

"I don't know," said Pooh rather dolefully.

"I thought this was *your* party."

"I thought it was *once*. But I suppose it isn't."

"I'd sooner it was yours than Eeyore's," said Piglet.

"So would I," said Pooh.

"H—hup!" said Roo again.

"AS—I—WAS—SAYING," said Eeyore loudly and sternly, "as I was saying when I was interrupted by various Loud Sounds, I feel that——"

"Here it is!" cried Christopher Robin excitedly. "Pass it down to silly old Pooh. It's for Pooh."

"For Pooh?" said Eeyore.

"Of course it is. The best bear in all the world."

"I might have known," said Eeyore. "After all, one can't complain. I have my friends. Somebody spoke to me only yesterday. And was it last week or the week before that Rabbit bumped into me and said 'Bother!' The Social Round. Always something going on."

Nobody was listening, for they were all saying "Open it, Pooh," "What is it, Pooh?" "I know what it is," "No, you don't" and other helpful remarks of this sort. And of course Pooh was opening it as quickly as ever he could, but without cutting the string, because you never know when a bit of string might be Useful. At last it was undone.

When Pooh saw what it was, he nearly fell down, he was so pleased. It was a Special Pencil Case. There were pencils in it marked "B" for Bear, and pencils marked "HB" for Helping Bear, and pencils marked "BB" for Brave Bear. There was a knife for sharpening the pencils, and india-rubber for rubbing out anything which you had spelt wrong, and a ruler for ruling lines for the words to walk on, and inches marked on the ruler in case you wanted to know how many inches anything was, and Blue Pencils and Red Pencils and Green Pencils for saying special things in blue and red and green. And all these lovely things were in little pockets of their own in a Special Case which shut with a click when you clicked it. And they were all for Pooh.

"Oh!" said Pooh.

"Oh, Pooh!" said everybody else except Eeyore.

"Thank-you," growled Pooh.

But Eeyore was saying to himself, "This writing business. Pencils and what-not. Over-rated, if you ask me. Silly stuff. Nothing in it."

Later on, when they had all said "Good-bye" and "Thank-you" to Christopher Robin, Pooh and Piglet walked home thoughtfully together in the golden evening, and for a long time they were silent.

"When you wake up in the morning, Pooh," said Piglet at last, "what's the first thing you say to yourself?"

"What's for breakfast?" said Pooh. "What do *you* say, Piglet?"

"I say, I wonder what's going to happen exciting *today*?" said Piglet.

Pooh nodded thoughtfully.

"It's the same thing," he said.

*   *   *

"And what did happen?" asked Christopher Robin.

"When?"

"Next morning."

"I don't know."

"Could you think and tell me and Pooh sometime?"

"If you wanted it very much."

"Pooh does," said Christopher Robin.

He gave a deep sigh, picked his bear up by the leg and walked off to the door, trailing Winnie-the-Pooh behind him. At the door he turned and said "Coming to see me have my bath?"

"I might," I said.

"Was Pooh's pencil case any better than mine?"

"It was just about the same," I said.

He nodded and went out . . . and in a moment I heard Winnie-the-Pooh—*bump, bump, bump*—going up the stairs behind him.

You gave me Christopher Robin, and then
   You breathed new life in Pooh.
Whatever of each has left my pen
   Goes homing back to you.
My book is ready, and comes to greet
   The mother it longs to see—
It would be my present to you, my sweet,
   If it weren't your gift to me.

THE HOUSE AT
POOH CORNER

Contradiction

AN INTRODUCTION is to introduce people, but Christopher Robin and his friends, who have already been introduced to you, are now going to say Good-bye. So this is the opposite. When we asked Pooh what the opposite of an Introduction was, he said "The what of a what?" which didn't help us as much as we had hoped, but luckily Owl kept his head and told us that the opposite of an Introduction, my dear Pooh, was a Contradiction; and, as he is very good at long words, I am sure that that's what it is.

Why we are having a Contradiction is because last week when Christopher Robin said to me, "What about that story you were going to tell me about what happened to Pooh when—" I happened to say very quickly, "What about nine times a hundred and seven?" And when we had done that one, we had one about cows going through a gate at two a minute, and there are three hundred in the field, so how many are left after an hour and a half? We find these very exciting, and when we have been excited quite enough, we curl up and go to sleep . . . and Pooh, sitting wakeful a little longer on his chair by our pillow, thinks Grand Thoughts to himself about Nothing, until he, too, closes his eyes and nods his head, and follows us on tip-toe into the Forest. There, still, we have magic adventures, more wonderful than any I have told you about; but now, when we wake up in the morning, they are gone before we can catch hold of them. How did the last one begin? "One day when Pooh was walking in the Forest, there were one hundred and seven cows on a gate. . . ." No, you see, we have lost it. It was the best, I think. Well, here are some of the other ones, all that we shall remember now. But, of course, it isn't really Good-bye, because the Forest will always be there . . . and anybody who is Friendly with Bears can find it.

A.A.M.

CHAPTER ONE

In Which

A House Is Built at Pooh Corner for Eeyore

ONE DAY when Pooh Bear had nothing else to do, he thought he would do something, so he went round to Piglet's house to see what Piglet was doing. It was still snowing as he stumped over the white forest track, and he expected to find Piglet warming his toes in front of his fire, but to his surprise he saw that the door was open, and the more he looked inside the more Piglet wasn't there.

"He's out," said Pooh sadly. "That's what it is. He's not in. I shall have to go a fast Thinking Walk by myself. Bother!"

But first he thought that he would knock very loudly just to make *quite* sure . . . and while he waited for Piglet not to answer, he jumped up and down to keep warm, and a hum came suddenly into his head, which seemed to him a Good Hum, such as is Hummed Hopefully to Others.

> The more it snows
>   (Tiddely pom),
> The more it goes
>   (Tiddely pom),
> The more it goes
>   (Tiddely pom),
>   On snowing.
> And nobody knows
>   (Tiddely pom),
> How cold my toes
>   (Tiddely pom),
> How cold my toes
>   (Tiddely pom),
>   Are growing.

"So what I'll do," said Pooh, "is I'll do this. I'll just go home first and see what the time is, and perhaps I'll put a muffler round my neck, and then I'll go and see Eeyore and sing it to him."

He hurried back to his own house; and his mind was so busy on the way with the hum that he was getting ready for Eeyore that, when he suddenly saw Piglet sitting in his best arm-chair, he could only stand there rubbing his head and wondering whose house he was in.

"Hallo, Piglet," he said. "I thought you were out."

"No," said Piglet, "it's you who were out, Pooh."

"So it was," said Pooh. "I knew one of us was."

He looked up at his clock, which had stopped at five minutes to eleven some weeks ago.

"Nearly eleven o'clock," said Pooh happily. "You're just in time for a little smackerel of something," and he put his head into the cupboard. "And then we'll go out, Piglet, and sing my song to Eeyore."

"Which song, Pooh?"

"The one we're going to sing to Eeyore," explained Pooh.

The clock was still saying five minutes to eleven when Pooh and Piglet set out on their way half an hour later. The wind had dropped, and the snow, tired of rushing round in circles trying to catch itself up, now fluttered gently down until it found a place on which to rest, and sometimes the place was Pooh's nose and sometimes it wasn't, and in a little while Piglet was wearing a white muffler round his neck and feeling more snowy behind the ears than he had ever felt before.

"Pooh," he said at last, and a little timidly, because he didn't want Pooh to think he was Giving In, "I was just wondering. How would it be if we went home now and *practised* your song, and then sang it to Eeyore to-morrow—or—or the next day, when we happen to see him."

"That's a very good idea, Piglet," said Pooh. "We'll practise it now as we go along. But it's no good going home to practise it, because it's a special Outdoor Song which Has To Be Sung In The Snow."

"Are you sure?" asked Piglet anxiously.

"Well, you'll see, Piglet, when you listen. Because this is how it begins. *The more it snows, tiddely pom——*"

"Tiddely what?" said Piglet.

"Pom," said Pooh. "I put that in to make it more hummy. *The more it goes, tiddely pom, the more——*"

"Didn't you say snows?"

"Yes, but that was *before*."

"Before the tiddely pom?"

"It was a *different* tiddely pom," said Pooh, feeling rather muddled now. "I'll sing it to you properly and then you'll see."

So he sang it again.

The more it
SNOWS-tiddely-pom,
The more it
GOES-tiddely-pom
The more it
GOES-tiddely-pom
On
Snowing.

And nobody
KNOWS-tiddely-pom,

> How cold my
> TOES-tiddely-pom
> How cold my
> TOES-tiddely-pom
> Are
> Growing.

He sang it like that, which is much the best way of singing it, and when he had finished, he waited for Piglet to say that, of all the Outdoor Hums for Snowy Weather he had ever heard, this was the best. And, after thinking the matter out carefully, Piglet said:

"Pooh," he said solemnly, "it isn't the *toes* so much as the *ears*."

By this time they were getting near Eeyore's Gloomy Place, which was where he lived, and as it was still very snowy behind Piglet's ears, and he was getting tired of it, they turned into a little pine wood, and sat down on the gate which led into it. They were out of the snow now, but it was very cold, and to keep themselves warm they sang Pooh's song right through six times, Piglet doing the tiddely-poms and Pooh doing the rest of it, and both of them thumping on the top of the gate with pieces of stick at the proper places. And in a little while they felt much warmer, and were able to talk again.

"I've been thinking," said Pooh, "and what I've been thinking is this. I've been thinking about Eeyore."

"What about Eeyore?"

"Well, poor Eeyore has nowhere to live."

"Nor he has," said Piglet.

"*You* have a house, Piglet, and I have a house, and they are very good houses. And Christopher Robin has a house, and Owl and Kanga and Rabbit have houses, and even Rabbit's friends and relations have houses or somethings, but poor Eeyore has nothing. So what I've been thinking is: Let's build him a house."

"That," said Piglet, "is a Grand Idea. Where shall we build it?"

"We will build it here," said Pooh, "just by this

wood, out of the wind, because this is where I thought of it. And we will call this Pooh Corner. And we will build an Eeyore House with sticks at Pooh Corner for Eeyore."

"There was a heap of sticks on the other side of the wood," said Piglet. "I saw them. Lots and lots. All piled up."

"Thank you, Piglet," said Pooh. "What you have just said will be a Great Help to us, and because of it I could call this place Poohanpiglet Corner if Pooh

Corner didn't sound better, which it does, being smaller and more like a corner. Come along."

So they got down off the gate and went around to the other side of the wood to fetch the sticks.

Christopher Robin had spent the morning indoors going to Africa and back, and he had just got off the boat and was wondering what it was like outside, when who should come knocking at the door but Eeyore.

"Hallo, Eeyore," said Christopher Robin, as he opened the door and came out. "How are *you*?"

"It's snowing still," said Eeyore gloomily.

"So it is."

"*And* freezing."

"Is it?"

"Yes," said Eeyore. "However," he said, brightening up a little, "we haven't had an earthquake lately."

"What's the matter, Eeyore?"

"Nothing, Christopher Robin. Nothing important. I suppose you haven't seen a house or whatnot anywhere about?"

"What sort of a house?"

"Just a house."

"Who lives there?"

"I do. At least I thought I did. But I suppose I don't. After all, we can't all have houses."

"But Eeyore, I didn't know. I always thought——"

"I don't know how it is, Christopher Robin, but what with all this snow and one thing and another, not to mention icicles and such-like, it isn't so Hot in my field about three o'clock in the morning as some people think it is. It isn't Close, if you know what I mean—not so as to be uncomfortable. It isn't Stuffy.

In fact, Christopher Robin," he went on in a loud whisper, "quite-between-ourselves-and-don't-tell-anybody, it's Cold."

"Oh, Eeyore!"

"And I said to myself: The others will be sorry if I'm getting myself all cold. They haven't got Brains, any of them, only grey fluff that's blown into their heads by mistake, and they don't Think, but if it goes on snowing for another six weeks or so, one of them will begin to say to himself: 'Eeyore can't be so very much too Hot about three o'clock in the morning.' And then it will Get About. And they'll be Sorry."

"Oh, Eeyore!" said Christopher Robin, feeling very sorry already.

"I don't mean you, Christopher Robin. You're different. So what it all comes to is that I built myself a house down by my little wood."

"Did you really? How exciting!"

"The really exciting part," said Eeyore in his most melancholy voice, "is that when I left it this morning it was there, and when I came back it wasn't. Not at all, very natural, and it was only Eeyore's house. But still I just wondered."

Christopher Robin didn't stop to wonder. He was already back in *his* house, putting on his waterproof hat, his waterproof boots and his waterproof macintosh as fast as he could.

"We'll go and look for it at once," he called out to Eeyore.

"Sometimes," said Eeyore, "when people have quite finished taking a person's house, there are one or two bits which they don't want and are rather glad for the person to take back, if you know what I mean. So I thought if we just went——"

"Come on," said Christopher Robin, and off they hurried, and in a very little time they got to the corner of the field by the side of the pine-wood, where Eeyore's house wasn't any longer.

"There!" said Eeyore. "Not a stick of it left! Of course, I've still got all this snow to do what I like with. One mustn't complain."

But Christopher Robin wasn't listening to Eeyore, he was listening to something else.

"Can't you hear it?" he asked.

"What is it? Somebody laughing?"

"Listen."

They both listened . . . and they heard a deep gruff voice saying in a singing voice that the more it snowed the more it went on snowing and a small high voice tiddely-pomming in between.

"It's Pooh," said Christopher Robin excitedly.

"Possibly," said Eeyore.

"*And* Piglet!" said Christopher Robin excitedly.

"Probably," said Eeyore. "What we *want* is a Trained Bloodhound."

The words of the song changed suddenly.

"*We've finished our HOUSE!*" sang the gruff voice.

"*Tiddely pom!*" sang the squeaky one.

"*It's a beautiful HOUSE. . . .*"

"*Tiddely pom. . . .*"

"*I wish it were MINE. . . .*"

"*Tiddely pom. . . .*"

"Pooh!" shouted Christopher Robin. . . .

The singers on the gate stopped suddenly.

"It's Christopher Robin!" said Pooh eagerly.

"He's round by the place where we got all those sticks from," said Piglet.

"Come on," said Pooh.

They climbed down their gate and hurried round the corner of the wood, Pooh making welcoming noises all the way.

"Why, here *is* Eeyore," said Pooh, when he had finished hugging Christopher Robin, and he nudged Piglet, and Piglet nudged him, and they thought to themselves what a lovely surprise they had got ready.

"Hallo, Eeyore."

"Same to you, Pooh Bear, and twice on Thursdays," said Eeyore gloomily.

Before Pooh could say: "Why Thursdays?" Christopher Robin began to explain the sad story of Eeyore's Lost House. And Pooh and Piglet listened, and their eyes seemed to get bigger and bigger.

"*Where* did you say it was?" asked Pooh.

"Just here," said Eeyore.

"Made of sticks?"

"Yes."

"Oh!" said Piglet.

"What?" said Eeyore.

"I just said 'Oh!'" said Piglet nervously. And so as

to seem quite at ease he hummed Tiddely-pom once or twice in a what-shall-we-do-now kind of way.

"You're sure it *was* a house?" said Pooh. "I mean, you're sure the house was just here?"

"Of course I am," said Eeyore. And he murmured to himself, "No brain at all some of them."

"Why, what's the matter, Pooh?" asked Christopher Robin.

"Well," said Pooh. . . . "The fact *is*," said Pooh. . . . "Well, the fact *is*," said Pooh. . . . "You see," said Pooh. . . . "It's like this," said Pooh, and something seemed to tell him that he wasn't explaining very well, and he nudged Piglet again.

"It's like this," said Piglet quickly. . . . "Only warmer," he added after deep thought.

"What's warmer?"

"The other side of the wood, where Eeyore's house is."

"*My* house?" said Eeyore. "My house was here."

"No," said Piglet firmly. "The other side of the wood."

"Because of being warmer," said Pooh.

"But I ought to *know*——"

"Come and look," said Piglet simply, and he led the way.

"There wouldn't be *two* houses," said Pooh. "Not so close together."

They came round the corner, and there was
Eeyore's house, looking as comfy as anything.

"There you are," said Piglet.

"Inside as well as outside," said Pooh proudly.

Eeyore went inside . . . and came out again.

"It's a remarkable thing," he said. "It *is* my house,
and I built it where I said I did, so the wind must have

blown it here. And the wind blew it right over the wood, and blew it down here, and here it is as good as ever. In fact, better in places."

"Much better," said Pooh and Piglet together.

"It just shows what can be done by taking a little trouble," said Eeyore. "Do you see, Pooh? Do you see, Piglet? Brains first and then Hard Work. Look at it! *That's* the way to build a house," said Eeyore proudly.

So they left him in it; and Christopher Robin went back to lunch with his friends Pooh and Piglet, and on the way they told him of the Awful Mistake they had made. And when he had finished laughing, they all sang the Outdoor Song for Snowy Weather the rest of the way home, Piglet, who was still not quite sure of his voice, putting in the tiddely-poms again.

"And I know it *seems* easy," said Piglet to himself, "but it isn't *every one* who could do it."

CHAPTER TWO

In Which

Tigger Comes to the Forest and Has Breakfast

WINNIE-THE-POOH woke up suddenly in the middle of the night and listened. Then he got out of bed, and lit his candle, and stumped across the room to see if anybody was trying to get into his honey-cupboard, and they weren't, so he stumped back again, blew out his candle, and got into bed. Then he heard the noise again.

"Is that you, Piglet?" he said.

But it wasn't.

"Come in, Christopher Robin," he said.

But Christopher Robin didn't.

"Tell me about it tomorrow, Eeyore," said Pooh sleepily.

But the noise went on.

"Worraworraworraworraworra," said Whatever-it-was, and Pooh found that he wasn't asleep after all.

"What can it be?" he thought. "There are lots of noises in the Forest, but this is a different one. It isn't a growl, and it isn't a purr, and it isn't a bark, and it isn't the noise-you-make-before-beginning-a-piece-of-poetry, but it's a noise of some kind, made by a strange animal. And he's making it outside my door. So I shall get up and ask him not to do it."

He got out of bed and opened his front door.

"Hallo!" said Pooh, in case there was anything out-side.

"Hallo!" said Whatever-it-was.

"Oh!" said Pooh. "Hallo!"

"Hallo!"

"Oh, *there* you are!" said Pooh. "Hallo!"

"Hallo!" said the Strange Animal, wondering how long this was going on.

Pooh was just going to say "Hallo!" for the fourth time when he thought that he wouldn't so he said: "Who is it?" instead.

"Me," said a voice.

"Oh!" said Pooh. "Well, come here."

So Whatever-it-was came here, and in the light of the candle he and Pooh looked at each other.

"I'm Pooh," said Pooh.

"I'm Tigger," said Tigger.

"Oh!" said Pooh, for he had never seen an animal like this before. "Does Christopher Robin know about you?"

"Of course he does," said Tigger.

"Well," said Pooh, "it's the middle of the night, which is a good time for going to sleep. And tomorrow morning we'll have some honey for breakfast. Do Tiggers like honey?"

"They like everything," said Tigger cheerfully.

"Then if they like going to sleep on the floor, I'll go back to bed," said Pooh, "and we'll do things in the morning. Good night." And he got back into bed and went fast asleep.

When he awoke in the morning, the first thing he saw was Tigger, sitting in front of the glass and looking at himself.

"Hallo!" said Pooh.

"Hallo!" said Tigger. "I've found somebody just like me. I thought I was the only one of them."

Pooh got out of bed, and began to explain what a looking-glass was, but just as he was getting to the interesting part, Tigger said:

"Excuse me a moment, but there's something climbing up your table," and with one loud *Worraworraworraworraworra* he jumped at the end of the tablecloth, pulled it to the ground, wrapped himself up in it three times, rolled to the other end of the room, and, after a terrible struggle, got his head into the daylight again, and said cheerfully: "Have I won?"

"That's my tablecloth," said Pooh, as he began to unwind Tigger.

"I wondered what it was," said Tigger.

"It goes on the table and you put things on it."

"Then why did it try to bite me when I wasn't looking?"

"I don't *think* it did," said Pooh.

"It tried," said Tigger, "but I was too quick for it."

Pooh put the cloth back on the table, and he put a large honey-pot on the cloth, and they sat down to breakfast. And as soon as they sat down, Tigger took a large mouthful of honey . . . and he looked up at the ceiling with his head on one side, and made ex-

ploring noises with his tongue and considering noises, and what-have-we-got-*here* noises . . . and then he said in a very decided voice:

"Tiggers don't like honey."

"Oh!" said Pooh, and tried to make it sound Sad and Regretful. "I thought they liked everything."

"Everything except honey," said Tigger.

Pooh felt rather pleased about this, and said that, as soon as he had finished his own breakfast, he would take Tigger round to Piglet's house, and Tigger could try some of Piglet's haycorns.

"Thank you, Pooh," said Tigger, "because haycorns is really what Tiggers like best."

So after breakfast they went round to see Piglet, and Pooh explained as they went that Piglet was a Very Small Animal who didn't like bouncing, and asked Tigger not to be too Bouncy just at first. And Tigger, who had been hiding behind trees and jumping out on Pooh's shadow when it wasn't looking, said that Tiggers were only bouncy before breakfast, and that as soon as they had had a few haycorns they became Quiet and Refined. So by and by they knocked at the door of Piglet's house.

"Hallo, Pooh," said Piglet.

"Hallo, Piglet. This is Tigger."

"Oh, is it?" said Piglet, and he edged round to the other side of the table. "I thought Tiggers were smaller than that."

"Not the big ones," said Tigger.

"They like haycorns," said Pooh, "so that's what we've come for, because poor Tigger hasn't had any breakfast yet."

Piglet pushed the bowl of haycorns towards Tigger, and said: "Help yourself," and then he got close up to Pooh and felt much braver, and said, "So you're Tigger? Well, well!" in a careless sort of voice. But Tigger said nothing because his mouth was full of haycorns. . . .

After a long munching noise he said:

"Ee-ers o i a-ors."

And when Pooh and Piglet said "What?" he said "Skoos ee," and went outside for a moment.

When he came back he said firmly:

"Tiggers don't like haycorns."

"But you said they liked everything except honey," said Pooh.

"Everything except honey and haycorns," explained Tigger.

When he heard this Pooh said, "Oh, I see!" and Piglet, who was rather glad that Tiggers didn't like haycorns, said, "What about thistles?"

"Thistles," said Tigger, "is what Tiggers like best."

"Then let's go along and see Eeyore," said Piglet.

So the three of them went; and after they had walked and walked and walked, they came to the part of the Forest where Eeyore was.

"Hallo, Eeyore!" said Pooh. "This is Tigger."

"What is?" said Eeyore.

"This," explained Pooh and Piglet together, and Tigger smiled his happiest smile and said nothing.

THE COMPLETE TALES OF POOH

Eeyore walked all round Tigger one way, and then turned and walked all round him the other way.

"What did you say it was?" he asked.

"Tigger."

"Ah!" said Eeyore.

"He's just come," explained Piglet.

"Ah!" said Eeyore again.

He thought for a long time and then said:

"When is he going?"

Pooh explained to Eeyore that Tigger was a great friend of Christopher Robin's, who had come to stay in the Forest, and Piglet explained to Tigger that he mustn't mind what Eeyore said because he was *always* gloomy; and Eeyore explained to Piglet that, on the contrary, he was feeling particularly cheerful this morning; and Tigger explained to anybody who was listening that he hadn't had any breakfast yet.

"I knew there was something," said Pooh. "Tiggers always eat thistles, so that was why we came to see you, Eeyore."

"Don't mention it, Pooh."

"Oh, Eeyore, I didn't mean that I didn't *want* to see you——"

"Quite—quite. But your new stripy friend—naturally, he wants his breakfast. What did you say his name was?"

"Tigger."

"Then come this way, Tigger."

Eeyore led the way to the most thistly-looking patch of thistles that ever was, and waved a hoof at it.

"A little patch I was keeping for my birthday," he said; "but, after all, what are birthdays? Here today and gone tomorrow. Help yourself, Tigger."

Tigger thanked him and looked a little anxiously at Pooh.

"Are these really thistles?" he whispered.

"Yes," said Pooh.

"What Tiggers like best?"

"That's right," said Pooh.

"I see," said Tigger.

So he took a large mouthful, and he gave a large crunch.

"*Ow!*" said Tigger.

He sat down and put his paw in his mouth.

"What's the matter?" asked Pooh.

"*Hot!*" mumbled Tigger.

"Your friend," said Eeyore, "appears to have bitten on a bee."

Pooh's friend stopped shaking his head to get the prickles out, and explained that Tiggers didn't like thistles.

"Then why bend a perfectly good one?" asked Eeyore.

"But you said," began Pooh—"you *said* that Tiggers like everything except honey and haycorns."

"*And* thistles," said Tigger, who was now running round in circles with his tongue hanging out.

Pooh looked at him sadly.

"What are we going to do?" he asked Piglet.

Piglet knew the answer to that, and he said at once that they must go and see Christopher Robin.

"You'll find him with Kanga," said Eeyore. He came close to Pooh, and said in a loud whisper:

"*Could* you ask your friend to do his exercises somewhere else? I shall be having lunch directly, and don't want it bounced on just before I begin. A trifling matter, and fussy of me, but we all have our little ways."

Pooh nodded solemnly and called to Tigger.

"Come along and we'll go and see Kanga. She's sure to have lots of breakfast for you."

Tigger finished his last circle and came up to Pooh and Piglet.

"Hot!" he explained with a large and friendly smile. "Come on!" and he rushed off.

Pooh and Piglet walked slowly after him. And as they walked Piglet said nothing, because he couldn't think of anything, and Pooh said nothing, because he was thinking of a poem. And when he had thought of it he began:

> What shall we do about
>   poor little Tigger?
> If he never eats nothing he'll
>   never get bigger.
> He doesn't like honey and haycorns
>   and thistles
> Because of the taste and because of
>   the bristles.
> And all the good things which an
>   animal likes
> Have the wrong sort of swallow or
>   too many spikes.

"He's quite big enough anyhow," said Piglet.

"He isn't *really* very big."

"Well, he *seems* so."

Pooh was thoughtful when he heard this, and then he murmured to himself:

> But whatever his weight in pounds,
>   shillings, and ounces,
> He always seems bigger
>   because of his bounces.

"And that's the whole poem," he said. "Do you like it, Piglet?"

"All except the shillings," said Piglet. "I don't think they ought to be there."

"They wanted to come in after the pounds," explained Pooh, "so I let them. It is the best way to write poetry, letting things come."

"Oh, I didn't know," said Piglet.

Tigger had been bouncing in front of them all this time, turning round every now and then to ask, "Is this the way?"—and now at last they came in sight of Kanga's house, and there was Christopher Robin. Tigger rushed up to him.

"Oh, there you are, Tigger!" said Christopher Robin. "I knew you'd be somewhere."

"I've been finding things in the Forest," said Tigger importantly. "I've found a pooh and a piglet and an eeyore, but I can't find any breakfast."

Pooh and Piglet came up and hugged Christopher Robin, and explained what had been happening.

"Don't *you* know what Tiggers like?" asked Pooh.

"I expect if I thought very hard I should," said Christopher Robin, "but I *thought* Tigger knew."

"I do," said Tigger. "Everything there is in the world except honey and haycorns and—what were those hot things called?"

"Thistles."

"Yes, and those."

"Oh, well then, Kanga can give you some break-fast."

So they went into Kanga's house, and when Roo had said, "Hallo, Pooh" and "Hallo, Piglet" once, and "Hallo, Tigger" twice, because he had never said it before and it sounded funny, they told Kanga what they wanted, and Kanga said very kindly, "Well, look in my cupboard, Tigger dear, and see what you'd like." Because she knew at once that, however big Tigger seemed to be, he wanted as much kindness as Roo.

"Shall I look, too?" said Pooh, who was beginning to feel a little eleven o'clockish. And he found a small tin of condensed milk, and something seemed to tell him that Tiggers didn't like this, so he took it into a corner by itself, and went with it to see that nobody interrupted it.

But the more Tigger put his nose into this and his paw into that, the more things he found which Tiggers didn't like. And when he had found everything in the cupboard, and couldn't eat any of it, he said to Kanga, "What happens now?"

But Kanga and Christopher Robin and Piglet were all standing round Roo, watching him have his Extract of Malt. And Roo was saying, "Must I?" and Kanga was saying "Now, Roo dear, you remember what you promised."

"What is it?" whispered Tigger to Piglet.

"His Strengthening Medicine," said Piglet. "He hates it."

So Tigger came closer, and he leant over the back of Roo's chair, and suddenly he put out his tongue, and took one large golollop, and, with a sudden jump of surprise, Kanga said, "Oh!" and then clutched at the spoon again just as it was disappearing, and pulled it safely back out of Tigger's mouth. But the Extract of Malt had gone.

"Tigger *dear*!" said Kanga.

"He's taken my medicine, he's taken my medicine, he's taken my medicine!" sang Roo happily, thinking it was a tremendous joke.

Then Tigger looked up at the ceiling, and closed his eyes, and his tongue went round and round his chops, in case he had left any outside, and a peaceful smile came over his face as he said, "So *that's* what Tiggers like!"

Which explains why he always lived at Kanga's house afterwards, and had Extract of Malt for breakfast, dinner, and tea. And sometimes, when Kanga thought he wanted strengthening, he had a spoonful or two of Roo's breakfast after meals as medicine.

"But *I* think," said Piglet to Pooh, "that he's been strengthened quite enough."

CHAPTER THREE

In Which

A Search Is Organdized, and Piglet Nearly Meets the Heffalump Again

POOH WAS SITTING in his house one day, counting his pots of honey, when there came a knock on the door.

"Fourteen," said Pooh. "Come in. Fourteen. Or was it fifteen? Bother. That's muddled me."

"Hallo, Pooh," said Rabbit.

"Hallo, Rabbit. Fourteen, wasn't it?"

"What was?"

"My pots of honey what I was counting."

"Fourteen, that's right."

"Are you sure?"

"No," said Rabbit. "Does it matter?"

"I just like to know," said Pooh humbly. "So as I can say to myself: 'I've got fourteen pots of honey left.' Or fifteen, as the case may be. It's sort of comforting."

"Well, let's call it sixteen," said Rabbit. "What I came to say was: Have you seen Small anywhere about?"

"I don't think so," said Pooh. And then, after thinking a little more, he said: "Who is Small?"

"One of my friends-and-relations," said Rabbit carelessly.

This didn't help Pooh much, because Rabbit had so many friends-and-relations, and of such different sorts and sizes, that he didn't know whether he ought to be looking for Small at the top of an oak-tree or in the petal of a buttercup.

"I haven't seen anybody today," said Pooh, "not so as to say 'Hallo, Small,' to. Did you want him for anything?"

"*I don't* want him," said Rabbit. "But it's always useful to know where a friend-and-relation *is*, whether you want him or whether you don't."

"Oh, I see," said Pooh. "Is he lost?"

"Well," said Rabbit, "nobody has seen him for a long time, so I suppose he is. Anyhow," he went on importantly, "I promised Christopher Robin I'd Organize a Search for him, so come on."

Pooh said good-bye affectionately to his fourteen pots of honey, and hoped they were fifteen; and he and Rabbit went out into the Forest.

"Now," said Rabbit, "this is a Search, and I've Organized it——"

"Done what to it?" said Pooh.

"Organized it. Which means—well, it's what you do to a Search, when you don't all look in the same place at once. So I want *you*, Pooh, to search by the Six Pine Trees first, and then work your way towards Owl's House, and look out for me there. Do you see?"

"No," said Pooh. "What——"

"Then I'll see you at Owl's House in about an hour's time."

"Is Piglet organdized too?"

"We all are," said Rabbit, and off he went.

As soon as Rabbit was out of sight, Pooh remembered that he had forgotten to ask who Small was, and whether he was the sort of friend-and-relation who settled on one's nose, or the sort who got trodden on by mistake, and as it was Too Late Now, he thought he would begin the Hunt by looking for Piglet, and asking him what they were looking for before he looked for it.

"And it's no good looking at the Six Pine Trees for Piglet," said Pooh to himself, "because he's been organdized in a special place of his own. So I shall have to look for the Special Place first. I wonder where it is." And he wrote it down in his head like this:

Order of Looking for Things

1. Special Place.   (*To find Piglet.*)
2. Piglet.   (*To find who Small is.*)
3. Small.   (*To find Small.*)
4. Rabbit.   (*To tell him I've found Small.*)
5. Small Again.   (*To tell him I've found Rabbit.*)

"Which makes it look like a bothering sort of day," thought Pooh, as he stumped along.

The next moment the day became very bothering indeed, because Pooh was so busy not looking where he was going that he stepped on a piece of the Forest which had been left out by mistake; and he only just had time to think to himself: "I'm flying. What Owl does. I wonder how you stop——" when he stopped.

Bump!

"Ow!" squeaked something.

"That's funny," thought Pooh. "I said 'Ow!' without really oo'ing."

"Help!" said a small, high voice.

"That's me again," thought Pooh. "I've had an Accident, and fallen down a well, and my voice has gone all squeaky and works before I'm ready for it, because I've done something to myself inside, Bother!"

"Help—help!"

"There you are! I say things when I'm not trying. So it must be a very bad Accident." And then he thought that perhaps when he did try to say things he wouldn't be able to; so, to make sure, he said loudly: "A Very Bad Accident to Pooh Bear."

"Pooh!" squeaked the voice.

"It's Piglet!" cried Pooh eagerly. "Where are you?"

"Underneath," said Piglet in an underneath sort of way.

"Underneath what?"

"You," squeaked Piglet. "Get up!"

"Oh!" said Pooh, and scrambled up as quickly as he could. "Did I fall on you, Piglet?"

"You fell on me," said Piglet, feeling himself all over.

"I didn't mean to," said Pooh sorrowfully.

"I didn't mean to be underneath," said Piglet sadly. "But I'm all right now, Pooh, and I *am* so glad it was you."

"What's happened?" said Pooh. "Where are we?"

"I think we're in a sort of Pit. I was walking along, looking for somebody, and then suddenly I wasn't any more, and just when I got up to see where I was, something fell on me. And it was you."

"So it was," said Pooh.

"Yes," said Piglet. "Pooh," he went on nervously, and came a little closer, "do you think we're in a trap?"

Pooh hadn't thought about it at all, but now he nodded. For suddenly he remembered how he and Piglet had once made a Pooh Trap for Heffalumps, and he guessed what had happened. He and Piglet had fallen into a Heffalump Trap for Poohs! That was what it was.

"What happens when the Heffalump comes?" asked Piglet tremblingly, when he had heard the news.

"Perhaps he won't notice *you*, Piglet," said Pooh encouragingly, "because you're a Very Small Animal."

"But he'll notice *you*, Pooh."

"He'll notice *me*, and I shall notice *him*," said Pooh, thinking it out. "We'll notice each other for a long time, and then he'll say: 'Ho-*ho*!'"

Piglet shivered a little at the thought of that "Ho-*ho*!" and his ears began to twitch.

"W-what will *you* say?" he asked.

Pooh tried to think of something he would say, but the more he thought, the more he felt that there *is* no real answer to "Ho-*ho*!" said by a Heffalump in the sort of voice this Heffalump was going to say it in.

"I shan't say anything," said Pooh at last. "I shall just hum to myself, as if I was waiting for something."

"Then perhaps he'll say, 'Ho-*ho*!' again?" suggested Piglet anxiously.

"He will," said Pooh.

Piglet's ears twitched so quickly that he had to lean them against the side of the Trap to keep them quiet.

"He will say it again," said Pooh, "and I shall go on humming. And that will Upset him. Because when you say 'Ho-*ho*' twice, in a gloating sort of way, and the other person only hums, you suddenly find, just as you begin to say it the third time—that—well, you find——"

"What?"

"That it isn't," said Pooh.

"Isn't what?"

Pooh knew what he meant, but, being a Bear of Very Little Brain, couldn't think of the words.

"Well, it just isn't," he said again.

"You mean it isn't ho-*ho*-ish any more?" said Piglet hopefully.

Pooh looked at him admiringly and said that that was what he meant—if you went on humming all the time, because you couldn't go on saying "Ho-*ho*!" for ever.

"But he'll say something else," said Piglet.

"That's just it. He'll say: 'What's all this?' And then

I shall say—and this is a very good idea, Piglet, which I've just thought of —*I* shall say: 'It's a trap for a Heffalump which I've made, and I'm waiting for the Heffalump to fall in.' And I shall go on humming. That will Unsettle him."

"Pooh!" cried Piglet, and now it was *his* turn to be the admiring one. "You've saved us!"

"Have I?" said Pooh, not feeling quite sure.

But Piglet was quite sure; and his mind ran on, and he saw Pooh and the Heffalump talking to each other, and he thought suddenly, and a little sadly, that it *would* have been rather nice if it had been Piglet and the Heffalump talking so grandly to each other, and not Pooh, much as he loved Pooh; because he really had more brain than Pooh, and the conversation would go better if he and not Pooh were doing one side of it, and it would be comforting afterwards in the evenings to look back on the day when he answered a Heffalump back as bravely as if the Heffalump wasn't there. It seemed so easy now. He knew just what he would say:

HEFFALUMP *(gloatingly):* "Ho-*ho*!"

PIGLET *(carelessly):* "Tra-la-la, tra-la-la."

HEFFALUMP *(surprised, and not quite so sure of himself):* "Ho-*ho*!"

PIGLET *(more carelessly still):* "Tiddle-um-tum, tiddle-um-tum."

HEFFALUMP *(beginning to say Ho-ho and turning it awkwardly into a cough):* "H'r'm! What's all this?"

PIGLET *(surprised):* "Hullo! This is a trap I've made, and I'm waiting for a Heffalump to fall into it."

HEFFALUMP *(greatly disappointed):* "Oh!" *(after a long silence):* "Are you sure?"

PIGLET: "Yes."

HEFFALUMP: "Oh!" *(nervously):* "I—I thought it was a trap *I'd* made to catch Piglets."

PIGLET *(surprised):* "Oh, no!"

HEFFALUMP: "Oh!" *(apologetically):* "I—I must have got it wrong, then."

PIGLET: "I'm afraid so." *(politely):* "I'm sorry." *(He goes on humming.)*

HEFFALUMP: "Well—well—I—well. I suppose I'd better be getting back?"

PIGLET *(looking up carelessly):* "Must you? Well, if you see Christopher Robin anywhere, you might tell him I want him."

HEFFALUMP *(eager to please):* "Certainly! Certainly!" *(He hurries off.)*

POOH *(who wasn't going to be there, but we find we can't do without him):* "Oh, Piglet, how brave and clever you are!"

PIGLET *(modestly):* "Not at all, Pooh." *(And then, when Christopher Robin comes, Pooh can tell him all about it.)*

While Piglet was dreaming this happy dream, and Pooh was wondering again whether it was fourteen or fifteen, the Search for Small was still going on all over the Forest. Small's real name was Very Small Beetle, but he was called Small for short, when he was spoken to at all, which hardly ever happened except when somebody said: "*Really*, Small!" He had been staying with Christopher Robin for a few seconds, and he started round a gorse-bush for exercise, but instead of coming back the other way, as expected, he hadn't, so nobody knew where he was.

"I expect he's just gone home," said Christopher Robin to Rabbit.

"Did he say Good-bye-and-thank-you-for-a-nice-time?" said Rabbit.

"He'd only just said how-do-you-do," said Christopher Robin.

"Ha!" said Rabbit. After thinking a little, he went on: "Has he written a letter saying how much he enjoyed himself, and how sorry he was he had to go so suddenly?"

Christopher Robin didn't think he had.

"Ha!" said Rabbit again, and looked very important. "This is Serious. He is Lost. We must begin the Search at once."

Christopher Robin, who was thinking of something else, said: "Where's Pooh?"—but Rabbit had gone. So he went into his house and drew a picture of Pooh going a long walk at about seven o'clock in the morning, and then he climbed to the top of his tree and climbed down again, and then he wondered what Pooh was doing, and went across the Forest to see.

It was not long before he came to the Gravel Pit, and he looked down, and there were Pooh and Piglet, with their backs to him, dreaming happily.

"Ho-*ho*!" said Christopher Robin loudly and suddenly.

Piglet jumped six inches in the air with Surprise and Anxiety, but Pooh went on dreaming.

"It's the Heffalump!" thought Piglet nervously. "Now, then!" He hummed in his throat a little, so that none of the words should stick, and then, in the

most delightfully easy way, he said: "Tra-la-la, tra-la-la," as if he had just thought of it. But he didn't look round, because if you look round and see a Very Fierce Heffalump looking down at you, sometimes you forget what you were going to say. "Rum-tum-tum-tiddle-um," said Christopher Robin in a voice like Pooh's. Because Pooh had once invented a song which went:

> Tra-la-la, tra-la-la,
> Tra-la-la, tra-la-la,
> Rum-tum-tum-tiddle-um.

So whenever Christopher Robin sings it, he always sings it in a Pooh-voice, which seems to suit it better.

"He's said the wrong thing," thought Piglet anxiously. "He ought to have said, 'Ho-*ho*!' again. Perhaps I had better say it for him." And, as fiercely as he could, Piglet said: "Ho-*ho*!"

"How *did* you get there, Piglet?" said Christopher Robin in his ordinary voice.

"This is Terrible," thought Piglet. "First he talks in Pooh's voice, and then he talks in Christopher Robin's voice, and he's doing it so as to Unsettle me." And being now Completely Unsettled, he said very quickly and squeakily: "This is a trap for Poohs, and I'm waiting to fall in it, ho-*ho*, what's all this, and then I say ho-*ho* again."

"*What?*" said Christopher Robin.

"A trap for ho-ho's," said Piglet huskily. "I've just made it, and I'm waiting for the ho-ho to come-come."

How long Piglet would have gone on like this I don't know, but at that moment Pooh woke up suddenly and decided that it was sixteen. So he got up; and as he turned his head so as to soothe himself in that awkward place in the middle of the back where something was tickling him, he saw Christopher Robin.

"Hallo!" he shouted joyfully.

"Hallo, Pooh."

Piglet looked up, and looked away again. And he

felt so Foolish and Uncomfortable that he had almost decided to run away to Sea and be a Sailor, when suddenly he saw something.

"Pooh!" he cried. "There's something climbing up your back."

"I thought there was," said Pooh.

"It's Small!" cried Piglet.

"Oh, *that's* who it is, is it?" said Pooh.

"Christopher Robin, I've found Small!" cried Piglet.

"Well done, Piglet," said Christopher Robin.

And at these encouraging words Piglet felt quite happy again, and decided not to be a Sailor after all. So when Christopher Robin had helped them out of the Gravel Pit, they all went off together hand-in-hand.

And two days later Rabbit happened to meet Eeyore in the Forest.

"Hallo, Eeyore," he said, "what are *you* looking for?"

"Small, of course," said Eeyore. "Haven't you any brain?"

"Oh, but didn't I tell you?" said Rabbit. "Small was found two days ago."

There was a moment's silence.

"Ha-ha," said Eeyore bitterly. "Merriment and what-not. Don't apologize. It's just what *would* happen."

CHAPTER FOUR

In Which

It Is Shown That Tiggers Don't Climb Trees

ONE DAY when Pooh was thinking, he thought he would go and see Eeyore, because he hadn't seen him since yesterday. And as he walked through the heather, singing to himself, he suddenly remembered that he hadn't seen Owl since the day before yesterday, so he thought that he would just look in at the Hundred Acre Wood on the way and see if Owl was at home.

Well, he went on singing, until he came to the part of the stream where the stepping-stones were, and when he was in the middle of the third stone he began to wonder how Kanga and Roo and Tigger were getting on, because they all lived together in a different part of the Forest. And he thought, "I haven't seen Roo for a long time, and if I don't see him today it will be a still longer time." So he sat down on the stone in the middle of the stream, and sang another verse of his song, while he wondered what to do.

The other verse of the song was like this:

> I could spend a happy morning
>   Seeing Roo,
> I could spend a happy morning
>   Being Pooh.
> For it doesn't seem to matter,
> If I don't get any fatter
> (And I *don't* get any fatter),
>   What I do.

The sun was so delightfully warm, and the stone, which had been sitting in it for a long time, was so warm, too, that Pooh had almost decided to go on being Pooh in the middle of the stream for the rest of the morning, when he remembered Rabbit.

"Rabbit," said Pooh to himself. "I *like* talking to Rabbit. He talks about sensible things. He doesn't use long, difficult words, like Owl. He uses short, easy words, like 'What about lunch?' and 'Help yourself, Pooh.' I suppose *really*, I ought to go and see Rabbit."

Which made him think of another verse:

> Oh, I like his way of talking,
> Yes, I do.
> It's the nicest way of talking
> Just for two.
> And a Help-yourself with Rabbit
> Though it may become a habit,
> Is a *pleasant* sort of habit
> For a Pooh.

So when he had sung this, he got up off his stone, walked back across the stream, and set off for Rabbit's house.

But he hadn't got far before he began to say to himself:

"Yes, but suppose Rabbit is out?"

"Or suppose I get stuck in his front door again, coming out, as I did once when his front door wasn't big enough?"

"Because I *know* I'm not getting fatter, but his front door may be getting thinner."

"So wouldn't it be better if——"

And all the time he was saying things like this he was going more and more westerly, without thinking . . . until suddenly he found himself at his own front door again.

And it was eleven o'clock.

Which was Time-for-a-little-something. . . .

Half an hour later he was doing what he had always really meant to do, he was stumping off to Piglet's house. And as he walked, he wiped his mouth with the back of his paw, and sang rather a fluffy song through the fur. It went like this:

> I could spend a happy morning
>   Seeing Piglet.
> And I couldn't spend a happy morning
>   Not seeing Piglet.
> And it doesn't seem to matter
> If I don't see Owl and Eeyore
>   (or any of the others),
> And I'm not going to see Owl or Eeyore
>   (or any of the others)
>   Or Christopher Robin.

Written down, like this, it doesn't seem a very good song, but coming through pale fawn fluff at about half-past eleven on a very sunny morning, it seemed to Pooh to be one of the best songs he had ever sung. So he went on singing it.

Piglet was busy digging a small hole in the ground outside his house.

"Hallo, Piglet," said Pooh.

"Hallo, Pooh," said Piglet, giving a jump of surprise. "I knew it was you."

"So did I," said Pooh. "What are you doing?"

"I'm planting a haycorn, Pooh, so that it can grow up into an oak-tree, and have lots of haycorns just outside the front door instead of having to walk miles and miles, do you see, Pooh?"

"Supposing it doesn't?" said Pooh.

"It will, because Christopher Robin says it will, so that's why I'm planting it."

"Well," said Pooh, "if I plant a honeycomb outside my house, then it will grow up into a beehive."

Piglet wasn't quite sure about this.

"Or a *piece* of a honeycomb," said Pooh, "so as not to waste too much. Only then I might only get a piece of a beehive, and it might be the wrong piece, where the bees were buzzing and not hunnying. Bother."

Piglet agreed that that would be rather bothering.

"Besides, Pooh, it's a very difficult thing, planting unless you know how to do it," he said; and he put the acorn in the hole he had made, and covered it up with earth,

and jumped on it.

"I do know," said Pooh, "because Christopher Robin gave me a mastershalum seed, and I planted it, and I'm going to have mastershalums all over the front door."

"I thought they were called nasturtiums," said Piglet timidly, as he went on jumping.

"No," said Pooh. "Not these. These are called mastershalums."

When Piglet had finished jumping, he wiped his paws on his front, and said, "What shall we do now?" and Pooh said, "Let's go and see Kanga and Roo and Tigger," and Piglet said, "Y-yes. L-let's"—because he was still a little anxious about Tigger, who was a Very Bouncy Animal, with a way of saying How-do-you-do, which always left your ears full of sand, even after Kanga had said, "Gently, Tigger dear," and had helped you up again. So they set off for Kanga's house.

Now it happened that Kanga had felt rather motherly that morning, and Wanting to Count Things—like Roo's vests, and how many pieces of soap there were left, and the two clean spots in Tigger's feeder; so she had sent them out with a packet of watercress sandwiches for Roo and a packet of extract-of-malt sandwiches for Tigger, to have a nice long morning in the Forest not getting into mischief. And off they had gone.

And as they went, Tigger told Roo (who wanted to know) all about the things that Tiggers could do.

"Can they fly?" asked Roo.

"Yes," said Tigger, "they're very good flyers, Tiggers are. Stornry good flyers."

"Oo!" said Roo. "Can they fly as well as Owl?"

"Yes," said Tigger. "Only they don't want to."

"Why don't they want to?"

"Well, they just don't like it, somehow."

Roo couldn't understand this, because he thought it would be lovely to be able to fly, but Tigger said it was difficult to explain to anybody who wasn't a Tigger himself.

"Well," said Roo, "can they jump as far as Kangas?"

"Yes," said Tigger. "When they want to."

"I *love* jumping," said Roo. "Let's see who can jump farthest, you or me."

"*I* can," said Tigger. "But we mustn't stop now, or we shall be late."

"Late for what?"

"For whatever we want to be in time for," said Tigger, hurrying on.

In a little while they came to the Six Pine Trees.

"I can swim," said Roo. "I fell into the river, and I swimmed. Can Tiggers swim?"

"Of course they can. Tiggers can do everything."

"Can they climb trees better than Pooh?" asked Roo, stopping under the tallest Pine Tree, and looking up at it.

"Climbing trees is what they do best," said Tigger. "Much better than Poohs."

"Could they climb this one?"

"They're always climbing trees like that," said Tigger. "Up and down all day."

"Oo, Tigger, are they *really*?"

"I'll show you," said Tigger bravely, "and you can sit on my back and watch me." For of all the things which he had said Tiggers could do, the only one he felt really certain about suddenly was climbing trees.

"Oo, Tigger, oo, Tigger, oo, Tigger!" squeaked Roo excitedly.

So he sat on Tigger's back and up they went.

And for the first ten feet Tigger said happily to himself, "Up we go!"

And for the next ten feet he said:

"I always *said* Tiggers could climb trees."

And for the next ten feet he said:

"Not that it's easy, mind you."

And for the next ten feet he said:

"Of course, there's the coming-down too. Back-wards."

And then he said:

"Which will be difficult . . ."

"Unless one fell . . ."

"When it would be . . ."

"EASY."

And at the word "easy" the branch he was standing on broke suddenly, and he just managed to clutch at the one above him as he felt himself going . . . and then slowly he got his chin over it . . . and then one back paw . . . and then the other . . . until at last he was sitting on it, breathing very quickly, and wishing that he had gone in for swimming instead.

Roo climbed off, and sat down next to him.

"Oo, Tigger," he said excitedly, "are we at the top?"

"No," said Tigger.

"Are we going to the top?"

"No," said Tigger.

"Oh," said Roo rather sadly. And then he went on hopefully: "That was a lovely bit just now, when you pretended we were going to fall-bump-to-the-bottom, and we didn't. Will you do that bit again?"

"NO," said Tigger.

Roo was silent for a little while, and then he said, "Shall we eat our sandwiches, Tigger?" And Tigger said, "Yes, where are they?" And Roo said, "At the bottom of the tree." And Tigger said, "I don't think we'd better eat them just yet." So they didn't.

By and by Pooh and Piglet came along. Pooh was telling Piglet in a singing voice that it didn't seem to matter, if he didn't get any fatter, and he didn't *think* he was getting any fatter, what he did; and Piglet was wondering how long it would be before his haycorn came up.

"Look, Pooh!" said Piglet suddenly. "There's something in one of the Pine Trees."

"So there is!" said Pooh, looking up wonderingly. "There's an Animal."

Piglet took Pooh's arm, in case Pooh was frightened.

"Is it One of the Fiercer Animals?" he said, looking the other way.

Pooh nodded.

"It's a Jagular," he said.

"What do Jagulars do?" asked Piglet, hoping that they wouldn't.

"They hide in the branches of trees, and drop on you as you go underneath," said Pooh. "Christopher Robin told me."

"Perhaps we better hadn't go underneath, Pooh. In case he dropped and hurt himself."

"They don't hurt themselves," said Pooh. "They're such very good droppers."

Piglet still felt that to be underneath a Very Good Dropper would be a Mistake, and he was just going to hurry back for something which he had forgotten when the Jagular called out to them.

"Help! Help!" it called.

"That's what Jagulars always do," said Pooh, much

interested. "They call 'Help! Help!' and then when you look up, they drop on you."

"I'm looking *down*," cried Piglet loudly, so as the Jagular shouldn't do the wrong thing by accident.

Something very excited next to the Jagular heard him, and squeaked:

"Pooh and Piglet! Pooh and Piglet!"

All of a sudden Piglet felt that it was a much nicer day than he had thought it was. All warm and sunny——

"Pooh!" he cried. "I believe it's Tigger and Roo!"

"So it is," said Pooh. "I thought it was a Jagular and another Jagular."

"Hallo, Roo!" called Piglet. "What are you doing?"

"We can't get down, we can't get down!" cried Roo. "Isn't it fun? Pooh, isn't it fun, Tigger and I are living in a tree, like Owl, and we're going to stay here for ever and ever. I can see Piglet's house. Piglet, I can see your house from here. Aren't we high? Is Owl's house as high up as this?"

"How did you get there, Roo?" asked Piglet.

"On Tigger's back! And Tiggers can't climb downwards, because their tails get in the way, only upwards, and Tigger forgot about that when we started, and he's only just remembered. So we've got to stay here for ever and ever—unless we go higher. What did you say, Tigger? Oh, Tigger says if we go higher we shan't be able to see Piglet's house so well, so we're going to stop here."

"Piglet," said Pooh solemnly, when he had heard all this, "what shall we do?" And he began to eat Tigger's sandwiches.

"Are they stuck?" asked Piglet anxiously.

Pooh nodded.

"Couldn't you climb up to them?"

"I might, Piglet, and I might bring Roo down on my back, but I couldn't bring Tigger down. So we must think of something else." And in a thoughtful way he began to eat Roo's sandwiches, too.

*   *   *

Whether he would have thought of anything before he had finished the last sandwich, I don't know, but he had just got to the last but one when there was a crackling in the bracken, and Christopher Robin and Eeyore came strolling along together.

"I shouldn't be surprised if it hailed a good deal tomorrow," Eeyore was saying. "Blizzards and what-not. Being fine today doesn't Mean Anything. It has no sig—what's that word? Well, it has none of that. It's just a small piece of weather."

"There's Pooh!" said Christopher Robin, who didn't much mind *what* it did tomorrow, as long as he was out in it. "Hallo, Pooh!"

"It's Christopher Robin!" said Piglet. "*He'll* know what to do."

They hurried up to him.

"Oh, Christopher Robin," began Pooh.

"And Eeyore," said Eeyore.

"Tigger and Roo are right up the Six Pine Trees, and they can't get down, and——"

"And I was just saying," put in Piglet, "that if only Christopher Robin——"

"*And* Eeyore——"

"If only you were here, then we could think of something to do."

Christopher Robin looked up at Tigger and Roo, and tried to think of something.

"*I* thought," said Piglet earnestly, "that if Eeyore stood at the bottom of the tree, and if Pooh stood on Eeyore's back, and if I stood on Pooh's shoulders——"

"And if Eeyore's back snapped suddenly, then we could all laugh. Ha ha! Amusing in a quiet way," said Eeyore, "but not really helpful."

"Well," said Piglet meekly, "*I* thought——"

"Would it break your back, Eeyore?" asked Pooh, very much surprised.

"That's what would be so interesting, Pooh. Not being quite sure till afterwards."

Pooh said "Oh!" and they all began to think again.

"I've got an idea!" cried Christopher Robin suddenly.

"Listen to this, Piglet," said Eeyore, "and then you'll know what we're trying to do."

"I'll take off my tunic and we'll each hold a corner, and then Roo and Tigger can jump into it, and it will be all soft and bouncy for them, and they won't hurt themselves."

"*Getting Tigger down,*" said Eeyore, "and *Not hurting anybody*. Keep those two ideas in your head, Piglet, and you'll be all right."

But Piglet wasn't listening, he was so agog at the thought of seeing Christopher Robin's blue braces again. He had only seen them once before, when he was much younger, and, being a little over-excited by them, had had to go to bed half an hour earlier than usual; and he had always wondered since if they were *really* as blue and as bracing as he had thought them.

So when Christopher Robin took his tunic off, and they were, he felt quite friendly to Eeyore again, and held the corner of the tunic next to him and smiled happily at him. And Eeyore whispered back: "I'm not saying there won't be an Accident *now*, mind you. They're funny things, Accidents. You never have them till you're having them."

When Roo understood what he had to do, he was wildly excited, and cried out: "Tigger, Tigger, we're going to jump! Look at me jumping, Tigger! Like flying, my jumping will be. Can Tiggers do it?" And he squeaked out: "I'm coming, Christopher Robin!" and he jumped—straight into the middle of the tunic. And he was going so fast that he bounced up again almost as high as where he was before—and went on bouncing and saying, "Oo!" for quite a long time— and then at last he stopped and said, "Oo, lovely!" And they put him on the ground.

"Come on, Tigger," he called out. "It's easy."

But Tigger was holding on to the branch and saying to himself: "It's all very well for Jumping Animals like Kangas, but it's quite different for Swimming Animals like Tiggers." And he thought of himself floating on his back down a river, or striking out from one island to another, and he felt that that was really the life for a Tigger.

"Come along," called Christopher Robin. "You'll be all right."

"Just wait a moment," said Tigger nervously. "Small piece of bark in my eye." And he moved slowly along his branch.

"Come on, it's easy!" squeaked Roo. And suddenly Tigger found how easy it was.

"Ow!" he shouted as the tree flew past him.

"Look out!" cried Christopher Robin to the others.

There was a crash, and a tearing noise, and a confused heap of everybody on the ground.

Christopher Robin and Pooh and Piglet picked themselves up first, and then they picked Tigger up, and underneath everybody else was Eeyore.

"Oh, Eeyore!" cried Christopher Robin. "Are you hurt?" And he felt him rather anxiously, and dusted him and helped him to stand up again.

Eeyore said nothing for a long time. And then he said: "Is Tigger there?"

Tigger was there, feeling Bouncy again already.

"Yes," said Christopher Robin. "Tigger's here."

"Well, just thank him for me," said Eeyore.

CHAPTER FIVE

In Which

Rabbit Has a Busy Day, and We Learn What Christopher Robin Does in the Mornings

IT WAS GOING to be one of Rabbit's busy days. As soon as he woke up he felt important, as if everything depended upon him. It was just the day for Organizing Something, or for Writing a Notice Signed Rabbit, or for Seeing What Everybody Else Thought About It. It was a perfect morning for hurrying round to Pooh, and saying, "Very well, then, I'll tell Piglet," and then going to Piglet, and saying, "Pooh thinks—but perhaps I'd better see Owl first." It was a Captainish sort of day, when everybody said, "Yes, Rabbit" and "No, Rabbit," and waited until he had told them.

He came out of his house and sniffed the warm spring morning as he wondered what he would do. Kanga's house was nearest, and at Kanga's house was Roo, who said "Yes, Rabbit" and "No, Rabbit" almost better than anybody else in the Forest; but there was another animal there nowadays, the strange and Bouncy Tigger; and he was the sort of Tigger who was always in front when you were showing him the way anywhere, and was generally out of sight when at last you came to the place and said proudly "Here we are!"

"No, not Kanga's," said Rabbit thoughtfully to himself, as he curled his whiskers in the sun; and, to make quite sure that he wasn't going there, he turned to the left and trotted off in the other direction, which was the way to Christopher Robin's house.

"After all," said Rabbit to himself, "Christopher Robin depends on Me. He's fond of Pooh and Piglet and Eeyore, and so am I, but they haven't any Brain. Not to notice. And he respects Owl, because you can't help respecting anybody who can spell TUESDAY, even if he doesn't spell it right; but spelling isn't everything. There are days when spelling Tuesday simply doesn't count. And Kanga is too busy looking after Roo, and Roo is too young and Tigger is too bouncy to be any help, so there's really nobody but Me, when you come to look at it. I'll go and see if there's anything he wants doing, and then I'll do it for him. It's just the day for doing things."

He trotted along happily, and by-and-by he crossed the stream and came to the place where his friends-and-relations lived. There seemed to be even more of them about than usual this morning, and having nodded to a hedgehog or two, with whom he was too busy to shake hands, and having said, "Good morning, good morning," importantly to some of the others, and "Ah, there you are," kindly, to the smaller ones, he waved a paw at them over his shoulder, and was gone; leaving such an air of excitement and I-don't-know-what behind him, that several members of the Beetle family, including Henry Rush, made their way at once to the Hundred Acre Wood and began climbing trees, in the hope of getting to the top before it happened, whatever it was, so that they might see it properly.

Rabbit hurried on by the edge of the Hundred Acre Wood, feeling more important every minute, and soon he came to the tree where Christopher Robin lived. He knocked at the door, and he called out once or twice, and then he walked back a little way and put his paw up to keep the sun out, and called to the top of the tree, and then he turned all round and shouted "Hallo!" and "I say!" "It's Rabbit!"—but nothing happened. Then he stopped and listened, and everything stopped and listened with him, and the Forest was very lone and still and peaceful in the sunshine, until suddenly a hundred miles above him a lark began to sing.

"Bother!" said Rabbit. "He's gone out."

He went back to the green front door, just to make sure, and he was turning away, feeling that his morning had got all spoilt, when he saw a piece of paper on the ground. And there was a pin in it, as if it had fallen off the door.

"Ha!" said Rabbit, feeling quite happy again. "Another notice!"

This is what it said:

GON OUT
BACKSON
BISY
BACKSON.
C. R.

"Ha!" said Rabbit again. "I must tell the others." And he hurried off importantly.

The nearest house was Owl's, and to Owl's House in the Hundred Acre Wood he made his way. He came to Owl's door, and he knocked and he rang, and he rang and he knocked, and at last Owl's head came out and said "Go away, I'm thinking—oh, it's you?" which was how he always began.

"Owl," said Rabbit shortly, "you and I have brains. The others have fluff. If there is any thinking to be done in this Forest—and when I say thinking I mean *thinking*—you and I must do it."

"Yes," said Owl. "I was."

"Read that."

Owl took Christopher Robin's notice from Rabbit and looked at it nervously. He could spell his own name WOL, and he could spell Tuesday so that you knew it wasn't Wednesday, and he could read quite comfortably when you weren't looking over his shoulder and saying "Well?" all the time, and he could——

"Well?" said Rabbit.

"Yes," said Owl, looking Wise and Thoughtful. "I see what you mean. Undoubtedly."

"Well?"

"Exactly," said Owl. "Precisely." And he added, after a little thought, "If you had not come to me, I should have come to you."

"Why?" asked Rabbit.

"For that very reason," said Owl, hoping that something helpful would happen soon.

"Yesterday morning," said Rabbit solemnly, "I went to see Christopher Robin. He was out. Pinned on his door was a notice."

"The same notice?"

"A different one. But the meaning was the same. It's very odd."

"Amazing," said Owl, looking at the notice again, and getting, just for a moment, a curious sort of feeling that something had happened to Christopher Robin's back. "What did you do?"

"Nothing."

"The best thing," said Owl wisely.

"Well?" said Rabbit again, as Owl knew he was going to.

"Exactly," said Owl.

For a little while he couldn't think of anything more; and then, all of a sudden, he had an idea.

"Tell me, Rabbit," he said, "the *exact* words of the first notice. This is very important. Everything depends on this. The *exact* words of the *first* notice."

"It was just the same as that one really."

Owl looked at him, and wondered whether to push him off the tree; but, feeling that he could always do it afterwards, he tried once more to find out what they were talking about.

"The exact words, please," he said, as if Rabbit hadn't spoken.

"It just said, 'Gon out. Backson.' Same as this, only this says 'Bisy Backson' too."

Owl gave a great sigh of relief.

"Ah!" said Owl. "*Now* we know where we are."

"Yes, but where's Christopher Robin?" said Rabbit. "That's the point."

Owl looked at the notice again. To one of his education the reading of it was easy. "Gone out, Backson. Bisy, Backson"—just the sort of thing you'd expect to see on a notice.

"It is quite clear what has happened, my dear Rabbit," he said. "Christopher Robin has gone out somewhere with Backson. He and Backson are busy together. Have you seen a Backson anywhere about in the Forest lately?"

"I don't know," said Rabbit. "That's what I came to ask you. What are they like?"

"Well," said Owl, "the Spotted or Herbaceous Backson is just a——"

"At least," he said, "it's really more of a——"

"Of course," he said, "it depends on the——"

"Well," said Owl, "the fact is," he said, "I don't know *what* they're like," said Owl frankly.

"Thank you," said Rabbit. And he hurried off to see Pooh.

Before he had gone very far he heard a noise. So he stopped and listened. This was the noise.

NOISE, BY POOH

Oh, the butterflies are flying,
Now the winter days are dying,
And the primroses are trying
　　To be seen.

And the turtle-doves are cooing,
And the woods are up and doing,
For the violets are blue-ing
　　In the green.

Oh, the honey-bees are gumming
On their little wings, and humming
That the summer, which is coming,
　　Will be fun.

And the cows are almost cooing,
And the turtle-doves are mooing,
Which is why a Pooh is poohing
　　In the sun.

For the spring is really springing;
You can see a skylark singing,
And the blue-bells, which are ringing,
　　Can be heard.

And the cuckoo isn't cooing,
But he's cucking and he's ooing,
And a Pooh is simply poohing
　　Like a bird.

"Hallo, Pooh," said Rabbit.

"Hallo, Rabbit," said Pooh dreamily.

"Did you make that song up?"

"Well, I sort of made it up," said Pooh. "It isn't Brain," he went on humbly, "because You Know Why, Rabbit; but it comes to me sometimes."

"Ah!" said Rabbit, who never let things come to him, but always went and fetched them. "Well, the point is, have you seen a Spotted or Herbaceous Backson in the Forest, at all?"

"No," said Pooh. "Not a—no," said Pooh. "I saw Tigger just now."

"That's no good."

"No," said Pooh. "I thought it wasn't."

"Have you seen Piglet?"

"Yes," said Pooh. "I suppose *that* isn't any good either?" he asked meekly.

"Well, it depends if he saw anything."

"He saw me," said Pooh.

Rabbit sat down on the ground next to Pooh and,

feeling much less important like that, stood up again.

"What it all comes to is this," he said. *"What does Christopher Robin do in the morning nowadays?"*

"What sort of thing?"

"Well, can you tell me anything you've seen him do in the morning? These last few days."

"Yes," said Pooh. "We had breakfast together yesterday. By the Pine Trees. I'd made up a little basket,

just a little, fair-sized basket,

an ordinary biggish sort of basket, full of——"

"Yes, yes," said Rabbit, "but I mean later than that. Have you seen him between eleven and twelve?"

"Well," said Pooh, "at eleven o'clock—at eleven o'clock—well, at eleven o'clock, you see, I generally get home about then. Because I have One or Two Things to Do."

"Quarter past eleven, then?"

"Well——" said Pooh.

"Half past."

"Yes," said Pooh. "At half past—or perhaps later —I might see him."

And now that he did think of it, he began to re-member that he *hadn't* seen Christopher Robin about so much lately. Not in the mornings. Afternoons, yes; evenings, yes; before breakfast, yes; just after break-fast, yes. And then, perhaps, "See you again, Pooh," and off he'd go.

"That's just it," said Rabbit. "Where?"

"Perhaps he's looking for something."

"What?" asked Rabbit.

"That's just what I was going to say," said Pooh. And then he added, "Perhaps he's looking for a—for a——"

"A Spotted or Herbaceous Backson?"

"Yes," said Pooh. "One of those. In case it isn't."

Rabbit looked at him severely.

"I don't think you're helping," he said.

"No," said Pooh. "I do try," he added humbly.

Rabbit thanked him for trying, and said that he would now go and see Eeyore, and Pooh could walk with him if he liked. But Pooh, who felt another verse of his song coming on him, said he would wait for Piglet, good-bye, Rabbit; so Rabbit went off.

But, as it happened, it was Rabbit who saw Piglet first. Piglet had got up early that morning to pick himself a bunch of violets; and when he had picked them and put them in a pot in the middle of his house, it suddenly came over him that nobody had ever picked Eeyore a bunch of violets, and the more he thought of this, the more he thought how sad it was to be an Animal who had never had a bunch of violets picked for him. So he hurried out again, saying to himself, "Eeyore, Violets," and then "Violets, Eeyore," in case he forgot, because it was that sort of day, and he picked a large bunch and trotted along, smelling them, and feeling very happy, until he came to the place where Eeyore was.

"Oh, Eeyore," began Piglet a little nervously, because Eeyore was busy.

Eeyore put out a paw and waved him away.

"Tomorrow," said Eeyore. "Or the next day."

Piglet came a little closer to see what it was. Eeyore had three sticks on the ground, and was looking at them. Two of the sticks were touching at one end, but not at the other, and the third stick was laid across them. Piglet thought that perhaps it was a Trap of some kind.

"Oh, Eeyore," he began again, "just——"

"Is that little Piglet?" said Eeyore, still looking hard at his sticks.

"Yes, Eeyore, and I——"

"Do you know what this is?"

"No," said Piglet.

"It's an A."

"Oh," said Piglet.

"Not O, A," said Eeyore severely. "Can't you *hear*, or do you think you have more education than Christopher Robin?"

"Yes," said Piglet. "No," said Piglet very quickly. And he came closer still.

"Christopher Robin said it was an A, and an A it is—until somebody treads on me," Eeyore added sternly.

Piglet jumped backwards hurriedly, and smelt at his violets.

"Do you know what A means, little Piglet?"

"No, Eeyore, I don't."

"It means Learning, it means Education, it means all the things that you and Pooh haven't got. That's what A means."

"Oh," said Piglet again. "I mean, does it?" he explained quickly.

"I'm telling you. People come and go in this Forest, and they say, 'It's only Eeyore, so it doesn't count.' They walk to and fro saying 'Ha ha!' But do they know anything about A? They don't. It's just three sticks to *them*. But to the Educated—mark this, little Piglet—to the Educated, not meaning Poohs and Piglets, it's a great and glorious A. Not," he added, "just something that anybody can come and *breathe* on."

Piglet stepped back nervously, and looked round for help.

"Here's Rabbit," he said gladly. "Hallo, Rabbit."

Rabbit came up importantly, nodded to Piglet, and said, "Ah, Eeyore," in the voice of one who would be saying "Good-bye" in about two more minutes.

"There's just one thing I wanted to ask you, Eeyore. What happens to Christopher Robin in the mornings nowadays?"

"What's this that I'm looking at?" said Eeyore, still looking at it.

"Three sticks," said Rabbit promptly.

"You see?" said Eeyore to Piglet. He turned to Rabbit. "I will now answer your question," he said solemnly.

"Thank you," said Rabbit.

"What does Christopher Robin do in the mornings? He learns. He becomes Educated. He instigo-rates—I *think* that is the word he mentioned, but I may be referring to something else—he instigorates Knowledge. In my small way I also, if I have the word right, am—am doing what he does. That, for instance, is——"

"An A," said Rabbit, "but not a very good one. Well, I must get back and tell the others."

Eeyore looked at his sticks and then he looked at Piglet.

"What did Rabbit say it was?" he asked.

"An A," said Piglet.

"Did you tell him?"

"No, Eeyore, I didn't. I expect he just knew."

"He *knew*? You mean this A thing is a thing *Rabbit* knew?"

"Yes, Eeyore. He's clever, Rabbit is."

"Clever!" said Eeyore scornfully, putting a foot heavily on his three sticks. "Education!" said Eeyore bitterly, jumping on his six sticks. "What *is* Learn-ing?" asked Eeyore as he kicked his twelve sticks into the air. "A thing *Rabbit* knows! Ha!"

"I think——" began Piglet nervously.

"Don't," said Eeyore.

"I think *Violets* are rather nice," said Piglet. And he laid his bunch in front of Eeyore and scampered off.

Next morning the notice on Christopher Robin's door said:

GONE OUT
BACK SOON
C. R.

Which is why all the animals in the Forest—except, of course, the Spotted and Herbaceous Backson— now know what Christopher Robin does in the mornings.

CHAPTER SIX

In Which

Pooh Invents a New Game and Eeyore Joins In

Y THE TIME it came to the edge of the Forest, the stream had grown up, so that it was almost a river, and, being grown-up, it did not run and jump and sparkle along as it used to do when it was younger, but moved more slowly. For it knew now where it was going, and it said to itself, "There is no hurry. We shall get there some day." But all the little streams higher up in the Forest went this way and that, quickly, eagerly, having so much to find out before it was too late.

There was a broad track, almost as broad as a road, leading from the Outland to the Forest, but before it could come to the Forest, it had to cross this river. So, where it crossed, there was a wooden bridge, almost as broad as a road, with wooden rails on each side of it. Christopher Robin could just get his chin to the top rail, if he wanted to, but it was more fun to stand on the bottom rail, so that he could lean right over, and watch the river slipping slowly away beneath him. Pooh could get his chin on the bottom rail if he wanted to, but it was more fun to lie down and get his head under it, and watch the river slipping slowly away beneath him. And this was the only way in which Piglet and Roo could watch the river at all, because they were too small to reach the bottom rail. So they would lie down and watch it . . . and it slipped away very slowly, being in no hurry to get there.

One day, when Pooh was walking towards this bridge, he was trying to make up a piece of poetry about fir-cones, because there they were, lying about on each side of him, and he felt singy. So he picked a fir-cone up, and looked at it, and said to himself, "This is a very good fir-cone, and something ought to rhyme to it." But he couldn't think of anything. And then this came into his head suddenly:

> Here is a myst'ry
> About a little fir-tree.
> Owl says it's *his* tree,
> And Kanga says it's *her* tree.

"Which doesn't make sense," said Pooh, "because Kanga doesn't live in a tree."

He had just come to the bridge; and not looking where he was going, he tripped over something, and the fir-cone jerked out of his paw into the river.

"Bother," said Pooh, as it floated slowly under the bridge, and he went back to get another fir-cone which had a rhyme to it. But then he thought that he would just look at the river instead, because it was a peaceful sort of day, so he lay down and looked at it, and it slipped slowly away beneath him . . . and suddenly, there was his fir-cone slipping away too.

"That's funny," said Pooh. "I dropped it on the other side," said Pooh, "and it came out on this side! I wonder if it would do it again?" And he went back for some more fir-cones.

It did. It kept on doing it. Then he dropped two in at once, and leant over the bridge to see which of them would come out first; and one of them did; but as they were both the same size, he didn't know if it was the one which he wanted to win, or the other one. So the next time he dropped one big one and one little one, and the big one came out first, which was what he had said it would do, and the little one came out last, which was what he had said it would do, so he had won twice . . . and when he went home for tea, he had won thirty-six and lost twenty-eight,

THE HOUSE AT POOH CORNER

which meant that he was—that he had—well, you take twenty-eight from thirty-six, and *that's* what he was. Instead of the other way round.

And that was the beginning of the game called Poohsticks, which Pooh invented, and which he and his friends used to play on the edge of the Forest. But they played with sticks instead of fir-cones, because they were easier to mark.

Now one day Pooh and Piglet and Rabbit and Roo were all playing Poohsticks together. They had dropped their sticks in when Rabbit said "Go!" and then they had hurried across to the other side of the bridge, and now they were all leaning over the edge, waiting to see whose stick would come out first. But it was a long time coming, because the river was very lazy that day, and hardly seemed to mind if it didn't ever get there at all.

"I can see mine!" cried Roo. "No, I can't, it's something else. Can you see yours, Piglet? I thought I could see mine, but I couldn't. There it is! No, it isn't. Can you see yours, Pooh?"

"No," said Pooh.

"I expect my stick's stuck," said Roo. "Rabbit, my stick's stuck. Is your stick stuck, Piglet?"

"They always take longer than you think," said Rabbit.

"How long do you *think* they'll take?" asked Roo.

"I can see yours, Piglet," said Pooh suddenly.

"Mine's a sort of greyish one," said Piglet, not daring to lean too far over in case he fell in.

"Yes, that's what I can see. It's coming over on to my side."

Rabbit leant over further than ever, looking for his, and Roo wriggled up and down, calling out "Come on, stick! Stick, stick, stick!" and Piglet got very excited because his was the only one which had been seen, and that meant that he was winning.

"It's coming!" said Pooh.

"Are you *sure* it's mine?" squeaked Piglet excitedly.

"Yes, because it's grey. A big grey one. Here it comes! A very—big—grey——Oh, no, it isn't, it's Eeyore."

And out floated Eeyore.

"Eeyore!" cried everybody.

Looking very calm, very dignified, with his legs in the air, came Eeyore from beneath the bridge.

"It's Eeyore!" cried Roo, terribly excited.

"Is that so?" said Eeyore, getting caught up by a little eddy, and turning slowly round three times. "I wondered."

"I didn't know you were playing," said Roo.

"I'm not," said Eeyore.

"Eeyore, what *are* you doing there?" said Rabbit.

"I'll give you three guesses, Rabbit. Digging holes in the ground? Wrong. Leaping from branch to branch of a young oak-tree? Wrong. Waiting for somebody to help me out of the river? Right. Give Rabbit time, and he'll always get the answer."

"But, Eeyore," said Pooh in distress, "what can we —I mean, how shall we—do you think if we——"

"Yes," said Eeyore. "One of those would be just the thing. Thank you, Pooh."

"He's going *round* and *round*," said Roo, much impressed.

"And why not?" said Eeyore coldly.

"I can swim too," said Roo proudly.

"Not round and round," said Eeyore. "It's much more difficult. I didn't want to come swimming at all today," he went on, revolving slowly. "But if, when in, I decide to practise a slight circular movement from right to left—or perhaps I should say," he added, as he got into another eddy, "from left to right, just as it happens to occur to me, it is nobody's business but my own."

There was a moment's silence while everybody thought.

"I've got a sort of idea," said Pooh at last, "but I don't suppose it's a very good one."

"I don't suppose it is either," said Eeyore.

"Go on, Pooh," said Rabbit. "Let's have it."

"Well, if we all threw stones and things into the

river on *one* side of Eeyore, the stones would make waves, and the waves would wash him to the other side."

"That's a very good idea," said Rabbit, and Pooh looked happy again.

"Very," said Eeyore. "When I want to be washed, Pooh, I'll let you know."

"Supposing we hit him by mistake?" said Piglet anxiously.

"Or supposing you missed him by mistake," said Eeyore. "Think of all the possibilities, Piglet, before you settle down to enjoy yourselves."

But Pooh had got the biggest stone he could carry, and was leaning over the bridge, holding it in his paws.

"I'm not throwing it, I'm dropping it, Eeyore," he explained. "And then I can't miss—I mean I can't hit you. *Could* you stop turning round for a moment, because it muddles me rather?"

"No," said Eeyore. "I *like* turning round."

Rabbit began to feel that it was time he took command.

"Now, Pooh," he said, "when I say 'Now!' you can drop it. Eeyore, when I say 'Now!' Pooh will drop his stone."

"Thank you very much, Rabbit, but I expect I shall know."

"Are you ready, Pooh? Piglet, give Pooh a little more room. Get back a bit there, Roo. Are you ready?"

"No," said Eeyore.

"Now!" said Rabbit.

Pooh dropped his stone. There was a loud splash, and Eeyore disappeared. . . .

It was an anxious moment for the watchers on the bridge. They looked and looked . . . and even the sight of Piglet's stick coming out a little in front of Rabbit's didn't cheer them up as much as you would have expected. And then, just as Pooh was beginning to think that he must have chosen the wrong stone or the wrong river or the wrong day for his Idea, something grey showed for a moment by the river bank . . . and it got slowly bigger and bigger . . . and at last it was Eeyore coming out.

With a shout they rushed off the bridge, and pushed and pulled at him; and soon he was standing among them again on dry land.

"Oh, Eeyore, you *are* wet!" said Piglet, feeling him.

Eeyore shook himself, and asked somebody to explain to Piglet what happened when you had been inside a river for quite a long time.

"Well done, Pooh," said Rabbit kindly. "That was a good idea of ours."

"What was?" asked Eeyore.

"Hooshing you to the bank like that."

"*Hooshing* me?" said Eeyore in surprise. "Hoosh-ing *me?* You didn't think I was *hooshed,* did you? I dived. Pooh dropped a large stone on me, and so as not to be struck heavily on the chest, I dived and swam to the bank."

"You didn't really," whispered Piglet to Pooh, so as to comfort him.

"I didn't *think* I did," said Pooh anxiously.

"It's just Eeyore," said Piglet. "*I* thought your Idea was a very good Idea."

Pooh began to feel a little more comfortable, be-cause when you are a Bear of Very Little Brain, and you Think of Things, you find sometimes that a Thing which seemed very Thingish inside you is quite different when it gets out into the open and has other people looking at it. And, anyhow, Eeyore *was* in the river, and now he *wasn't,* so he hadn't done any harm.

"How did you fall in, Eeyore?" asked Rabbit, as he dried him with Piglet's handkerchief.

"I didn't," said Eeyore.

"But how——"

"I was BOUNCED," said Eeyore.

"Oo," said Roo excitedly, "did somebody push you?"

"Somebody BOUNCED me. I was just thinking by the side of the river—thinking, if any of you know what that means, when I received a loud BOUNCE."

"Oh, Eeyore!" said everybody.

"Are you sure you didn't slip?" asked Rabbit wisely.

"Of course I slipped. If you're standing on the slippery bank of a river, and somebody BOUNCES you loudly from behind, you slip. What did you think I did?"

"But who did it?" asked Roo.

Eeyore didn't answer.

"I expect it was Tigger," said Piglet nervously.

"But, Eeyore," said Pooh, "was it a Joke, or an Accident? I mean——"

"I didn't stop to ask, Pooh. Even at the very bottom of the river I didn't stop to say to myself, '*Is* this a Hearty Joke, or is it the Merest Accident?' I just floated to the surface, and said to myself, 'It's wet.' If you know what I mean."

"And where was Tigger?" asked Rabbit.

Before Eeyore could answer, there was a loud noise behind them, and through the hedge came Tigger himself.

"Hallo, everybody," said Tigger cheerfully.

"Hallo, Tigger," said Roo.

Rabbit became very important suddenly.

"Tigger," he said solemnly, "what happened just now?"

"Just when?" said Tigger a little uncomfortably.

"When you bounced Eeyore into the river."

"I didn't bounce him."

"You bounced me," said Eeyore gruffly.

"I didn't really. I had a cough, and I happened to be behind Eeyore, and I said 'Grrrr—oppp—ptschschschz.'"

"Why?" said Rabbit, helping Piglet up, and dusting him. "It's all right, Piglet."

"It took me by surprise," said Piglet nervously.

"That's what I call bouncing," said Eeyore. "Taking people by surprise. Very unpleasant habit. I don't mind Tigger being in the Forest," he went on, "because it's a large Forest, and there's plenty of room to bounce in it. But I don't see why he should come into *my* little corner of it, and bounce there. It isn't as if there was anything very wonderful about my little corner. Of course for people who like cold, wet, ugly bits it *is* something rather special, but otherwise it's just a corner, and if anybody feels bouncy——"

"I didn't bounce, I coughed," said Tigger crossly.

"Bouncy or coffy, it's all the same at the bottom of the river."

"Well," said Rabbit, "all I can say is—well, here's Christopher Robin, so *he* can say it."

Christopher Robin came down from the Forest to the bridge, feeling all sunny and careless, and just as if twice nineteen didn't matter a bit, as it didn't on such a happy afternoon, and he thought that if he stood on the bottom rail of the bridge, and leant over, and watched the river slipping slowly away beneath him, then he would suddenly know everything that there was to be known, and he would be able to tell Pooh, who wasn't quite sure about some of it. But when he got to the bridge and saw all the animals there, then he knew that it wasn't that kind of afternoon, but the other kind, when you wanted to *do* something.

"It's like this, Christopher Robin," began Rabbit. "Tigger——"

"No, I didn't," said Tigger.

"Well, anyhow, there I was," said Eeyore.

"But I don't think he meant to," said Pooh.

"He just *is* bouncy," said Piglet, "and he can't help it."

"Try bouncing *me*, Tigger," said Roo eagerly. "Eeyore, Tigger's going to try *me*. Piglet, do you think——"

"Yes, yes," said Rabbit, "we don't all want to speak at once. The point is, what does Christopher Robin think about it?"

"All I did was I coughed," said Tigger.

"He bounced," said Eeyore.

"Well, I sort of boffed," said Tigger.

"Hush!" said Rabbit, holding up his paw. "What does Christopher Robin think about it all? That's the point."

"Well," said Christopher Robin, not quite sure what it was all about, "*I* think——"

"Yes?" said everybody.

"*I* think we all ought to play Poohsticks."

So they did. And Eeyore, who had never played it before, won more times than anybody else; and Roo fell in twice, the first time by accident and the second time on purpose, because he suddenly saw Kanga

coming from the Forest, and he knew he'd have to go to bed anyhow. So then Rabbit said he'd go with them; and Tigger and Eeyore went off together, because Eeyore wanted to tell Tigger How to Win at Poohsticks, which you do by letting your stick drop in a twitchy sort of way, if you understand what I mean, Tigger; and Christopher Robin and Pooh and Piglet were left on the bridge by themselves.

For a long time they looked at the river beneath them, saying nothing, and the river said nothing too, for it felt very quiet and peaceful on this summer afternoon.

"Tigger is all right *really*," said Piglet lazily.

"Of course he is," said Christopher Robin.

"Everybody is *really*," said Pooh. "That's what *I* think," said Pooh. "But I don't suppose I'm right," he said.

"Of course you are," said Christopher Robin.

CHAPTER SEVEN

In Which

Tigger Is Unbounced

ONE DAY Rabbit and Piglet were sitting outside Pooh's front door listening to Rabbit, and Pooh was sitting with them. It was a drowsy summer afternoon, and the Forest was full of gentle sounds, which all seemed to be saying to Pooh, "Don't listen to Rabbit, listen to me." So he got into a comfortable position for not listening to Rabbit, and from time to time he opened his eyes to say "Ah!" and then closed them again to say "True," and from time to time Rabbit said, "You see what I mean, Piglet," very earnestly, and Piglet nodded earnestly to show that he did.

"In fact," said Rabbit, coming to the end of it at last, "Tigger's getting so Bouncy nowadays that it's time we taught him a lesson. Don't you think so, Piglet?"

273

Piglet said that Tigger *was* very Bouncy, and that if they could think of a way of unbouncing him, it would be a Very Good Idea.

"Just what I feel," said Rabbit. "What do *you* say, Pooh?"

Pooh opened his eyes with a jerk and said, "Extremely."

"Extremely what?" asked Rabbit.

"What you were saying," said Pooh. "Undoubtably."

Piglet gave Pooh a stiffening sort of nudge, and Pooh, who felt more and more that he was somewhere else, got up slowly and began to look for himself.

"But how shall we do it?" asked Piglet. "What sort of a lesson, Rabbit?"

"That's the point," said Rabbit.

The word "lesson" came back to Pooh as one he had heard before somewhere.

"There's a thing called Twy-stymes," he said. "Christopher Robin tried to teach it to me once, but it didn't."

"What didn't?" said Rabbit.

"Didn't what?" said Piglet.

Pooh shook his head.

"I don't know," he said. "It just didn't. What are we talking about?"

"Pooh," said Piglet reproachfully, "haven't you been listening to what Rabbit was saying?"

"I listened, but I had a small piece of fluff in my ear. Could you say it again, please, Rabbit?"

Rabbit never minded saying things again, so he asked where he should begin from; and when Pooh had said from the moment when the fluff got in his ear, and Rabbit had asked when that was, and Pooh had said he didn't know because he hadn't heard properly, Piglet settled it all by saying that what they were trying to do was, they were just trying to think of a way to get the bounces out of Tigger, because however much you liked him, you couldn't deny it, he *did* bounce.

"Oh, I see," said Pooh.

"There's too much of him," said Rabbit, "that's what it comes to."

Pooh tried to think, and all he could think of was something which didn't help at all. So he hummed it very quietly to himself.

> If Rabbit
> Was bigger
> And fatter
> And stronger,
> Or bigger
> Than Tigger,
> If Tigger was smaller,
> Then Tigger's bad habit
> Of bouncing at Rabbit
> Would matter
> No longer,
> If Rabbit
> Was taller.

"What was Pooh saying?" asked Rabbit. "Any good?"

"No," said Pooh sadly. "No good."

"Well, I've got an idea," said Rabbit, "and here it is. We take Tigger for a long explore, somewhere where he's never been, and we lose him there, and next morning we find him again, and—mark my words—he'll be a different Tigger altogether."

"Why?" said Pooh.

"Because he'll be a Humble Tigger. Because he'll be a Sad Tigger, a Melancholy Tigger, a Small and

THE HOUSE AT POOH CORNER

Sorry Tigger, and Oh-Rabbit-I-*am*-glad-to-see-you Tigger. That's why."

"Will he be glad to see me and Piglet, too?"

"Of course."

"That's good," said Pooh.

"I should hate him to go *on* being Sad," said Piglet doubtfully.

"Tiggers never go on being Sad," explained Rabbit. "They get over it with Astonishing Rapidity. I asked Owl, just to make sure, and he said that that's what they always get over it with. But if we can make Tigger feel Small and Sad just for five minutes, we shall have done a good deed."

"Would Christopher Robin think so?" asked Piglet.

"Yes," said Rabbit. "He'd say 'You've done a good deed, Piglet. I would have done it myself, only I happened to be doing something else. Thank you, Piglet.' And Pooh, of course."

Piglet felt very glad about this, and he saw at once that what they were going to do to Tigger was a good thing to do, and as Pooh and Rabbit were doing it with him, it was a thing which even a Very Small Animal could wake up in the morning and be comfortable about doing. So the only question was, where should they lose Tigger?

"We'll take him to the North Pole," said Rabbit,

"because it was a very long explore finding it, so it will be a very long explore for Tigger unfinding it again."

It was now Pooh's turn to feel very glad, because it was he who had first found the North Pole, and when they got there, Tigger would see a notice which said, "Discovered by Pooh, Pooh found it," and then Tigger would know, which perhaps he didn't know, the sort of Bear Pooh was. *That* sort of Bear.

So it was arranged that they should start next morning, and that Rabbit, who lived near Kanga and Roo and Tigger, should now go home and ask Tigger what he was doing tomorrow, because if he wasn't doing anything, what about coming for an explore and getting Pooh and Piglet to come too? And if Tigger said "Yes" that would be all right, and if he said "No"——

"He won't," said Rabbit. "Leave it to me." And he went off busily.

The next day was quite a different day. Instead of being hot and sunny, it was cold and misty. Pooh didn't mind for himself, but when he thought of all the honey the bees wouldn't be making, a cold and misty day always made him feel sorry for them. He said so to Piglet when Piglet came to fetch him, and Piglet said that he wasn't thinking of that so much, but of how cold and miserable it would be being lost all day and night on the top of the Forest. But when he and Pooh had got to Rabbit's house, Rabbit said it was just the day for them, because Tigger always bounced on ahead of everybody, and as soon as he got out of sight, they would hurry away in the other direction, and he would never see them again.

"Not never?" said Piglet.

"Well, not until we find him again, Piglet. Tomorrow, or whenever it is. Come on. He's waiting for us."

When they got to Kanga's house, they found that Roo was waiting too, being a great friend of Tigger's, which made it Awkward; but Rabbit whispered "Leave this to me" behind his paw to Pooh, and went up to Kanga.

"I don't think Roo had better come," he said. "Not today."

"Why not?" said Roo, who wasn't supposed to be listening.

"Nasty cold day," said Rabbit, shaking his head. "And you were coughing this morning."

"How do you know?" asked Roo indignantly.

"Oh, Roo, you never told me," said Kanga reproachfully.

"It was a Biscuit Cough," said Roo, "not one you tell about."

"I think not today, dear. Another day."

"Tomorrow?" said Roo hopefully.

"We'll see," said Kanga.

"You're always seeing, and nothing ever happens," said Roo sadly.

"Nobody could see on a day like this, Roo," said Rabbit. "I don't expect we shall get very far, and then this afternoon we'll all—we'll all—we'll—ah, Tigger, there you are. Come on. Good-bye, Roo! This afternoon we'll—come on, Pooh! All ready? That's right. Come on."

So they went. At first Pooh and Rabbit and Piglet walked together, and Tigger ran round them in circles, and then, when the path got narrower, Rabbit, Piglet and Pooh walked one after another, and Tigger ran round them in oblongs, and by-and-by, when the gorse got very prickly on each side of the path, Tigger ran up and down in front of them, and sometimes he bounced into Rabbit and sometimes he didn't. And as they got higher, the mist got thicker, so that Tigger kept disappearing, and then when you thought he wasn't there, there he was again, saying "I say, come on," and before you could say anything, there he wasn't.

Rabbit turned round and nudged Piglet.

"The next time," he said. "Tell Pooh."

"The next time," said Piglet to Pooh.

"The next what?" said Pooh to Piglet.

Tigger appeared suddenly, bounced into Rabbit, and disappeared again. "Now!" said Rabbit. He jumped into a hollow by the side of the path, and Pooh and Piglet jumped after him. They crouched in the bracken, listening. The Forest was very silent when you stopped and listened to it. They could see nothing and hear nothing.

"H'sh!" said Rabbit.

"I am," said Pooh.

There was a pattering noise . . . then silence again.

"Hallo!" said Tigger, and he sounded so close suddenly that Piglet would have jumped if Pooh hadn't accidentally been sitting on most of him.

"Where are you?" called Tigger.

Rabbit nudged Pooh, and Pooh looked about for Piglet to nudge, but couldn't find him, and Piglet went on breathing wet bracken as quietly as he could, and felt very brave and excited.

"That's funny," said Tigger.

There was a moment's silence, and then they heard him pattering off again. For a little longer they waited, until the Forest had become so still that it almost frightened them, and then Rabbit got up and stretched himself.

"Well?" he whispered proudly. "There we are! Just as I said."

"I've been thinking," said Pooh, "and I think——"

"No," said Rabbit. "Don't. Run. Come on." And they all hurried off, Rabbit leading the way.

"Now," said Rabbit, after they had gone a little way, "we can talk. What were you going to say, Pooh?"

"Nothing much. Why are we going along here?"

"Because it's the way home."

"Oh!" said Pooh.

"I *think* it's more to the right," said Piglet nervously. "What do *you* think, Pooh?"

Pooh looked at his two paws. He knew that one of them was the right, and he knew that when you had decided which one of them was the right, then the other one was the left, but he never could remember how to begin.

"Well," he said slowly——

"Come on," said Rabbit. "I know it's this way."

They went on. Ten minutes later they stopped again.

"It's very silly," said Rabbit, "but just for the moment I——Ah, of course. Come on. . . ."

"Here we are," said Rabbit ten minutes later. "No, we're not. . . ."

"Now," said Rabbit ten minutes later, "I think we ought to be getting—or are we a little bit more to the right than I thought? . . ."

"It's a funny thing," said Rabbit ten minutes later, "how everything looks the same in a mist. Have you noticed it, Pooh?"

Pooh said that he had.

"Lucky we know the Forest so well, or we might get lost," said Rabbit half an hour later, and he gave the careless laugh which you give when you know the Forest so well that you can't get lost.

Piglet sidled up to Pooh from behind.

"Pooh!" he whispered.

"Yes, Piglet?"

"Nothing," said Piglet, taking Pooh's paw. "I just wanted to be sure of you."

When Tigger had finished waiting for the others to

catch him up, and they hadn't, and when he had got tired of having nobody to say, "I say, come on" to, he thought he would go home. So he trotted back; and the first thing Kanga said when she saw him was "There's a good Tigger. You're just in time for your Strengthening Medicine," and she poured it out for him. Roo said proudly, "I've *had* mine," and Tigger swallowed his and said, "So have I," and then he and Roo pushed each other about in a friendly way, and Tigger accidentally knocked over one or two chairs by accident, and Roo accidentally knocked over one on purpose, and Kanga said, "Now then, run along."

"Where shall we run along to?" asked Roo.

"You can go and collect some fir-cones for me," said Kanga, giving them a basket.

So they went to the Six Pine Trees, and threw fir-cones at each other until they had forgotten what they came for, and they left the basket under the trees and went back to dinner. And it was just as they were finishing dinner that Christopher Robin put his head in at the door.

"Where's Pooh?" he asked.

"Tigger dear, where's Pooh?" said Kanga. Tigger explained what had happened at the same time that Roo was explaining about his Biscuit Cough and Kanga was telling them not both to talk at once, so it was some time before Christopher Robin guessed that Pooh and Piglet and Rabbit were all lost in the mist on the top of the Forest.

"It's a funny thing about Tiggers," whispered Tigger to Roo, "how Tiggers *never* get lost."

"Why don't they, Tigger?"

"They just don't," explained Tigger. "That's how it is."

"Well," said Christopher Robin, "we shall have to go and find them, that's all. Come on, Tigger."

"I shall have to go and find them," explained Tigger to Roo.

"May I find them too?" asked Roo eagerly.

"I think not today, dear," said Kanga. "Another day."

"Well, if they're lost tomorrow, may I find them?"

"We'll see," said Kanga, and Roo, who knew what *that* meant, went into a corner, and practised jumping out at himself, partly because he wanted to practise this, and partly because he didn't want Christopher

Robin and Tigger to think that he minded when they went off without him.

"The fact is," said Rabbit, "we've missed our way somehow."

They were having a rest in a small sand-pit on the top of the Forest. Pooh was getting rather tired of that sand-pit, and suspected it of following them about, because whichever direction they started in, they always ended up at it, and each time, as it came through the mist at them, Rabbit said triumphantly, "Now I know where we are!" and Pooh said sadly, "So do I," and Piglet said nothing. He had tried to think of something to say, but the only thing he could think of was, "Help, help!" and it seemed silly to say that, when he had Pooh and Rabbit with him.

"Well," said Rabbit, after a long silence in which nobody thanked him for the nice walk they were having, "we'd better get on, I suppose. Which way shall we try?"

"How would it be," said Pooh slowly, "if, as soon as we're out of sight of this Pit, we try to find it again?"

"What's the good of that?" said Rabbit.

"Well," said Pooh, "we keep looking for Home and not finding it, so I thought that if we looked for this Pit, we'd be sure not to find it, which would be a Good Thing, because then we might find something that we *weren't* looking for, which might be just what we *were* looking for, really."

"I don't see much sense in that," said Rabbit.

"No," said Pooh humbly, "there isn't. But there was *going* to be when I began it. It's just that something happened to it on the way."

"If I walked away from this Pit, and then walked back to it, of *course* I should find it."

"Well, I thought perhaps you wouldn't," said Pooh. "I just thought."

"Try," said Piglet suddenly. "We'll wait here for you."

Rabbit gave a laugh to show how silly Piglet was, and walked into the mist. After he had gone a hundred yards, he turned and walked back again . . . and after Pooh and Piglet had waited twenty minutes for him, Pooh got up.

"I just thought," said Pooh. "Now then, Piglet, let's go home."

"But, Pooh," cried Piglet, all excited, "do you know the way?"

"No," said Pooh. "But there are twelve pots of honey in my cupboard, and they've been calling to me for hours. I couldn't hear them properly before, because Rabbit *would* talk, but if nobody says anything except those twelve pots, I *think*, Piglet, I shall know where they're calling from. Come on."

They walked off together; and for a long time Piglet said nothing, so as not to interrupt the pots; and then suddenly he made a squeaky noise . . . and an oo-noise . . . because now he began to know where he was; but he still didn't dare to say so out loud, in case he wasn't. And just when he was getting so sure of himself that it didn't matter whether the pots went on calling or not, there was a shout from in front of them, and out of the mist came Christopher Robin.

"Oh, there you are," said Christopher Robin carelessly, trying to pretend that he hadn't been Anxious.

"Here we are," said Pooh.

"Where's Rabbit?"

"I don't know," said Pooh.

"Oh—well, I expect Tigger will find him. He's sort of looking for you all."

"Well," said Pooh, "I've got to go home for something, and so has Piglet, because we haven't had it yet, and——"

"I'll come and watch you," said Christopher Robin.

So he went home with Pooh, and watched him for quite a long time . . . and all the time he was watching, Tigger was tearing round the Forest making loud yapping noises for Rabbit. And at last a very Small and Sorry Rabbit heard him. And the Small and Sorry Rabbit rushed through the mist at the noise, and it suddenly turned into Tigger; a Friendly Tigger, a

Grand Tigger, a Large and Helpful Tigger, a Tigger who bounced, if he bounced at all, in just the beautiful way a Tigger ought to bounce.

"Oh, Tigger, I *am* glad to see you," cried Rabbit.

CHAPTER EIGHT

In Which

Piglet Does a Very Grand Thing

ALF WAY between Pooh's house and Piglet's house was a Thoughtful Spot where they met sometimes when they had decided to go and see each other, and as it was warm and out of the wind they would sit down there for a little and wonder what they would do now that they *had* seen each other. One day when they had decided not to do anything, Pooh made up a verse about it, so that everybody should know what the place was for.

> This warm and sunny Spot
>   Belongs to Pooh.
> And here he wonders what
>   He's going to do.
> Oh, bother, I forgot—
>   It's Piglet's too.

Now one autumn morning when the wind had blown all the leaves off the trees in the night, and was trying to blow the branches off, Pooh and Piglet were sitting in the Thoughtful Spot and wondering.

"What *I* think," said Pooh, "is I think we'll go to Pooh Corner and see Eeyore, because perhaps his house has been blown down, and perhaps he'd like us to build it again."

"What *I* think," said Piglet, "is I think we'll go and see Christopher Robin, only he won't be there, so we can't."

"Let's go and see everybody," said Pooh. "Because when you've been walking in the wind for miles, and you suddenly go into somebody's house, and he says, 'Hallo, Pooh, you're just in time for a little smackerel of something,' and you are, then it's what I call a Friendly Day."

Piglet thought that they ought to have a Reason for going to see everybody, like Looking for Small or Organizing an Expotition, if Pooh could think of something.

Pooh could.

"We'll go because it's Thursday," he said, "and we'll go to wish everybody a Very Happy Thursday. Come on, Piglet."

They got up; and when Piglet had sat down again, because he didn't know the wind was so strong, and had been helped up by Pooh, they started off. They went to Pooh's house first, and luckily Pooh was at home just as they got there, so he asked them in, and they had some, and then they went on to Kanga's house, holding on to each other, and shouting "Isn't it?" and "What?" and "I can't hear." By the time they got to Kanga's house they were so buffeted that they stayed to lunch. Just at first it seemed rather cold outside afterwards, so they pushed on to Rabbit's as quickly as they could.

"We've come to wish you a Very Happy Thursday," said Pooh, when he had gone in and out once or twice just to make sure that he *could* get out again.

"Why, what's going to happen on Thursday?" asked Rabbit, and when Pooh had explained, and Rabbit, whose life was made up of Important Things, said, "Oh, I thought you'd really come about something," they sat down for a little . . . and by-and-by Pooh and Piglet went on again. The wind was behind them now, so they didn't have to shout.

"Rabbit's clever," said Pooh thoughtfully.

"Yes," said Piglet, "Rabbit's clever."

"And he has Brain."

"Yes," said Piglet, "Rabbit has Brain."

There was a long silence.

"I suppose," said Pooh, "that that's why he never understands anything."

Christopher Robin was at home by this time, because it was the afternoon, and he was so glad to see them that they stayed there until very nearly tea-time, and then they had a Very Nearly tea, which is one you forget about afterwards, and hurried on to Pooh Corner, so as to see Eeyore before it was too late to have a Proper Tea with Owl.

"Hallo, Eeyore," they called out cheerfully.

"Ah!" said Eeyore. "Lost your way?"

"We just came to see you," said Piglet. "And to see how your house was. Look, Pooh, it's still standing!"

"I know," said Eeyore. "Very odd. Somebody ought to have come down and pushed it over."

"We wondered whether the wind would blow it down," said Pooh.

"Ah, that's why nobody's bothered, I suppose. I thought perhaps they'd forgotten."

"Well, we're very glad to see you, Eeyore, and now we're going on to see Owl."

"That's right. You'll like Owl. He flew past a day

or two ago and noticed me. He didn't actually say anything, mind you, but he knew it was me. Very friendly of him, I thought. Encouraging."

Pooh and Piglet shuffled about a little and said, "Well, good-bye, Eeyore" as lingeringly as they could, but they had a long way to go, and wanted to be getting on.

"Good-bye," said Eeyore. "Mind you don't get blown away, little Piglet. You'd be missed. People would say 'Where's little Piglet been blown to?'— really wanting to know. Well, good-bye. And thank you for happening to pass me."

"Good-bye," said Pooh and Piglet for the last time, and they pushed on to Owl's house.

The wind was against them now, and Piglet's ears

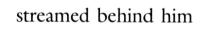

streamed behind him

like banners

as he fought his way along, and it seemed hours before he got them into the shelter of the Hundred Acre Wood and they stood up straight again, to listen, a little nervously, to the roaring of the gale among the tree-tops.

"Supposing a tree fell down, Pooh, when we were underneath it?"

"Supposing it didn't," said Pooh after careful thought.

Piglet was comforted by this, and in a little while they were knocking and ringing very cheerfully at Owl's door.

"Hallo, Owl," said Pooh. "I hope we're not too late for——I mean, how are you, Owl? Piglet and I just came to see how you were, because it's Thursday."

"Sit down, Pooh, sit down, Piglet," said Owl kindly. "Make yourselves comfortable."

They thanked him, and made themselves as comfortable as they could.

"Because, you see, Owl," said Pooh, "we've been hurrying, so as to be in time for—so as to see you before we went away again."

Owl nodded solemnly.

"Correct me if I am wrong," he said, "but am I right in supposing that it is a very Blusterous day outside?"

"Very," said Piglet, who was quietly thawing his

ears, and wishing that he was safely back in his own house.

"I thought so," said Owl. "It was on just such a blusterous day as this that my Uncle Robert, a portrait of whom you see upon the wall on your right, Piglet, while returning in the late forenoon from a——What's that?"

There was a loud cracking noise.

"Look out!" cried Pooh. "Mind the clock! Out of the way, Piglet! Piglet, I'm falling on you!"

"Help!" cried Piglet.

Pooh's side of the room was slowly tilting upwards

and his chair began sliding down on Piglet's. The clock slithered gently along the mantelpiece, collecting vases on the way, until they all crashed together on to what had once been the floor, but was now trying to see what it looked like as a wall. Uncle Robert, who was going to be the new hearthrug, and was bringing the rest of his wall with him as carpet, met Piglet's chair just as Piglet was expecting to leave it, and for a little while it became very difficult to remember which was really the north. Then there was another loud crack . . . Owl's room collected itself feverishly . . . and there was silence.

In a corner of the room, the table-cloth began to

wriggle.

Then it wrapped itself into a ball and rolled

across the room.

Then it jumped up and down once or twice, and put out two ears. It rolled across the room again, and unwound itself.

"Pooh," said Piglet nervously.

"Yes?" said one of the chairs.

"Where are we?"

"I'm not quite sure," said the chair.

"Are we—are we in Owl's House?"

"I think so, because we were just going to have tea, and we hadn't had it."

"Oh!" said Piglet. "Well, did Owl *always* have a letter-box in his ceiling?"

"Has he?"

"Yes, look."

"I can't," said Pooh. "I'm face downwards under something, and that, Piglet, is a very bad position for looking at ceilings."

"Well, he has, Pooh."

"Perhaps he's changed it," said Pooh. "Just for a change."

There was a disturbance behind the table in the other corner of the room, and Owl was with them again.

"Ah, Piglet," said Owl, looking very much annoyed, "where's Pooh?"

"I'm not quite sure," said Pooh.

Owl turned at his voice, and frowned at as much of Pooh as he could see.

"Pooh," said Owl severely, "did *you* do that?"

"No," said Pooh humbly. "I don't *think* so."

"Then who did?"

"I think it was the wind," said Piglet. "I think your house has blown down."

"Oh, is that it? I thought it was Pooh."

"No," said Pooh.

"If it was the wind," said Owl, considering the matter, "then it wasn't Pooh's fault. No blame can be attached to him." With these kind words he flew up to look at his new ceiling.

"Piglet!" called Pooh in a loud whisper.

Piglet leant down to him.

"Yes, Pooh?"

"*What* did he say was attached to me?"

"He said he didn't blame you."

"Oh! I thought he meant——Oh, I see."

"Owl!" said Piglet, "come down and help Pooh."

Owl, who was admiring his letter-box, flew down again. Together they pushed and pulled at the arm-chair, and in a little while Pooh came out from underneath, and was able to look round him again.

"Well!" said Owl. "This is a nice state of things!"

"What are we going to do, Pooh? Can you think of anything?" asked Piglet.

"Well, I *had* just thought of something," said Pooh. "It was just a little thing I thought of." And he began to sing:

> I lay on my chest
> And I thought it best
> To pretend I was having an evening rest;
> I lay on my tum
> And I tried to hum
> But nothing particular seemed to come.
> My face was flat
> On the floor, and that
> Is all very well for an acrobat;
> But it doesn't seem fair
> To a Friendly Bear
> To stiffen him out with a basket-chair.
> And a sort of sqoze
> Which grows and grows
> Is not too nice for his poor old nose,
> And a sort of squch
> Is much too much
> For his neck and his mouth
>   and his ears and such.

"That was all," said Pooh.

Owl coughed in an unadmiring sort of way, and said that, if Pooh was sure that *was* all, they could now give their minds to the Problem of Escape.

"Because," said Owl, "we can't go out by what used to be the front door. Something's fallen on it."

"But how else *can* you go out?" asked Piglet anxiously.

"That is the Problem, Piglet, to which I am asking Pooh to give his mind."

Pooh sat on the floor which had once been a wall, and gazed up at the ceiling which had once been another wall, with a front door in it which had once been a front door, and tried to give his mind to it.

"Could you fly up to the letter-box with Piglet on your back?" he asked.

"No," said Piglet quickly. "He couldn't."

Owl explained about the Necessary Dorsal Muscles. He had explained this to Pooh and Christopher Robin once before, and had been waiting ever since for a chance to do it again, because it is a thing which you can easily explain twice before anybody knows what you are talking about.

"Because you see, Owl, if we could get Piglet into the letter-box, he might squeeze through the place where the letters come, and climb down the tree and run for help."

Piglet said hurriedly that he had been getting bigger lately, and couldn't *possibly*, much as he would like to, and Owl said that he had had his letter-box made bigger lately in case he got bigger letters, so perhaps Piglet *might*, and Piglet said, "But you said the necessary you-know-whats *wouldn't*," and Owl said, "No, they *won't*, so it's no good thinking about it," and Piglet said, "Then we'd better think of something else," and began to at once.

But Pooh's mind had gone back to the day when he had saved Piglet from the flood, and everybody had admired him so much; and as that didn't often happen he thought he would like it to happen again. And suddenly, just as it had come before, an idea came to him.

"Owl," said Pooh, "I have thought of something."

"Astute and Helpful Bear," said Owl.

Pooh looked proud at being called a stout and helpful bear, and said modestly that he just happened to think of it. You tied a piece of string to Piglet, and you flew up to the letter-box with the other end in your beak, and you pushed it through the wire and brought it down to the floor, and you and Pooh pulled hard at this end, and Piglet went slowly up at the other end. And there you were.

"And there Piglet is," said Owl. "If the string doesn't break."

"Supposing it does?" asked Piglet, wanting to know.

"Then we try another piece of string."

This was not very comforting to Piglet, because however many pieces of string they tried pulling up with, it would always be the same him coming down; but still, it did seem the only thing to do. So with one last look back in his mind at all the happy hours he had spent in the Forest *not* being pulled up to the ceiling by a piece of string, Piglet nodded bravely at Pooh and said that it was a Very Clever pup-pup-pup Clever pup-pup Plan.

"It won't break," whispered Pooh comfortingly, "because you're a Small Animal, and I'll stand under-neath, and if you save us all, it will be a Very Grand Thing to talk about afterwards, and perhaps I'll make up a Song, and people will say 'It was so grand what Piglet did that a Respectful Pooh Song was made about it.'"

Piglet felt much better after this, and when every-thing was ready, and he found himself slowly going up to the ceiling, he was so proud that he would have called out "Look at *me*!" if he hadn't been afraid that Pooh and Owl would let go of their end of the string and look at him.

"Up we go!" said Pooh cheerfully.

"The ascent is proceeding as expected," said Owl helpfully. Soon it was over. Piglet opened the letter-box and climbed in. Then, having untied himself, he

began to squeeze into the slit, through which in the

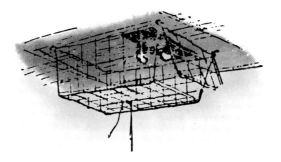

old days when front doors *were* front doors, many an unexpected letter that WOL had written to himself, had come slipping.

He squeezed and he squoze, and then with one last

sqooze he was out. Happy and excited he turned round to squeak a last message to the prisoners.

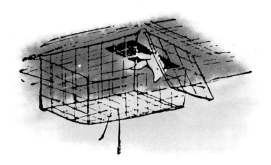

"It's all right," he called through the letter-box. "Your tree is blown right over, Owl, and there's a branch across the door, but Christopher Robin and I can move it, and we'll bring a rope for Pooh, and I'll go and tell him now, and I can climb down quite easily, I mean it's dangerous but I can do it all right, and Christopher Robin and I will be back in about half-an-hour. Good-bye, Pooh!" And without waiting to hear Pooh's answering "Good-bye, and thank you, Piglet," he was off.

"Half-an-hour," said Owl, settling himself comfortably. "That will just give me time to finish that story I was telling you about my Uncle Robert—a portrait of whom you see underneath you. Now let me see, where was I? Oh, yes. It was on just such a blusterous day as this that my Uncle Robert——"

Pooh closed his eyes.

CHAPTER NINE

In Which

Eeyore Finds the Wolery and Owl Moves Into It

POOH HAD WANDERED into the Hundred Acre Wood, and was standing in front of what had once been Owl's House. It didn't look at all like a house now; it looked like a tree which had been blown down; and as soon as a house looks like that, it is time you tried to find another one. Pooh had had a Mysterious Missage underneath his front door that morning, saying, "I AM SCERCHING FOR A NEW HOUSE FOR OWL SO HAD YOU RABBIT," and while he was wondering what it meant, Rabbit had come in and read it for him.

"I'm leaving one for all the others," said Rabbit, "and telling them what it means, and they'll all search too. I'm in a hurry, good-bye." And he had run off.

Pooh followed slowly. He had something better to do than to find a new house for Owl; he had to make up a Pooh song about the old one. Because he had promised Piglet days and days ago that he would, and whenever he and Piglet had met since, Piglet didn't actually say anything, but you knew at once why he didn't; and if anybody mentioned Hums or Trees or String or Storms-in-the-Night, Piglet's nose went all pink at the tip and he talked about something quite different in a hurried sort of way.

"But it isn't Easy," said Pooh to himself, as he looked at what had once been Owl's House. "Be-cause Poetry and Hums aren't things which you get, they're things which get *you*. And all you can do is to go where they can find you."

He waited hopefully. . . .

"Well," said Pooh after a long wait, "I shall begin *'Here lies a tree'* because it does, and then I'll see what happens."

This is what happened.

Here lies a tree which Owl (a bird)
Was fond of when it stood on end,
And Owl was talking to a friend
Called Me (in case you hadn't heard)
When something Oo occurred.

For lo! the wind was blusterous
And flattened out his favourite tree;
And things looks bad for him and we—
Looked bad, I mean, for he and us—
I've never known them wuss.

Then Piglet (PIGLET) thought a thing:
"Courage!" he said. "There's always hope.
I want a thinnish piece of rope.
Or, if there isn't any bring
A thickish piece of string."

So to the letter-box he rose,
While Pooh and Owl said "Oh!"
and "Hum!"
And where the letters always come
(Called "LETTERS ONLY") Piglet sqoze
His head and then his toes.

O gallant Piglet (PIGLET)! Ho!
Did Piglet tremble? Did he blinch?
No, No, he struggled inch by inch
Through LETTERS ONLY, as I know
Because I saw him go.

He ran and ran, and then he stood
And shouted, "Help for Owl, a bird
And Pooh, a bear!" until he heard
The others coming through the wood
As quickly as they could.

"Help-help and Rescue!" Piglet cried
And showed the others where to go.
Sing ho! for Piglet (PIGLET) ho!
And soon the door was opened wide
And we were both outside!

Sing ho! for Piglet, ho!
Ho!

"So there it is," said Pooh, when he had sung this to himself three times. "It's come different from what I thought it would, but it's come. Now I must go and sing it to Piglet."

I AM SCERCHING FOR A NEW HOUSE FOR OWL SO HAD YOU RABBIT.

"What's all this?" said Eeyore.
Rabbit explained.

"What's the matter with his old house?" asked Eeyore.

Rabbit explained.

"Nobody tells me," said Eeyore. "Nobody keeps me Informed. I make it seventeen days come Friday since anybody spoke to me."

"It certainly isn't seventeen days——"

"Come Friday," explained Eeyore.

"And today's Saturday," said Rabbit. "So that would make it eleven days. And I was here myself a week ago."

"Not conversing," said Eeyore. "Not first one and then the other. You said 'Hallo' and Flashed Past. I saw your tail in the distance as I was meditating my reply. I *had* thought of saying 'What?'—but, of course, it was then too late."

"Well, I was in a hurry."

"No Give and Take," Eeyore went on. "No Exchange of Thought: *'Hallo—What'*—— I mean, it gets you nowhere, particularly if the other person's tail is only just in sight for the second half of the conversation."

"It's your fault, Eeyore. You've never been to see any of us. You just stay here in this one corner of the Forest waiting for the others to come to *you*. Why don't you go to *them* sometimes?"

Eeyore was silent for a little while, thinking.

"There may be something in what you say, Rabbit," he said at last. "I must move about more. I must come and go."

"That's right, Eeyore. Drop in on any of us at any time, when you feel like it."

"Thank-you, Rabbit. And if anybody says in a Loud Voice 'Bother, it's Eeyore,' I can drop out again."

Rabbit stood on one leg for a moment.

"Well," he said, "I must be going."

"Good-bye," said Eeyore.

"What? Oh, good-bye. And if you do come across a house for Owl, you must let us know."

"I will give my mind to it," said Eeyore.

Rabbit went.

Pooh had found Piglet, and they were walking back to the Hundred Acre Wood together.

"Piglet," said Pooh a little shyly, after they had walked for some time without saying anything.

"Yes, Pooh?"

"Do you remember when I said that a Respectful Pooh Song might be written about You Know What?"

"Did you, Pooh?" said Piglet, getting a little pink round the nose. "Oh, yes, I believe you did."

"It's been written, Piglet."

The pink went slowly up Piglet's nose to his ears, and settled there.

"Has it, Pooh?" he asked huskily. "About—about

——That Time When?——Do you mean really written?"

"Yes, Piglet."

The tips of Piglet's ears glowed suddenly, and he tried to say something; but even after he had husked once or twice, nothing came out. So Pooh went on.

"There are seven verses in it."

"Seven?" said Piglet as carelessly as he could. "You don't often get *seven* verses in a Hum, do you, Pooh?"

"Never," said Pooh. "I don't suppose it's *ever* been heard of before."

"Do the Others know yet?" asked Piglet, stopping for a moment to pick up a stick and throw it away.

"No," said Pooh. "And I wondered which you would like best. For me to hum it now, or to wait till we find the others, and then hum it to all of you."

Piglet thought for a little.

"I think what I'd like best, Pooh, is I'd like you to hum it to me *now*—and—and *then* to hum it to all of us. Because then Everybody would hear it, but I could say 'Oh, yes, Pooh's told me,' and pretend not to be listening."

So Pooh hummed it to him, all the seven verses and Piglet said nothing, but just stood and glowed.

Never before had anyone sung ho for Piglet (PIG-LET) ho all by himself. When it was over, he wanted to ask for one of the verses over again, but didn't quite like to. It was the verse beginning "O gallant Piglet," and it seemed to him a very thoughtful way of beginning a piece of poetry.

"Did I really do all that?" he said at last.

"Well," said Pooh, "in poetry—in a piece of poetry—well, you *did* it, Piglet, because the poetry says you did. And that's how people know."

"Oh!" said Piglet. "Because I—I thought I did blinch a little. Just at first. And it says, 'Did he blinch no no.' That's why."

"You only blinched inside," said Pooh, "and that's the bravest way for a Very Small Animal not to blinch that there is."

Piglet sighed with happiness, and began to think about himself. He was BRAVE. . . .

When they got to Owl's old house, they found everybody else there except Eeyore. Christopher Robin

was telling them what to do, and Rabbit was telling them again directly afterwards, in case they hadn't heard, and then they were all doing it. They had got a rope and were pulling Owl's chairs and pictures and things out of his old house so as to be ready to put them into his new one. Kanga was down below tying the things on, and calling out to Owl, "You won't want this dirty old dish-cloth any more, will you, and

what about this carpet, it's all in holes," and Owl was calling back indignantly, "Of course I do! It's just a question of arranging the furniture properly, and it isn't a dish-cloth, it's my shawl." Every now and then Roo fell in and came back on the rope with the next article, which flustered Kanga a little because she never knew where to look for him. So she got cross with Owl and said that his house was a Disgrace, all damp and dirty, and it was quite time it did tumble down. Look at that horrid bunch of toadstools growing out of the floor there! So Owl looked down, a little surprised because he didn't know about this, and then gave a short sarcastic laugh, and explained that that was his sponge, and that if people didn't know a perfectly ordinary bath-sponge when they saw it, things were coming to a pretty pass. *"Well!"* said Kanga, and Roo fell in quickly, crying, "I *must* see Owl's sponge! Oh, there it is! Oh, Owl! Owl, it isn't a sponge, it's a spudge! Do you know what a spudge is, Owl? It's when your sponge gets all——" and Kanga said, "Roo, dear!" very quickly, because that's *not* the way to talk to anybody who can spell TUES-DAY.

But they were all quite happy when Pooh and Piglet came along, and they stopped working in order to have a little rest and listen to Pooh's new song. So then they all told Pooh how good it was and Piglet said carelessly, "It *is* good, isn't it? I mean as a song."

"And what about the new house?" asked Pooh. "Have you found it, Owl?"

"He's found a name for it," said Christopher Robin, lazily nibbling at a piece of grass, "so now all he wants is the house."

"I am calling it this," said Owl importantly, and he showed them what he had been making. It was a square piece of board with the name of the house painted on it.

THE WOLERY

It was at this exciting moment that something came through the trees, and bumped into Owl. The board fell to the ground, and Piglet and Roo bent over it eagerly.

"Oh, it's you," said Owl crossly.

"Hallo, Eeyore!" said Rabbit. "*There* you are!

Where have *you* been?" Eeyore took no notice of them.

"Good morning, Christopher Robin," he said, brushing away Roo and Piglet, and sitting down on THE WOLERY. "Are we alone?"

"Yes," said Christopher Robin, smiling to himself. "I have been told—the news has worked through to my corner of the Forest—the damp bit down on the right which nobody wants—that a certain Person is looking for a house. I have found one for him."

"Ah, well done," said Rabbit kindly.

Eeyore looked round slowly at him, and then turned back to Christopher Robin.

"We have been joined by something," he said in a loud whisper. "But no matter. We can leave it behind. If you will come with me, Christopher Robin, I will show you the house."

Christopher Robin jumped up.

"Come on, Pooh," he said.

"Come on, Tigger!" cried Roo.

"Shall we go, Owl?" said Rabbit.

"Wait a moment," said Owl, picking up his noticeboard, which had just come into sight again.

Eeyore waved them back.

"Christopher Robin and I are going for a Short Walk," he said, "not a Jostle. If he likes to bring Pooh and Piglet with him, I shall be glad of their company, but one must be able to Breathe."

"That's all right," said Rabbit, rather glad to be left in charge of something. "We'll go on getting the things out. Now then, Tigger, where's that rope? What's the matter, Owl?"

Owl, who had just discovered that his new address was THE SMUDGE, coughed at Eeyore sternly, but said nothing, and Eeyore, with most of THE WOLERY behind him, marched off with his friends.

So, in a little while, they came to the house which Eeyore had found, and for some minutes before they came to it, Piglet was nudging Pooh, and Pooh was nudging Piglet, and they were saying, "It is!" and "It can't be!" and "It is, *really*!" to each other.

And when they got there, it really was.

"There!" said Eeyore proudly, stopping them outside Piglet's house. "And the name on it, and everything!"

"Oh!" cried Christopher Robin, wondering whether to laugh or what.

"Just the house for Owl. Don't you think so, little Piglet?"

And then Piglet did a Noble Thing, and he did it in a sort of dream, while he was thinking of all the wonderful words Pooh had hummed about him.

"Yes, it's just the house for Owl," he said grandly. "And I hope he'll be very happy in it." And then he gulped twice, because he had been very happy in it himself.

"What do *you* think, Christopher Robin?" asked Eeyore a little anxiously, feeling that something wasn't quite right.

Christopher Robin had a question to ask first, and he was wondering how to ask it.

"Well," he said at last, "it's a very nice house, and if your own house is blown down, you *must* go somewhere else, mustn't you, Piglet? What would *you* do, if *your* house was blown down?"

Before Piglet could think, Pooh answered for him.

"He'd come and live with me," said Pooh, "wouldn't you, Piglet?"

Piglet squeezed his paw.

"Thank you, Pooh," he said, "I should love to."

CHAPTER TEN

In Which

Christopher Robin and Pooh Come to an Enchanted Place, and We Leave Them There

CHRISTOPHER ROBIN was going away. Nobody knew why he was going; nobody knew where he was going; indeed, nobody even knew why he knew that Christopher Robin *was* going away. But somehow or other everybody in the Forest felt that it was happening at last. Even Smallest-of-All, a friend-and-relation of Rabbit's who thought he had once seen Christopher Robin's foot, but couldn't be sure because perhaps it was something else, even S.-of-A. told himself that Things were going to be Different; and Late and Early, two other friends-and-relations, said, "Well, Early?" and "Well, Late?" to each other in such a hopeless sort of way that it really didn't seem any good waiting for the answer.

One day when he felt that he couldn't wait any longer, Rabbit brained out a Notice, and this is what it said:

"Notice a meeting of everybody will meet at the House at Pooh Corner to pass a Rissolution By Order Keep to the Left Signed Rabbit."

He had to write this out two or three times before he could get the rissolution to look like what he thought it was going to when he began to spell it: but, when at last it was finished, he took it round to everybody and read it out to them. And they all said they would come.

"Well," said Eeyore that afternoon, when he saw them all walking up to his house, "this *is* a surprise. Am *I* asked too?"

"Don't mind Eeyore," whispered Rabbit to Pooh. "I told him all about it this morning."

Everybody said "How-do-you-do" to Eeyore, and Eeyore said that he didn't, not to notice, and then they sat down; and as soon as they were all sitting down, Rabbit stood up again.

"We all know why we're here," he said, "but I have asked my friend Eeyore——"

"That's Me," said Eeyore. "Grand."

"I have asked him to Propose a Rissolution." And he sat down again. "Now then, Eeyore," he said.

"Don't Bustle me," said Eeyore, getting up slowly. "Don't now-then me." He took a piece of paper from behind his ear, and unfolded it. "Nobody knows anything about this," he went on. "This is a Surprise." He coughed in an important way, and began again: "What-nots and Etceteras, before I begin, or perhaps I should say, before I end, I have a piece of Poetry to read to you. Hitherto—hitherto—a long word meaning—well, you'll see what it means directly—hitherto, as I was saying, all the Poetry in the Forest has been written by Pooh, a Bear with a Pleasing

Manner but a Positively Startling Lack of Brain. The Poem which I am now about to read to you was written by Eeyore, or Myself, in a Quiet Moment. If somebody will take Roo's bull's-eye away from him, and wake up Owl, we shall all be able to enjoy it. I call it—POEM."

This was it.

Christopher Robin is going.
At least I think he is.
Where?
Nobody knows.
But he is going—
I mean he goes
(To rhyme with "knows")
Do we care?
(To rhyme with "where")
We do
Very much.
(I haven't got a rhyme for that
  "is" in the second line yet.
  Bother.)
(Now I haven't got a rhyme for
  bother. Bother.)
Those two bothers will have
  to rhyme with each other
  Buther.
The fact is this is more difficult
  than I thought,
I ought—
(Very good indeed)

I ought
To begin again,
But it is easier
To stop.
Christopher Robin, good-bye,
I
(Good)
I
And all your friends
Sends—
I mean all your friend
Send—
(Very awkward this, it keeps
going wrong)
Well, anyhow, we send
Our love
END.

"If anybody wants to clap," said Eeyore when he had read this, "now is the time to do it."

They all clapped.

"Thank you," said Eeyore. "Unexpected and gratifying, if a little lacking in Smack."

WOL

Piglet

"It's much better than mine," said Pooh admiringly, and he really thought it was.

eOR

"Well," explained Eeyore modestly, "it was meant to be."

Rabbit

"The rissolution," said Rabbit, "is that we all sign it, and take it to Christopher Robin."

So it was signed PooH, PIGLET, WOL, EOR, RABBIT, KANGA,

BLOT,

SMUDGE,

and they all went off to Christopher Robin's house

with it. "Hallo, everybody," said Christopher Robin
—"Hallo, Pooh."

They all said "Hallo," and felt awkward and un-
happy suddenly, because it was a sort of good-bye
they were saying, and they didn't want to think about
it. So they stood around, and waited for somebody
else to speak, and they nudged each other, and said
"Go on," and gradually Eeyore was nudged to the
front, and the others crowded behind him.

"What is it, Eeyore?" asked Christopher Robin.
Eeyore swished his tail from side to side, so as to
encourage himself, and began.

"Christopher Robin," he said, "we've come to say
—to give you—it's called—written by—but we've
all—because we've heard, I mean we all know—
well, you see, it's—we—you—well, that, to put it as
shortly as possible, is what it is." He turned round
angrily on the others and said, "Everybody crowds
round so in this Forest. There's no Space. I never saw
a more Spreading lot of animals in my life, and all
in the wrong places. Can't you *see* that Christopher Robin wants to be alone? I'm going." And he
humped off.

Not quite knowing why, the others began edging
away, and when Christopher Robin had finished reading POEM, and was looking up to say, "Thank you,"
only Pooh was left.

"It's a comforting sort of thing to have," said

Christopher Robin, folding up the paper, and putting it in his pocket. "Come on, Pooh," and he walked off quickly.

"Where are we going?" said Pooh, hurrying after him, and wondering whether it was to be an Explore or a What-shall-I-do-about-you-know-what.

335

"Nowhere," said Christopher Robin.

So they began going there, and after they had walked a little way Christopher Robin said:

"What do you like doing best in the world, Pooh?"

"Well," said Pooh, "what I like best——" and then he had to stop and think. Because although Eating Honey *was* a very good thing to do, there was a moment just before you began to eat it which was better than when you were, but he didn't know what it was called. And then he thought that being with Christopher Robin was a very good thing to do, and having Piglet near was a very friendly thing to have; and so, when he had thought it all out, he said, "What I like best in the whole world is Me and Piglet going to see You, and You saying 'What about a little something?' and Me saying, 'Well, I shouldn't mind a little something, should you, Piglet,' and it being a hummy sort of day outside, and birds singing."

"I like that too," said Christopher Robin, "but what I like *doing* best is Nothing."

"How do you do Nothing?" asked Pooh, after he had wondered for a long time.

"Well, it's when people call out at you just as you're going off to do it, What are you going to do, Christopher Robin, and you say, Oh, nothing, and then you go and do it."

"Oh, I see," said Pooh.

"This is a nothing sort of thing that we're doing now."

"Oh, I see," said Pooh again.

"It means just going along, listening to all the things you can't hear, and not bothering."

"Oh!" said Pooh.

They walked on, thinking of This and That, and by-and-by they came to an enchanted place on the very top of the Forest called Galleons Lap, which is sixty-something trees in a circle; and Christopher Robin knew that it was enchanted because nobody had ever been able to count whether it was sixty-three or sixty-four, not even when he tied a piece of string round each tree after he had counted it. Being enchanted, its floor was not like the floor of the Forest, gorse and bracken and heather, but close-set grass, quiet and smooth and green. It was the only place in the Forest where you could sit down carelessly, without getting up again almost at once and looking for somewhere else. Sitting there they could see the whole world spread out until it reached the sky, and whatever there was all the world over was with them in Galleons Lap.

Suddenly Christopher Robin began to tell Pooh about some of the things: People called Kings and Queens and something called Factors, and a place called Europe, and an island in the middle of the sea

where no ships came, and how you make a Suction
Pump (if you want to), and when Knights were

Knighted, and what comes from Brazil. And Pooh, his back against one of the sixty-something trees, and his paws folded in front of him, said "Oh!" and "I didn't know," and thought how wonderful it would be to have a Real Brain which could tell you things. And by-and-by Christopher Robin came to an end of the things, and was silent, and he sat there looking out over the world, and wishing it wouldn't stop.

But Pooh was thinking too, and he said suddenly to Christopher Robin:

"Is it a very Grand thing to be an Afternoon, what you said?"

"A what?" said Christopher Robin lazily, as he listened to something else.

"On a horse," explained Pooh.

"A Knight?"

"Oh, was that it?" said Pooh. "I thought it was a ——Is it as Grand as a King and Factors and all the other things you said?"

"Well, it's not as grand as a King," said Christopher Robin, and then, as Pooh seemed disappointed, he added quickly, "but it's grander than Factors."

"Could a Bear be one?"

"Of course he could!" said Christopher Robin. "I'll make you one." And he took a stick and touched Pooh on the shoulder, and said, "Rise, Sir Pooh de Bear, most faithful of all my Knights."

So Pooh rose and sat down and said "Thank you," which is the proper thing to say when you have been made a Knight, and he went into a dream again, in which he and Sir Pomp and Sir Brazil and Factors lived together with a horse, and were faithful Knights (all except Factors, who looked after the horse) to Good King Christopher Robin . . . and every now and then he shook his head, and said to himself "I'm not getting it right." Then he began to think of all

341

the things Christopher Robin would want to tell him when he came back from wherever he was going to, and how muddling it would be for a Bear of Very Little Brain to try and get them right in his mind. "So, perhaps," he said sadly to himself, "Christopher Robin won't tell me any more," and he wondered if being a Faithful Knight meant that you just went on being faithful without being told things.

Then, suddenly again, Christopher Robin, who was still looking at the world, with his chin in his hands, called out "Pooh!"

"Yes?" said Pooh.

"When I'm—when——Pooh!"

"Yes, Christopher Robin?"

"I'm not going to do Nothing any more."

"Never again?"

"Well, not so much. They don't let you."

Pooh waited for him to go on, but he was silent again.

"Yes, Christopher Robin?" said Pooh helpfully.

"Pooh, when I'm—*you* know—when I'm *not*

doing Nothing, will you come up here sometimes?"

"Just Me?"

"Yes, Pooh."

"Will you be here too?"

"Yes, Pooh, I will be, *really*. I *promise* I will be, Pooh."

"That's good," said Pooh.

"Pooh, *promise* you won't forget about me, ever. Not even when I'm a hundred."

Pooh thought for a little.

"How old shall *I* be then?"

"Ninety-nine."

Pooh nodded.

"I promise," he said.

Still with his eyes on the world Christopher Robin put out a hand and felt for Pooh's paw.

"Pooh," said Christopher Robin earnestly, "if I— if I'm not quite——" he stopped and tried again— "Pooh, *whatever* happens, you *will* understand, won't you?"

"Understand what?"

"Oh, nothing." He laughed and jumped to his feet. "Come on!"

"Where?" said Pooh.

"Anywhere," said Christopher Robin.

* * *

So they went off together. But wherever they go, and whatever happens to them on the way, in that enchanted place on the top of the Forest, a little boy and his Bear will always be playing.

to
CHRISTOPHER ROBIN MILNE
or
as he prefers to call himself
BILLY MOON
this book
which owes so much to him
is now
humbly offered

WHEN WE WERE
VERY YOUNG

Just Before We Begin

AT ONE TIME (but I have changed my mind now) I thought I was going to write a little Note at the top of each of these poems, in the manner of Mr. William Wordsworth, who liked to tell his readers where he was staying, and which of his friends he was walking with, and what he was thinking about, when the idea of writing his poem came to him. You will find some lines about a swan here, if you get as far as that, and I should have explained to you in the Note that Christopher Robin, who feeds this swan in the mornings, has given him the name of "Pooh." This is a very fine name for a swan, because, if you call him and he doesn't come (which is a thing swans are good at), then you can pretend that you were just saying "Pooh!" to show how little you wanted him. Well, I should have told you that there are six cows who come down to Pooh's lake every afternoon to drink, and of course they say "Moo" as they come. So I thought to myself one fine day, walking with my friend Christopher Robin, "Moo rhymes with Pooh! Surely there is a bit of poetry to be got out of that?" Well, then, I began to think about the swan on his lake; and at first I thought how lucky it was that his name was Pooh; and then I didn't think about that any more . . . and the poem came quite differently from what I intended . . . and all I can say for it now is that, if it hadn't been for Christopher Robin, I shouldn't have written it; which, indeed, is all I can say for any of the others. So this is why these verses go about together, because they are all friends of Christopher Robin; and if I left out one because it was not quite like the one before, then I should have to leave out the one before because it was not quite like the next, which would be disappointing for them.

Then there is another thing. You may wonder sometimes who is supposed to be saying the verses. Is it the Author, that strange but uninteresting person, or is it Christopher Robin, or some other boy or girl, or Nurse, or Hoo? If I had followed Mr. Wordsworth's plan I could have explained this each time; but, as it is, you will have to decide for yourselves. If you are not quite sure, then it is probably Hoo. I don't know if you have ever met Hoo, but he is one of those curious children who look four on Monday, and eight on Tuesday, and are really twenty-eight on Saturday, and you never know whether it is the day when he can pronounce his "r's." He had a great deal to do with these verses. In fact, you might almost say that this book is entirely the unaided work of Christopher Robin, Hoo, and Mr. Shepard, who drew the pictures. They have said "Thank you" politely to each other several times, and now they say it to you for taking them into your house. "Thank you so much for asking us. We've come."

A.A.M.

Corner-of-the-Street

Down by the corner of the street,
   Where the three roads meet,
     And the feet
Of the people as they pass go "Tweet-tweet-tweet—"
Who comes tripping round the corner of the street?
   One pair of shoes which are Nurse's;
   One pair of slippers which are Percy's . . .
     Tweet! Tweet! Tweet!

353

Buckingham Palace

They're changing guard at Buckingham Palace—
Christopher Robin went down with Alice.
Alice is marrying one of the guard.
"A soldier's life is terrible hard,"
                    Says Alice.

They're changing guard at Buckingham Palace—
Christopher Robin went down with Alice.
We saw a guard in a sentry-box.
"One of the sergeants looks after their socks,"
                    Says Alice.

They're changing guard at Buckingham Palace—
Christopher Robin went down with Alice.
We looked for the King, but he never came.
"Well, God take care of him, all the same,"
                    Says Alice.

They're changing guard at Buckingham Palace—
Christopher Robin went down with Alice.
They've great big parties inside the grounds.
"I wouldn't be King for a hundred pounds,"
                    Says Alice.

They're changing guard at Buckingham Palace—
Christopher Robin went down with Alice.
A face looked out, but it wasn't the King's.
"He's much too busy a-signing things,"
                    Says Alice.

They're changing guard at Buckingham Palace—
Christopher Robin went down with Alice.
"Do you think the King knows all about *me*?"
"Sure to, dear, but it's time for tea,"
                    Says Alice.

Happiness

John had
Great Big
Waterproof
Boots on;
John had a
Great Big
Waterproof
Hat;
John had a
Great Big
Waterproof
Mackintosh—
And that
(Said John)
Is
That.

The Christening

What shall I call
   My dear little dormouse?
His eyes are small,
   But his tail is e-nor-mouse.

I sometimes call him Terrible John,
'Cos his tail goes on—
And on—
And on.
And I sometimes call him Terrible Jack,
'Cos his tail goes on to the end of his back.
And I sometimes call him Terrible James,
'Cos he says he likes me calling him names. . . .

   But I think I shall call him Jim,
   'Cos I *am* so fond of him.

Puppy and I

I met a man as I went walking;
We got talking,
Man and I.
"Where are you going to, Man?" I said
(I said to the Man as he went by).
"Down to the village, to get some bread.
Will you come with me?" "No, not I."

I met a Horse as I went walking;
We got talking,
Horse and I.
"Where are you going to, Horse, today?"
(I said to the Horse as he went by).
"Down to the village to get some hay.
Will you come with me?" "No, not I."

I met a Woman as I went walking;
We got talking,
Woman and I.
"Where are you going to, Woman, so early?"
(I said to the Woman as she went by).
"Down to the village to get some barley.
Will you come with me?" "No, not I."

I met some Rabbits as I went walking;
We got talking,
Rabbits and I.
"Where are you going in your brown fur coats?"
(I said to the Rabbits as they went by).
"Down to the village to get some oats.
Will you come with us?" "No, not I."

I met a Puppy as I went walking;
We got talking,
Puppy and I.
"Where are you going this nice fine day?"
(I said to the Puppy as he went by).
"Up in the hills to roll and play."
"*I'll* come with you, Puppy," said I.

Twinkletoes

When the sun
Shines through the leaves of the apple-tree,
When the sun
Makes shadows of the leaves of the apple-tree,
Then I pass
On the grass
From one leaf to another,
From one leaf to its brother,
Tip-toe, tip-toe!
Here I go!

The Four Friends

Ernest was an elephant, a great big fellow,
    Leonard was a lion with a six-foot tail,
George was a goat, and his beard was yellow,
    And James was a very small snail.

Leonard had a stall, and a great big strong one,
    Ernest had a manger, and its walls were thick,
George found a pen, but I think it was the wrong
    one,
    And James sat down on a brick.

Ernest started trumpeting, and cracked his manger,
  Leonard started roaring, and shivered his stall,
James gave the huffle of a snail in danger
    And nobody heard him at all.

Ernest started trumpeting and raised such a rumpus,
  Leonard started roaring and trying to kick,
James went a journey with the goat's new compass
    And he reached the end of his brick.

Ernest was an elephant and very well-intentioned,
  Leonard was a lion with a brave new tail,
George was a goat, as I think I have mentioned,
    But James was only a snail.

Lines and Squares

Whenever I walk in a London street,
I'm ever so careful to watch my feet;
 And I keep in the squares,
 And the masses of bears,
Who wait at the corners all ready to eat
The sillies who tread on the lines of the street,
 Go back to their lairs,
 And I say to them, "Bears,
 Just look how I'm walking in all of the squares!"

And the little bears growl to each other,
   "He's mine,
As soon as he's silly and steps on a line."
And some of the bigger bears try to pretend
That they came round the corner to look
   for a friend;
And they try to pretend that nobody cares
Whether you walk on the lines or squares.
But only the sillies believe their talk;
It's ever so portant how you walk.
And it's ever so jolly to call out, "Bears,
Just watch me walking in all the squares!"

Brownie

In a corner of the bedroom is a great big curtain,
    Someone lives behind it, but I don't know who;
I think it is a Brownie, but I'm not quite certain.
    (Nanny isn't certain, too.)
I looked behind the curtain, but he went so
        quickly—
    Brownies never wait to say, "How do you do?"
They wriggle off at once because they're all so
        tickly.
    (Nanny says they're tickly too.)

Independence

I never did, I never did, I never *did* like
      "Now take care, dear!"
  I never did, I never did, I never *did* want
      "Hold-my-hand";
I never did, I never did, I never *did* think much of
      "Not up there, dear!"
  It's no good saying it. They don't understand.

367

Nursery Chairs

One of the chairs is South America,
One of the chairs is a ship at sea,
One is a cage for a great big lion,
And one is a chair for Me.

THE FIRST CHAIR

When I go up the Amazon,
I stop at night and fire a gun
  To call my faithful band.
And Indians in twos and threes,
Come silently between the trees,
  And wait for me to land.
And if I do not want to play
With any Indians today,
  I simply wave my hand.
And then they turn and go away—
  They always understand.

THE SECOND CHAIR

I'm a great big lion in my cage,
　And I often frighten Nanny with a roar.
　　Then I hold her very tight, and
　　Tell her not to be so frightened—
And she doesn't be so frightened any more.

THE THIRD CHAIR

When I am in my ship, I see
    The other ships go sailing by.
A sailor leans and calls to me
    As his ship goes sailing by.
Across the sea he leans to me,
    Above the winds I hear him cry:
"Is this the way to Round-the-World?"
    He calls as he goes by.

THE FOURTH CHAIR

Whenever I sit in a high chair
   For breakfast or dinner or tea,
I try to pretend that it's *my* chair,
   And that I am a baby of three.

Shall I go off to South America?
   Shall I put out in my ship to sea?
Or get in my cage and be lions and tigers?
   Or—shall I be only Me?

THE COMPLETE POEMS OF POOH

Market Square

I had a penny,
A bright new penny,
I took my penny
    To the market square.
I wanted a rabbit,
A little brown rabbit,
And I looked for a rabbit
    'Most everywhere.

For I went to the stall where they sold sweet
    lavender.
("Only a penny for a bunch of lavender!")
"Have you got a rabbit, 'cos I don't want
    lavender?"
      But they hadn't got a rabbit, not anywhere
        there.

I had a penny,
And I had another penny,
I took my pennies
    To the market square.
I did want a rabbit,
A little baby rabbit,
And I looked for rabbits
    'Most everywhere.

And I went to the stall where they sold fresh
    mackerel.
(*"Now then! Tuppence for a fresh-caught mackerel!"*)
"Have you got a rabbit, 'cos I don't like
    mackerel?"
      But they hadn't got a rabbit, not anywhere
        there.

THE COMPLETE POEMS OF POOH

I found a sixpence,
A little white sixpence.
I took it in my hand
   To the market square.
I was buying my rabbit
(I do like rabbits),
And I looked for my rabbit
   'Most everywhere.

So I went to the stall where they sold fine
   saucepans.
("Walk up, walk up, sixpence for a saucepan!")
"Could I have a rabbit, 'cos we've got two
   saucepans?"
   But they hadn't got a rabbit, not anywhere
    there.

I had nuffin',
No, I hadn't got nuffin',
So I didn't go down
   To the market square;
But I walked on the common,
The old-gold common . . .
And I saw little rabbits
'Most everywhere!

So I'm sorry for the people who sell fine saucepans,
I'm sorry for the people who sell fresh mackerel,
I'm sorry for the people who sell sweet lavender,
   'Cos they haven't got a rabbit, not anywhere
     there!

Daffodowndilly

She wore her yellow sun-bonnet,
  She wore her greenest gown;
She turned to the south wind
  And curtsied up and down.
She turned to the sunlight
  And shook her yellow head,
And whispered to her neighbour:
  "Winter is dead."

Water-Lilies

Where the water-lilies go
To and fro,
Rocking in the ripples of the water,
Lazy on a leaf lies the Lake King's daughter,
And the faint winds shake her.
Who will come and take her?
I will! I will!
Keep still! Keep still!
Sleeping on a leaf lies the Lake King's daughter. . . .
Then the wind comes skipping
To the lilies on the water;
And the kind winds wake her.
Now who will take her?
With a laugh she is slipping
Through the lilies on the water.
Wait! Wait!
Too late, too late!
Only the water-lilies go
To and fro,
Dipping, dipping,
To the ripples of the water.

381

Disobedience

James James
Morrison Morrison
Weatherby George Dupree
Took great
Care of his Mother,
Though he was only three.
James James
Said to his Mother,
"Mother," he said, said he:
"You must never go down to the end of the town,
    if you don't go down with me."

James James
Morrison's Mother
Put on a golden gown,
James James
Morrison's Mother
Drove to the end of the town.
James James
Morrison's Mother
Said to herself, said she:
"I can get right down to the end of the town
    and be back in time for tea."

King John
Put up a notice,
"LOST or STOLEN or STRAYED!
JAMES JAMES
MORRISON'S MOTHER
SEEMS TO HAVE BEEN MISLAID.
LAST SEEN
WANDERING VAGUELY:
QUITE OF HER OWN ACCORD,
SHE TRIED TO GET DOWN TO THE END
        OF THE TOWN—FORTY SHILLINGS
        REWARD!"

James James
Morrison Morrison
(Commonly known as Jim)
Told his
Other relations
Not to go blaming *him*.
James James
Said to his Mother,
"Mother," he said, said he:
"You must *never* go down to the end of the town
without consulting me."

James James
Morrison's mother
Hasn't been heard of since.
King John
Said he was sorry,
So did the Queen and Prince.
King John
(Somebody told me)
Said to a man he knew:
"If people go down to the end of the town, well,
    what can *anyone* do?"

  (Now then, very softly)

J. J.
M. M.
W. G. Du P.
Took great
C/o his M*****
Though he was only 3.
J. J.
Said to his M*****
"M*****," he said, said he:
"You-must-never-go-down-to-the-end-of-the-town-
    if-you-don't-go-down-with ME!"

385

Spring Morning

Where am I going? I don't quite know.
Down to the stream where the king-cups
    grow—
Up on the hill where the pine-trees blow—
Anywhere, anywhere. *I* don't know.

Where am I going? The clouds sail by,
Little one, baby ones, over the sky.
Where am I going? The shadows pass,
Little ones, baby ones, over the grass.

If you were a cloud, and sailed up there,
You'd sail on water as blue as air,
And you'd see me here in the fields and say:
"Doesn't the sky look green today?"

Where am I going? The high rooks call:
"It's awful fun to be born at all."
Where am I going? The ring-doves coo:
"We do have beautiful things to do."

If you were a bird, and lived on high,
You'd lean on the wind when the wind came by,
You'd say to the wind when it took you away:
"*That's* where I wanted to go today!"

Where am I going? I don't quite know.
What does it matter where people go?
Down to the wood where the blue-bells grow—
Anywhere, anywhere. *I* don't know.

The Island

If I had a ship,
I'd sail my ship,
I'd sail my ship
Through Eastern seas;
Down to a beach where the slow waves
    thunder—
The green curls over and the white falls
    under—
Boom! Boom! Boom!
On the sun-bright sand.

Then I'd leave my ship and I'd land,
And climb the steep white sand,
And climb to the trees,
The six dark trees,
The coco-nut trees on the cliff's green crown—
Hands and knees
To the coco-nut trees,
Face to the cliff as the stones patter down,
Up, up, up, staggering, stumbling,
Round the corner where the rock is crumbling
Round this shoulder,
Over this boulder,
Up to the top where the six trees stand. . . .

And there would I rest, and lie,
My chin in my hands, and gaze
At the dazzle of sand below,
And the green waves curling slow,
And the grey-blue distant haze
Where the sea goes up to the sky. . . .

And I'd say to myself as I looked so lazily down at
    the sea:
"There's nobody else in the world, and the world
    was made for me."

The Three Foxes

Once upon a time there were three little foxes
Who didn't wear stockings, and they didn't wear
    sockses,
But they all had handkerchiefs to blow their noses,
And they kept their handkerchiefs in cardboard
    boxes.

They lived in the forest in three little houses,
And they didn't wear coats, and they didn't wear
    trousies.
They ran through the woods on their little bare
    tootsies,
And they played "Touch Last" with a family of
    mouses.

They didn't go shopping in the High Street
    shopses,
But caught what they wanted in the woods and
    copses.
They all went fishing, and they caught three
    wormses,
They went out hunting, and they caught three
    wopses.

391

They went to a Fair, and they all won prizes—
Three plum-puddingses and three mince-pieses.
They rode on elephants and swang on swingses,
And hit three coco-nuts at coco-nut shieses.

That's all that I know of the three little foxes
Who kept their handkerchiefs in cardboard boxes.
They lived in the forest in three little houses,
But they didn't wear coats and they didn't wear
    trousies,
And they didn't wear stockings and they didn't
    wear sockses.

Politeness

If people ask me,
I always tell them:
"Quite well, thank you, I'm very glad to say."
If people ask me,
I always answer,
"Quite well, thank you, how are you today?"
I always answer,
I always tell them,
If they ask me
Politely. . . .
BUT SOMETIMES

                    I wish

                            That they wouldn't.

Jonathan Jo

Jonathan Jo
Has a mouth like an "O"
And a wheelbarrow full of surprises;
    If you ask for a bat,
    Or for something like that,
He has got it, whatever the size is.

If you're wanting a ball,
    It's no trouble at all;
Why, the more that you ask for, the merrier—
    Like a hoop and a top,
    And a watch that won't stop,
And some sweets, and an Aberdeen terrier.

Jonathan Jo
    Has a mouth like an "O"
But this is what makes him so funny:
    If you give him a smile,
    Only once in a while,
Then he never expects any money!

395

At the Zoo

There are lions and roaring tigers, and enormous
   camels and things,
There are biffalo-buffalo-bisons, and a great big
   bear with wings,
There's a sort of a tiny potamus, and a tiny
   nosserus too—
But *I* gave buns to the elephant when *I* went down
   to the Zoo!

There are badgers and bidgers and bodgers, and a
      Superintendent's House,
There are masses of goats, and a Polar, and different
      kinds of mouse,
And I think there's a sort of a something which is
      called a wallaboo—
But *I* gave buns to the elephant when *I* went down
      to the Zoo!

If you try to talk to the bison, he never quite
      understands;
You can't shake hands with a mingo—he doesn't
      like shaking hands.
And lions and roaring tigers *hate* saying, "How do
      you do?"—
But *I* give buns to the elephant when *I* go down to
      the Zoo!

Rice Pudding

What is the matter with Mary Jane?
She's crying with all her might and main,
And she won't eat her dinner—rice pudding
    again—
What *is* the matter with Mary Jane?

What is the matter with Mary Jane?
I've promised her dolls and a daisy-chain,
And a book about animals—all in vain—
What *is* the matter with Mary Jane?

What is the matter with Mary Jane?
She's perfectly well, and she hasn't a pain;
But, look at her, now she's beginning again!—
What *is* the matter with Mary Jane?

What is the matter with Mary Jane?
I've promised her sweets and a ride in the train,
And I've begged her to stop for a bit and explain—
What *is* the matter with Mary Jane?

What is the matter with Mary Jane?
She's perfectly well, and she hasn't a pain,
And it's lovely rice pudding for dinner again!—
What *is* the matter with Mary Jane?

Missing

Has anybody seen my mouse?

I opened his box for half a minute,
Just to make sure he was really in it,
And while I was looking, he jumped outside!
I tried to catch him, I tried, I tried. . . .
I think he's somewhere about the house.
Has *anyone* seen my mouse?

Uncle John, have you seen my mouse?

Just a small sort of mouse, a dear little brown one
He came from the country, he wasn't a town one,
So he'll feel all lonely in a London street;
Why, what could he possibly find to eat?

He must be somewhere. I'll ask Aunt Rose:
Have *you* seen a mouse with a woffelly nose?
Oh, somewhere about—
He's just got out. . . .

Hasn't *anybody* seen my mouse?

The King's Breakfast

The King asked
The Queen, and
The Queen asked
The Dairymaid:
"Could we have some butter for
The Royal slice of bread?"
The Queen asked
The Dairymaid,
The Dairymaid
Said, "Certainly,
I'll go and tell
The cow
Now
Before she goes to bed."

The Dairymaid
She curtsied,
And went and told
The Alderney:
"Don't forget the butter for
The Royal slice of bread."

The Alderney
Said sleepily:
"You'd better tell
His Majesty
That many people nowadays
Like marmalade
Instead."

The Dairymaid
Said, "Fancy!"
And went to
Her Majesty.
She curtsied to the Queen, and
She turned a little red:
"Excuse me,
Your Majesty,
For taking of
The liberty,
But marmalade is tasty, if
It's very
Thickly
Spread."

The Queen said
"Oh!"
And went to
His Majesty:
"Talking of the butter for
The Royal slice of bread,
Many people
Think that
Marmalade
Is nicer.
Would you like to try a little
Marmalade
Instead?"

The King said,
"Bother!"
And then he said,
"Oh, dear me!"
The King sobbed, "Oh, deary me!"
And went back to bed.
"Nobody,"
He whimpered,
"Could call me
A fussy man;
I *only* want
A little bit
Of butter for
My bread!"

The Queen said,
"There, there!"
And went to
The Dairymaid.
The Dairymaid
Said, "There, there!"
And went to the shed.
The cow said,
"There, there!

I didn't really
Mean it;
Here's milk for his porringer
And butter for his bread."

The Queen took
The butter
And brought it to
His Majesty;
The King said,
"Butter, eh?"
And bounced out of bed.
"Nobody," he said,
As he kissed her
Tenderly,
"Nobody," he said,
As he slid down
The banisters,
"Nobody,
My darling,
Could call me
A fussy man—
BUT
I do like a little bit of butter to my bread!"

Hoppity

Christopher Robin goes
Hoppity, hoppity,

Hoppity, hoppity, hop.
Whenever I tell him
Politely to stop it, he
Says he can't possibly stop.

If he stopped hopping,
    he couldn't go anywhere,
Poor little Christopher
Couldn't go anywhere. . . .
That's why he *always* goes
Hoppity, hoppity,
Hoppity,
Hoppity,
Hop.

410

At Home

I want a soldier
(A soldier in a busby),
I want a soldier to come and play with me.
I'd give him cream-cakes
(Big ones, sugar ones),
I'd give him cream-cakes and cream for his tea.

I want a soldier
(A tall one, a red one),
I want a soldier who plays on the drum.
Daddy's going to get one
(He's written to the shopman)
Daddy's going to get one as soon as he can
    come.

The Wrong House

I went into a house, and it wasn't a house,
   It has big steps and a great big hall;
But it hasn't got a garden,
     A garden,
     A garden,
It isn't like a house at all.

I went into a house, and it wasn't a house,
  It has a big garden and a great high wall;
But it hasn't got a may-tree,
        A may-tree,
        A may-tree,
  It isn't like a house at all.

I went into a house and it wasn't a house—
  Slow white petals from the may-tree fall;
But it hasn't got a blackbird,
        A blackbird,
        A blackbird,
  It isn't like a house at all.

I went into a house, and I thought it was a house,
  I could hear from the may-tree the blackbird
        call. . . .
But nobody listened to it,
        Nobody
        Liked it,
  Nobody wanted it at all.

Summer Afternoon

Six brown cows walk down to drink
   (All the little fishes blew bubbles at the may-fly).
Splash goes the first as he comes to the brink,
   Swish go the tails of the five who follow. . . .
Twelve brown cows bend drinking there
   (All the little fishes went waggle-tail, waggle-tail)—
Six from the water and six from the air;
   Up and down the river darts a blue-black
     swallow.

The Dormouse
and the Doctor

There once was a Dormouse who lived in a bed
Of delphiniums (blue) and geraniums (red),
And all the day long he'd a wonderful view
Of geraniums (red) and delphiniums (blue).

A Doctor came hurrying round, and he said:
"Tut-tut, I am sorry to find you in bed.
Just say 'Ninety-nine,' while I look at your
    chest. . . .
Don't you find that chrysanthemums answer the
    best?"

415

The Dormouse looked round at the view and
    replied
(When he'd said "Ninety-nine") that he'd tried
    and he'd tried,
And much the most answering things that he
    knew
Were geraniums (red) and delphiniums (blue).

The Doctor stood frowning and shaking his head,
And he took up his shiny silk hat as he said:
"What the patient requires is a change," and he
    went
To see some chrysanthemum people in Kent.

The Dormouse lay there, and he gazed at the view
Of geraniums (red) and delphiniums (blue),
And he knew there was nothing he wanted instead
Of delphiniums (blue) and geraniums (red).

The Doctor came back and, to show what he
    meant,
He had brought some chrysanthemum cuttings
    from Kent.
"Now *these*," he remarked, "give a *much* better
    view
Than geraniums (red) and delphiniums (blue)."

They took out their spades and they dug up the
    bed
Of delphiniums (blue) and geraniums (red),
And they planted chrysanthemums (yellow and
    white).
"And *now*," said the Doctor, "we'll *soon* have you
    right."

The Dormouse looked out, and he said with a sigh:
"I suppose all these people know better than I.
It was silly, perhaps, but I *did* like the view
Of geraniums (red) and delphiniums (blue)."

The Doctor came round and examined his chest,
And ordered him Nourishment, Tonics, and Rest,
"How very effective," he said as he shook
The thermometer, "all these chrysanthemums look!"

417

The Dormouse turned over to shut out the sight
Of the endless chrysanthemums (yellow and white).
"How lovely," he thought, "to be back in a bed
Of delphiniums (blue) and geraniums (red)."

The Doctor said, "Tut! It's another attack!"
And ordered him Milk and Massage-of-the-back,
And Freedom-from-worry and Drives-in a car,
And murmured, "How sweet your chrysanthemums
      are!"

The Dormouse lay there with his paws to his eyes
And imagined himself such a pleasant surprise:
"I'll *pretend* the chrysanthemums turn to a bed
Of delphiniums (blue) and geraniums (red)!"

The Doctor next morning was rubbing his hands,
And saying, "There's nobody quite understands
These cases as I do! The cure has begun!
How fresh the chrysanthemums look in the sun!"

The Dormouse lay happy, his eyes were so tight
He could see no chrysanthemums, yellow or white,
And all that he felt at the back of his head
Were delphiniums (blue) and geraniums (red).

And that is the reason (Aunt Emily said)
If a Dormouse gets in a chrysanthemum bed,
You will find (so Aunt Emily says) that he lies
Fast asleep on his front with his paws to his eyes.

419

Shoes and Stockings

There's a cavern in the mountain
    where the old men meet
(Hammer, hammer, hammer . . .
Hammer, hammer, hammer . . .)
They make gold slippers for my lady's feet
(Hammer, hammer, hammer . . .
Hammer, hammer, hammer . . .)
My lady is marrying her own true knight,
White her gown, and her veil is white,
But she must have slippers on her dainty feet.
Hammer, hammer, hammer . . .
Hammer.

There's a cottage by the river
    where the old wives meet
(Chatter, chatter, chatter . . .
Chatter, chatter, chatter . . .)

They weave gold stockings for my lady's feet
(Chatter, chatter, chatter . . .
Chatter, chatter, chatter . . .)
My lady is going to her own true man,
Youth to youth, since the world began,
But she must have stockings on her dainty feet.
Chatter, chatter, chatter . . .
Chatter.

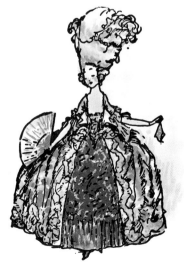

421

Sand-Between-the-Toes

I went down to the shouting sea,
Taking Christopher down with me,
For Nurse had given us sixpence each—
And down we went to the beach.

    We had sand in the eyes and the ears and
        the nose,
    And sand in the hair, and sand-between-
        the-toes.
    Whenever a good nor' wester blows,
    Christopher is certain of
    Sand-between-the-toes.

The sea was galloping grey and white;
Christopher clutched his sixpence tight;
We clambered over the humping sand—
And Christopher held my hand.

> We had sand in the eyes and the ears and
>   the nose,
> And sand in the hair, and sand-between-
>   the-toes.
> Whenever a good nor' wester blows,
> Christopher is certain of
> Sand-between-the-toes.

There was a roaring in the sky;
The sea-gulls cried as they blew by;
We tried to talk, but had to shout—
Nobody else was out.

> When we got home, we had sand in the hair,
> In the eyes and the ears and everywhere;
> Whenever a good nor' wester blows,
> Christopher is found with
> Sand-between-the-toes.

Knights and Ladies

There is in my old picture-book
A page at which I like to look,
Where knights and squires come riding down
The cobbles of some steep old town,
And ladies from beneath the eaves
Flutter their bravest handkerchiefs,
Or, smiling proudly, toss down gages. . . .
But that was in the Middle Ages.
It wouldn't happen now; but still,
Whenever I look up the hill
Where, dark against the green and blue,
The firs come marching, two by two,
I wonder if perhaps I *might*
See suddenly a shining knight
Winding his way from blue to green—
Exactly as it would have been
Those many, many years ago. . . .

Perhaps I might. You never know.

Little Bo-Peep
and Little Boy Blue

"What have you done with your sheep,
     Little Bo-Peep?
What have you done with your sheep,
     Bo-Peep?"
"Little Boy Blue, what fun!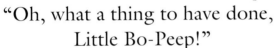
I've lost them, every one!"
"Oh, what a thing to have done,
     Little Bo-Peep!"

"What have you done with your sheep,
     Little Boy Blue?
What have you done with your sheep,
     Boy Blue?"
"Little Bo-Peep, my sheep
Went off, when I was asleep."
"I'm sorry about your sheep,
     Little Boy Blue."

"What are you going to do,
      Little Bo-Peep?
What are you going to do,
      Bo-Peep?"
"Little Boy Blue, you'll see
They'll all come home to tea."
"They wouldn't do that for me,
      Little Bo-Peep."

"What are you going to do,
      Little Boy Blue?
What are you going to do,
      Boy Blue?"
"Little Bo-Peep, I'll blow
My horn for an hour or so."
"Isn't that rather slow,
      Little Boy Blue?"

"Whom are you going to marry,
     Little Bo-Peep?
Whom are you going to marry,
     Bo-Peep?"
"Little Boy Blue, Boy Blue,
I'd like to marry you."
"I think I should like it too,
     Little Bo-Peep."

"Where are we going to live,
      Little Boy Blue?
Where are we going to live,
      Boy Blue?"
"Little Bo-Peep, Bo-Peep,
Up in the hills with the sheep."
"And you'll love your little Bo-Peep,
      Little Boy Blue?"

"I'll love you for ever and ever,
      Little Bo-Peep.
I'll love you for ever and ever,
      Bo-Peep."
"Little Boy Blue, my dear,
Keep near, keep very near."
"I shall be always here,
      Little Bo-Peep."

The Mirror

Between the woods the afternoon
Is fallen in a golden swoon,
The sun looks down from quiet skies
To where a quiet water lies,
   And silent trees stoop down to trees.

And there I saw a white swan make
Another white swan in the lake;
And, breast to breast, both motionless,
They waited for the wind's caress . . .
   And all the water was at ease.

THE COMPLETE POEMS OF POOH

Halfway Down

Halfway down the stairs
Is a stair
Where I sit.
There isn't any
Other stair
Quite like
It.
I'm not at the bottom,
I'm not at the top;
So this is the stair
Where
I always
Stop.

Halfway up the stairs
Isn't up,
And isn't down.
It isn't in the nursery,
It isn't in the town.
And all sorts of funny thoughts
Run round my head:
"It isn't really
Anywhere!
It's somewhere else
Instead!"

The Invaders

In careless patches through the wood
The clumps of yellow primrose stood,
And sheets of white anemones,
Like driven snow against the trees,
Had covered up the violet,
But left the blue-bell bluer yet.

Along the narrow carpet ride,
With primroses on either side,
Between their shadows and the sun,
The cows came slowly, one by one,
Breathing the early morning air
And leaving it still sweeter there.

And, one by one, intent upon
Their purposes, they followed on
In ordered silence . . . and were gone.

But all the little wood was still,
As if it waited so, until
Some blackbird on an outpost yew,
Watching the slow procession through,
Lifted his yellow beak at last
To whistle that the line had passed. . . .
Then all the wood began to sing
Its morning anthem to the spring.

Before Tea

Emmeline
Has not been seen
For more than a week. She slipped between
The two tall trees at the end of the green. . . .
We all went after her. *"Emmeline!"*

"Emmeline,
I didn't mean—
I only said that your hands weren't clean."
We went to the trees at the end of the green. . . .
But Emmeline
Was not to be seen.

Emmeline
Came slipping between
The two tall trees at the end of the green.
We all ran up to her. "Emmeline!
Where have you been?
Where have you been?
Why, it's more than a week!" And Emmeline
Said, "Sillies, I went and saw the Queen.
She says my hands are *purfickly* clean!"

Teddy Bear

A bear, however hard he tries,
Grows tubby without exercise.
Our Teddy Bear is short and fat
Which is not to be wondered at;
He gets what exercise he can
By falling off the ottoman,
But generally seems to lack
The energy to clamber back.

Now tubbiness is just the thing
Which gets a fellow wondering;
And Teddy worried lots about
The fact that he was rather stout.
He thought: "If only I were thin!
But how does anyone begin?"
He thought: "It really isn't fair
To grudge me exercise and air."

For many weeks he pressed in vain
His nose against the window-pane,
And envied those who walked about
Reducing their unwanted stout.
None of the people he could see
"Is quite" (he said) "as fat as me!"
Then, with a still more moving sigh,
"I mean" (he said) "as fat as I!"

Now Teddy, as was only right,
Slept in the ottoman at night,
And with him crowded in as well
More animals than I can tell;
Not only these, but books and things,
Such as a kind relation brings—
Old tales of "Once upon a time,"
And history retold in rhyme.

One night it happened that he took
A peep at an old picture-book,
Wherein he came across by chance
The picture of a King of France
(A stoutish man) and, down below,
These words: "King Louis So and So,
Nicknamed 'The Handsome'"! There he sat,
And (think of it!) the man was fat!

Our bear rejoiced like anything
To read about this famous King,
Nicknamed "The Handsome." There he sat,
And certainly the man was fat.

437

Nicknamed "The Handsome." Not a doubt
The man was definitely stout.
Why then, a bear (for all his tub)
Might yet be named "The Handsome Cub"!

"Might yet be named." Or did he mean
That years ago he "might have been"?
For now he felt a slight misgiving:
"Is Louis So and So still living?
Fashions in beauty have a way
Of altering from day to day.
Is 'Handsome Louis' with us yet?
Unfortunately I forget."

Next morning (nose to window-pane)
The doubt occurred to him again.
One question hammered in his head:
"Is he alive or is he dead?"
Thus, nose to pane, he pondered; but
The lattice window, loosely shut,
Swung open. With one startled "Oh!"
Our Teddy disappeared below.

There happened to be passing by
A plump man with a twinkling eye,
Who, seeing Teddy in the street,
Raised him politely to his feet,
And murmured kindly in his ear
Soft words of comfort and of cheer:
"Well, well!" "Allow me!" "Not at all."
"Tut-tut! A very nasty fall."

Our Teddy answered not a word;
It's doubtful if he even heard.
Our bear could only look and look:
The stout man in the picture-book!
That "handsome" King—could this be he,
This man of adiposity?
"Impossible," he thought. "But still,
No harm in asking. Yes I will!"

"Are you," he said, "by any chance
His Majesty the King of France?"
The other answered, "I am that,"
Bowed stiffly, and removed his hat;
Then said, "Excuse me," with an air,
"But is it Mr. Edward Bear?"
And Teddy, bending very low,
Replied politely, "Even so!"

They stood beneath the window there,
The King and Mr. Edward Bear,
And, handsome, if a trifle fat,
Talked carelessly of this and that. . . .
Then said His Majesty, "Well, well,
I must get on," and rang the bell.
"Your bear, I think," he smiled. "Good-day!"
And turned, and went upon his way.

A bear, however hard he tries,
Grows tubby without exercise.
Our Teddy Bear is short and fat,
Which is not to be wondered at.
But do you think it worries him
To know that he is far from slim?
No, just the other way about—
He's *proud* of being short and stout.

Bad Sir Brian Botany

Sir Brian had a battleaxe with great big
    knobs on;
He went among the villagers and blipped them
    on the head.
On Wednesday and on Saturday, but mostly on
    the latter day,
He called at all the cottages, and this is what
    he said:

    "I am Sir Brian!" *(ting-ling)*
       "I am Sir Brian!" *(rat-tat)*
    "I am Sir Brian, as bold as a lion—
       Take *that!*—and *that*—and *that*!"

441

Sir Brian had a pair of boots with great big spurs
    on,
A fighting pair of which he was particularly fond.
On Tuesday and on Friday, just to make the street
    look tidy,
He'd collect the passing villagers and kick them in
    the pond.

"I am Sir Brian!" *(sper-lash)*
    "I am Sir Brian!" *(sper-losh!)*
"I am Sir Brian, as bold as a lion—
    Is anyone else for a wash?"

Sir Brian woke one morning, and he couldn't find
    his battleaxe;
He walked into the village in his second pair of
    boots.
He had gone a hundred paces, when the street was
    full of faces,
And the villagers were round him with ironical
    salutes.

"You are Sir Brian? Indeed!
    You are Sir Brian? Dear, dear!
You are Sir Brian, as bold as a lion?
    Delighted to meet you here!"

Sir Brian went a journey, and he found a lot of
    duckweed;

They pulled him out and dried him, and they
    blipped him on the head.
They took him by the breeches, and they hurled
    him into ditches,
And they pushed him under waterfalls, and this
    is what they said:

"You are Sir Brian—don't laugh,
    You are Sir Brian—don't cry;
You are Sir Brian, as bold as a lion—
    Sir Brian, the lion, good-bye!"

Sir Brian struggled home again, and chopped up
    his battleaxe,
Sir Brian took his fighting boots, and threw them
    in the fire.
He is quite a different person now he hasn't got his
    spurs on,
And he goes about the village as B. Botany, Esquire.

    "I am Sir Brian? Oh, *no!*
        I am Sir Brian? Who's he?
    I haven't got any title, I'm Botany—
        Plain Mr. Botany (B)."

In the Fashion

A lion has a tail and a very fine tail,
And so has an elephant, and so has a whale,
And so has a crocodile, and so has a quail—
    They've all got tails but me.

If I had sixpence I would buy one;
I'd say to the shopman, "Let me try one";
I'd say to the elephant, "This is *my* one."
    They'd all come round to see.

Then I'd say to the lion, "Why, *you've* got a tail!
And so has the elephant, and so has the whale!
And, look! There's a crocodile! *He's* got a tail!
    "You've all got tails like me!"

The Alchemist

There lives an old man at the top of the street,
And the end of his beard reaches down to his feet,
And he's just the one person I'm longing to meet.
    I think that he sounds so exciting;
For he talks all the day to his tortoiseshell cat,
And he asks about this, and explains about that,
And at night he puts on a big wide-awake* hat
    And sits in the writing-room, writing.

He has worked all his life (and he's terribly old)
At a wonderful spell which says, "Lo, and behold!
Your nursery fender is gold!"—and it's gold!
    (Or the tongs, or the rod for the curtain);
But somehow he hasn't got hold of it quite,
Or the liquid you pour on it first isn't right,
So that's why he works at it night after night
    Till he knows he can do it for certain.

        *So as not to go to sleep.

Growing Up

I've got shoes with grown up laces,
I've got knickers and a pair of braces,
I'm all ready to run some races.
  Who's coming out with me?

I've got a nice new pair of braces,
I've got shoes with new brown laces,
I know wonderful paddly places.
  Who's coming out with me?

Every morning my new grace is,
"Thank you, God, for my nice braces:
I can tie my new brown laces."
  Who's coming out with me?

If I Were King

I often wish I were a King,
And then I could do anything.

If only I were King of Spain,
I'd take my hat off in the rain.

If only I were King of France,
I wouldn't brush my hair for aunts.

I think, if I were King of Greece,
I'd push things off the mantelpiece.

If I were King of Norroway,
I'd ask an elephant to stay.

If I were King of Babylon,
I'd leave my button gloves undone.

If I were King of Timbuctoo,
I'd think of lovely things to do.

If I were King of anything,
I'd tell the soldiers, "I'm the King!"

Vespers

Little Boy kneels at the foot of the bed,
Droops on the little hands little gold head.
Hush! Hush! Whisper who dares!
Christopher Robin is saying his prayers.

God bless Mummy. I know that's right.
Wasn't it fun in the bath tonight?
The cold's so cold, and the hot's so hot.
Oh! *God bless Daddy*—I quite forgot.

If I open my fingers a little bit more,
I can see Nanny's dressing-gown on the door.
It's a beautiful blue, but it hasn't a hood.
Oh! *God bless Nanny and make her good.*

Mine has a hood, and I lie in bed,
And pull the hood right over my head,
And I shut my eyes, and I curl up small,
And nobody knows that I'm there at all.

Oh! *Thank you, God, for a lovely day.*
And what was the other I had to say?
I said "Bless Daddy," so what can it be?
Oh! Now I remember. *God bless Me.*

Little Boy kneels at the foot of the bed,
Droops on the little hands little gold head.
Hush! Hush! Whisper who dares!
Christopher Robin is saying his prayers.

to
ANNE DARLINGTON
now she is seven
and
because she is
so
SPESHAL

NOW
WE ARE SIX

Introduction

WHEN YOU ARE reciting poetry, which is a thing we
never do, you find sometimes, just as you are beginning, that Uncle John is still telling Aunt Rose that if he can't
find his spectacles he won't be able to hear properly, and does
she know where they are; and by the time everybody has
stopped looking for them, you are at the last verse, and in
another minute they will be saying, "Thank-you, thank-you,"
without really knowing what it was all about. So, next time, you
are more careful; and, just before you begin you say, *"Er-h'r'm!"*
very loudly, which means, "Now then, here we are"; and
everybody stops talking and looks at you: which is what you
want. So then you get in the way of saying it whenever you
are asked to recite . . . and sometimes it is just as well, and
sometimes it isn't. . . . And by and by you find yourself saying
it without thinking. Well, this bit which I am writing now,
called Introduction, is really the *er-h'r'm* of the book, and I
have put it in, partly so as not to take you by surprise, and
partly because I can't do without it now. There are some very
clever writers who say that it is quite easy not to have an
er-h'r'm, but I don't agree with them. I think it is much
easier not to have all the rest of the book.

What I want to explain in the Introduction is this. We have
been nearly three years writing this book. We began it when
we were very young . . . and now we are six. So, of course,
bits of it seem rather babyish to us, almost as if they had

slipped out of some other book by mistake. On page whatever-it-is there is a thing which is simply three-ish, and when we read it to ourselves just now we said, "Well, well, well," and turned over rather quickly. So we want you to know that the name of the book doesn't mean that this is us being six all the time, but that it is about as far as we've got at present, and we half think of stopping there.

A.A.M.

P.S. Pooh wants us to say that he thought it was a different book; and he hopes you won't mind, but he walked through it one day, looking for his friend Piglet, and sat down on some of the pages by mistake.

Solitude

I have a house where I go
   When there's too many people,
I have a house where I go
   Where no one can be;
I have a house where I go,
Where nobody ever says "No";
Where no one says anything—so
   There is no one but me.

King John's Christmas

King John was not a good man—
 He had his little ways.
And sometimes no one spoke to him
 For days and days and days.
And men who came across him,
 When walking in the town,
Gave him a supercilious stare,
Or passed with noses in the air—
And bad King John stood dumbly there,
 Blushing beneath his crown.

King John was not a good man,
 And no good friends had he.
He stayed in every afternoon . . .
 But no one came to tea.

And, round about December,
   The cards upon his shelf
Which wished him lots of Christmas cheer,
And fortune in the coming year,
Were never from his near and dear,
   But only from himself.

King John was not a good man,
   Yet had his hopes and fears.
They'd given him no present now
   For years and years and years.
But every year at Christmas,
   While minstrels stood about,
Collecting tribute from the young
For all the songs they might have sung,
He stole away upstairs and hung
   A hopeful stocking out.

King John was not a good man,
   He lived his life aloof;
Alone he thought a message out
   While climbing up the roof.
He wrote it down and propped it
   Against the chimney stack:
"TO ALL AND SUNDRY—NEAR AND FAR—
F. CHRISTMAS IN PARTICULAR."
And signed it not "Johannes R."
   But very humbly, "JACK."

461

"I want some crackers,
    And I want some candy;
I think a box of chocolates
    Would come in handy;
I don't mind oranges,
    I do like nuts!
And I SHOULD like a pocket-knife
    That really cuts.
And, oh! Father Christmas, if you love me at all,
Bring me a big, red, india-rubber ball!"

King John was not a good man—
    He wrote this message out,
And gat him to his room again,
    Descending by the spout.
And all that night he lay there,
    A prey to hopes and fears.
"I think that's him a-coming now."
    (Anxiety bedewed his brow.)
"He'll bring one present, anyhow—
    The first I've had for years."

"Forget about the crackers,
    And forget about the candy;
I'm sure a box of chocolates
    Would never come in handy;
I don't like oranges,
    I don't want nuts,
And I HAVE got a pocket-knife
    That almost cuts.
But, oh! Father Christmas, if you love me at all,
Bring me a big, red, india-rubber ball!"

King John was not a good man—
    Next morning when the sun
Rose up to tell a waiting world
    That Christmas had begun,
And people seized their stockings,
    And opened them with glee,
And crackers, toys and games appeared,
And lips with sticky sweets were smeared,
King John said grimly: "As I feared,
    Nothing again for me!"

463

"I did want crackers,
 And I did want candy;
I know a box of chocolates
 Would come in handy;
I do love oranges,
 I did want nuts.
I haven't got a pocket-knife—
 Not one that cuts.
And, oh! if Father Christmas had loved me at all,
He would have brought a big, red, india-rubber
 ball!"

King John stood by the window,
 And frowned to see below
The happy bands of boys and girls
 All playing in the snow.
A while he stood there watching,
 And envying them all . . .
When through the window big and red
There hurtled by his royal head,
And bounced and fell upon the bed,
 An india-rubber ball!

AND, OH, FATHER CHRISTMAS,
MY BLESSINGS ON YOU FALL
 FOR BRINGING HIM
 A BIG, RED,
 INDIA-RUBBER
 BALL!

Busy

I think I am a Muffin Man. I haven't got a
    bell,
I haven't got the muffin things that muffin people
    sell.

Perhaps I am a Postman. No, I think I am a
    Tram.
I'm feeling rather funny and I don't know *what* I
    am—

        BUT
Round about
And *round* about
And *round* about I go—
All around the table,
The table in the nursery—

465

Round about
And *round* about
And *round* about I go;

I think I am a Traveller escaping from a Bear;

I think I am an Elephant,
Behind another Elephant
Behind *another* Elephant who isn't really there. . . .

SO
Round about
And *round* about
And *round* about and *round* about
And *round* about
And *round* about
I go.

I think I am a Ticket Man who's selling tickets—
    please,

I think I am a Doctor who is visiting a Sneeze;

Perhaps I'm just a Nanny who is walking with a
    pram
I'm feeling rather funny and I don't know *what* I
    am—

    BUT
  Round about
  And *round* about
  And *round* about I go—
  All around the table,
  The table in the nursery—

Round about
And *round* about
And *round* about I go:

I think I am a Puppy, so I'm hanging out my
    tongue;

I think I am a Camel who
Is looking for a Camel who
Is looking for a Camel who is looking for its
    Young. . . .

SO
Round about
And *round* about
And *round* about and *round* about
And *round* about
And *round* about
    I go.

Sneezles

Christopher Robin
Had wheezles
And sneezles,
They bundled him
Into
His bed.
They gave him what goes
With a cold in the nose,
And some more for a cold
In the head.
They wondered
If wheezles
Could turn
Into measles,
If sneezles
Would turn
Into mumps;

They examined his chest
For a rash,
And the rest
Of his body for swellings and lumps.
They sent for some doctors
In sneezles
And wheezles
To tell them what ought
To be done.

All sorts of conditions
Of famous physicians
Came hurrying round
At a run.
They all made a note
Of the state of his throat,
They asked if he suffered from thirst;
They asked if the sneezles
Came *after* the wheezles,
Or if the first sneeze
Came first.

Binker's always talking, 'cos I'm teaching him
    to speak:
He sometimes likes to do it in a funny sort
    of squeak,
And he sometimes likes to do it in a hoodling sort
    of roar . . .
And I have to do it for him 'cos his throat is
    rather sore.

  Oh, Daddy is clever, he's a clever sort of man,
  And Mummy knows all that anybody can,
  And Nanny is Nanny, and I call her Nan—
        But they don't
        Know
        Binker.

Binker's brave as lions when we're running in
    the park;
Binker's brave as tigers when we're lying in
    the dark;
Binker's brave as elephants. He never, never
    cries . . .
Except (like other people) when the soap gets in
    his eyes.

Oh, Daddy is Daddy, he's a Daddy sort of
    man,
And Mummy is as Mummy as anybody can,
And Nanny is Nanny, and I call her Nan . . .
        But they're not
        Like
        Binker.

Binker isn't greedy, but he does like things to eat,
So I have to say to people when they're giving
    me a sweet,
"Oh, Binker wants a chocolate, so could you give
    me two?"
And then I eat it for him, 'cos his teeth are rather
    new.

Well, I'm very fond of Daddy, but he hasn't time
      to play,
And I'm very fond of Mummy, but she sometimes
      goes away,
And I'm often cross with Nanny when she wants
      to brush my hair . . .

But Binker's always Binker, and is certain to
      be there.

Cherry Stones

Tinker, Tailor,

Soldier, Sailor,

Rich Man, Poor Man,

Ploughboy, Thief—

And what about a Cowboy,
Policeman, Jailer,
Engine-driver,
Or Pirate Chief?
What about a Postman—or a Keeper at the Zoo?
What about the Circus Man who lets the people
    through?
And the man who takes the pennies for the round-
    abouts and swings,
Or the man who plays the organ, and the other
    man who sings?
What about a Conjuror with rabbits in his pockets?
What about a Rocket Man who's always making
    rockets?
Oh, there's such a lot of things to do and such a lot
    to be

That there's always lots of cherries on my little
    cherry-tree!

477

The Knight Whose Armour Didn't Squeak

Of all the Knights in Appledore
    The wisest was Sir Thomas Tom.
He multiplied as far as four,
    And knew what nine was taken from
To make eleven. He could write
A letter to another Knight.

No other Knight in all the land
    Could do the things which he could do
Not only did he understand
    The way to polish swords, but knew
What remedy a Knight should seek
Whose armour had begun to squeak.

And, if he didn't fight too much,
    It wasn't that he did not care
For blips and buffetings and such,
    But felt that it was hardly fair
To risk, by frequent injuries,
A brain as delicate as his.

His castle (Castle Tom) was set
    Conveniently on a hill;
And daily, when it wasn't wet,
    He paced the battlements until
Some smaller Knight who couldn't swim
Should reach the moat and challenge him.

479

Or sometimes, feeling full of fight,
    He hurried out to scour the plain;
And, seeing some approaching Knight,
    He either hurried home again,
Or hid; and, when the foe was past,
Blew a triumphant trumpet-blast.

One day when good Sir Thomas Tom
    Was resting in a handy ditch,
The noises he was hiding from,
    Though very much the noises which
He'd always hidden from before,
Seemed somehow less. . . . Or was it more?

The trotting horse, the trumpet's blast,
    The whistling sword, the armour's squeak,
These, and especially the last,
    Had clattered by him all the week.
Was this the same, or was it not?
Something was different. But what?

Sir Thomas raised a cautious ear
    And listened as Sir Hugh went by,

And suddenly he seemed to hear
    (Or not to hear) the reason why
This stranger made a nicer sound
Than other Knights who lived around.

Sir Thomas watched the way he went—
 His rage was such he couldn't speak,
For years they'd called him down in Kent
 The Knight Whose Armour Didn't Squeak!
Yet here and now he looked upon
Another Knight whose squeak had gone.

He rushed to where his horse was tied;
 He spurred it to a rapid trot.
The only fear he felt inside
 About his enemy was not
"How sharp his sword?" "How stout his
  heart?"
But "Has he got too long a start?"

Sir Hugh was singing, hand on hip,
 When something sudden came along,
And caught him a terrific blip
 Right in the middle of his song.
"A thunderstorm!" he thought. "Of course!"
And toppled gently off his horse.

Then said the good Sir Thomas Tom,
    Dismounting with a friendly air,
"Allow me to extract you from
    The heavy armour that you wear.
At times like these the bravest Knight
May find his armour much too tight."

A hundred yards or so beyond
    The scene of brave Sir Hugh's defeat
Sir Thomas found a useful pond,
    And, careful not to wet his feet,
He brought the armour to the brink
And flung it in . . . and watched it sink.

So ever after, more and more,
   The men of Kent would proudly speak
Of Thomas Tom of Appledore,
   "The Knight Whose Armour Didn't Squeak"
Whilst Hugh, the Knight who gave him best,
Squeaks just as badly as the rest.

Buttercup Days

Where is Anne?
  Head above the buttercups,
Walking by the stream,
  Down among the buttercups.
Where is Anne?
Walking with her man,
Lost in a dream,
  Lost among the buttercups.

What has she got in that little brown head?
Wonderful thoughts which can never be said.
What has she got in that firm little fist of hers?
Somebody's thumb, and it feels like Christopher's.

Where is Anne?
Close to her man.
Brown head, gold head,
  In and out the buttercups.

The Charcoal-Burner

The charcoal-burner has tales to tell.
He lives in the Forest,
Alone in the Forest;
He sits in the Forest,
Alone in the Forest.
And the sun comes slanting between
    the trees,
And rabbits come up, and they give him
    good-morning,
And rabbits come up and say, "Beautiful
    morning. . . ."

And the moon swings clear of the tall black
　　trees,
And owls fly over and wish him good-night,
Quietly over to wish him good-night. . . .

And he sits and thinks of the things they
　　know,
He and the Forest, alone together—
The springs that come and the summers
　　that go,
Autumn dew on bracken and heather,
The drip of the Forest beneath the snow. . . .
All the things they have seen,
All the things they have heard:
An April sky swept clean and the song of
　　a bird . . .
Oh, the charcoal-burner has tales to tell!
And he lives in the Forest and knows us
　　well.

Us Two

Wherever I am, there's always Pooh,
There's always Pooh and Me.
Whatever I do, he wants to do,
"Where are you going today?" says Pooh:
"Well, that's very odd 'cos I was too.
Let's go together," says Pooh, says he.
"Let's go together," says Pooh.

"What's twice eleven?" I said to Pooh.
("Twice what?" said Pooh to Me.)
"I *think* it ought to be twenty-two."
"Just what I think myself," said Pooh.
"It wasn't an easy sum to do,
But that's what it is," said Pooh, said he.
"That's what it is," said Pooh.

"Let's look for dragons," I said to Pooh.
"Yes, let's," said Pooh to Me.
We crossed the river and found a few—
"Yes, those are dragons all right," said Pooh.
"As soon as I saw their beaks I knew.
That's what they are," said Pooh, said he.
"That's what they are," said Pooh.

"Let's frighten the dragons," I said to Pooh.
"That's right," said Pooh to Me.
"*I'm* not afraid," I said to Pooh,
And I held his paw and I shouted "Shoo!
Silly old dragons!"—and off they flew.

"I wasn't afraid," said Pooh, said he,
"I'm *never* afraid with you."

So wherever I am, there's always Pooh,
There's always Pooh and Me.
"What would I do?" I said to Pooh,
"If it wasn't for you," and Pooh said: "True,
It isn't much fun for One, but Two
Can stick together," says Pooh, says he.
"That's how it is," says Pooh.

The Old Sailor

There was once an old sailor my grandfather knew
Who had so many things which he wanted to do
That, whenever he thought it was time to begin,
He couldn't because of the state he was in.

He was shipwrecked, and lived on an island
    for weeks,

And he wanted a hat,

         and he wanted some breeks;
And he wanted some nets, or a line and some
    hooks
For turtles and things which you read of
    in books.

And, thinking of this, he remembered a thing
Which he wanted (for water) and that was a spring;
And he thought that to talk to he'd look for,
    and keep
(If he found it) a goat, or some chickens
    and sheep.

Then, because of the weather, he wanted a hut
With a door (to come in by) which opened and shut
(With a jerk, which was useful if snakes were about),
And a very strong lock to keep savages out.

He began on the fish-hooks, and when he'd begun
He decided he couldn't because of the sun.
So he knew what he ought to begin with, and that
Was to find, or to make, a large sun-stopping hat.

He was making the hat with some leaves from
    a tree,
When he thought, "I'm as hot as a body can be,
And I've nothing to take for my terrible thirst;
So I'll look for a spring, and I'll look for it *first*."

Then he thought as he started, "Oh, dear and
    oh, dear!
I'll be lonely tomorrow with nobody here!"
So he made in his note-book a couple of notes:
"I must first find some chickens"

and *"No, I mean goats."*

He had just seen a goat (which he knew by
    the shape)
When he thought, "But I must have a boat
    for escape.

But a boat means a sail, which means needles
    and thread;
So I'd better sit down and make needles instead."

He began on a needle, but thought as he worked,
That, if this was an island where savages lurked,
Sitting safe in his hut he'd have nothing to fear,
Whereas now they might suddenly breathe in
    his ear!

So he thought of his hut . . . and he thought of
    his boat,
And his hat and his breeks, and his chickens
    and goat,
And the hooks (for his food) and the spring (for
    his thirst) . . .
But he *never* could think which he ought to
    do first.

And so in the end he did nothing at all,
But basked on the shingle wrapped up in
    a shawl.
And I think it was dreadful the way
    he behaved—
He did nothing but basking until he
    was saved!

The Engineer

Let it rain!
Who cares?
I've a train
Upstairs,
With a brake
Which I make
From a string
Sort of thing,
Which works
In jerks,
'Cos it drops
In the spring,

Which stops
With the string,
And the wheels
All stick
So quick
That it feels
Like a thing
That you make
With a brake,
Not string. . . .

So that's what I make,
When the day's all wet.
It's a good sort of brake
But it hasn't worked yet.

Journey's End

Christopher, Christopher, where are you going,
    Christopher Robin?
    "Just up to the top of the hill,
    Upping and upping until
    I am right on the top of the hill,"
    Said Christopher Robin.

Christopher, Christopher, why are you going,
            Christopher Robin?
There's nothing to see, so when
You've got to the top, what then?
"Just down to the bottom again,"
            Said Christopher Robin.

Furry Bear

If I were a bear,
    And a big bear too,
I shouldn't much care
    If it froze or snew;
I shouldn't much mind
    If it snowed or friz—
I'd be all fur-lined
    With a coat like his!

For I'd have fur boots and a brown fur wrap,
And brown fur knickers and a big fur cap.
I'd have a fur muffle-ruff to cover my jaws,
And brown fur mittens on my big brown paws.
With a big brown furry-down up to my head,
I'd sleep all the winter in a big fur bed.

Forgiven

I found a little beetle, so that Beetle was
    his name,
And I called him Alexander and he answered
    just the same.
I put him in a match-box, and I kept him
    all the day . . .
And Nanny let my beetle out—

    Yes, Nanny let my beetle out—

    She went and let my beetle out—

    And Beetle ran away.

She said she didn't mean it, and I never said
    she did,
She said she wanted matches and she just took off
    the lid,
She said that she was sorry, but it's difficult
    to catch
An excited sort of beetle you've mistaken for
    a match.

She said that she was sorry, and I really mustn't
    mind,
As there's lots and lots of beetles which she's
    certain we could find
If we looked about the garden for the holes where
    beetles hid—
And we'd get another match-box and write
    BEETLE on the lid.

We went to all the places which a beetle might
      be near,
And we made the sort of noises which a beetle
      likes to hear,
And I saw a kind of something, and I gave a sort
      of shout:
"A beetle-house and Alexander Beetle coming out!"

It was Alexander Beetle I'm as certain as can be
And he had a sort of look as if he thought it must
      be ME,

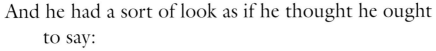

And he had a sort of look as if he thought he ought
      to say:
"I'm very, very sorry that I tried to run away."

And Nanny's very sorry too for you-know-what-
      she-did,
And she's writing ALEXANDER very blackly on
      the lid.
So Nan and Me are friends, because it's difficult
      to catch
An excited Alexander you've mistaken for a match.

505

The Emperor's Rhyme

The King of Peru
(Who was Emperor too)
    Had a sort of a rhyme
        Which was useful to know,
If he felt very shy
When a stranger came by,
    Or they asked him the time
        When his watch didn't go;
Or supposing he fell
(By mistake) down a well,
Or he tumbled when skating
    And sat on his hat,
Or perhaps wasn't told,
Till his porridge was cold,
    That his breakfast was waiting—
        Or something like that;
Oh, whenever the Emperor
Got into a temper, or
    Felt himself sulky or sad,

He would murmur and murmur,
Until he felt firmer,
    This curious rhyme which he had:

Eight eights are sixty-four;
    Multiply by seven.
When it's done,
Carry one,
    And take away eleven.
Nine nines are eighty-one;
    Multiply by three.
If it's more,
Carry four,
    And then it's time for tea.

So whenever the Queen
Took his armour to clean,
    And she didn't remember
        To use any starch;
Or his birthday (in May)
Was a horrible day,
    Being wet as November
        And windy as March;
Or, if sitting in state
With the Wise and the Great,
    He just happened to hiccup
        While signing his name,
Or the Queen gave a cough,
When his crown tumbled off
    As he bent down to pick up
        A pen for the same;

Oh, whenever the Emperor
Got into a temper, or
   Felt himself awkward and shy,
He would whisper and whisper,
Until he felt crisper,
   This odd little rhyme to the sky:

Eight eights are eighty-one;
   Multiply by seven.
If it's more,
Carry four,
   And take away eleven.
Nine nines are sixty-four;
   Multiply by three.
When it's done,
Carry one,
   And then it's time for tea.

Knight-in-Armour

Whenever I'm a shining Knight,
I buckle on my armour tight;
And then I look about for things,
Like Rushings-Out, and Rescuings,
And Savings from the Dragon's Lair,
And fighting all the Dragons there.
And sometimes when our fights begin,
I think I'll let the Dragons win . . .
And then I think perhaps I won't,
Because they're Dragons, and I don't.

THE COMPLETE POEMS OF POOH

Come Out with Me

There's sun on the river and sun on the hill . . .
You can hear the sea if you stand quite still!
There's eight new puppies at Roundabout Farm—
And I saw an old sailor with only one arm!

    But every one says, "Run along!"
      (Run along, run along!)
  All of them say, "Run along! I'm busy as can be."
      Every one says, "Run along,
      There's a little darling!"
  If I'm a little darling, why don't they run with me?

There's wind on the river and wind on the hill . . .
There's a dark dead water-wheel under the mill!
I saw a fly which had just been drowned—
And I know where a rabbit goes into the ground!

    But every one says, "Run along!"
      (Run along, run along!)
  All of them say, "Yes, dear," and never notice me.
      Every one says, "Run along,
      There's a little darling!"
  If I'm a little darling, why won't they come and see?

Down by the Pond

I'm fishing.
Don't talk, anybody, don't come near!
Can't you see that the fish might hear?
He thinks I'm playing with a piece of string;
He thinks I'm another sort of funny sort of thing,
    But he doesn't know I'm fishing—
    He doesn't know I'm fishing.
    That's what I'm doing—
    Fishing.

No, I'm not, I'm newting.
Don't cough, anybody, don't come by!
Any small noise makes a newt feel shy.
He thinks I'm a bush, or a new sort of tree;
He thinks it's somebody, but doesn't think it's Me,
And he doesn't know I'm newting—
No, he doesn't know I'm newting.
That's what I'm doing—
Newting.

The Little Black Hen

Berryman and Baxter,
  Prettiboy and Penn
And old Farmer Middleton
  Are five big men . . .
And all of them were after
  The Little Black Hen.

She ran quickly,
  They ran fast;
Baxter was first, and
  Berryman was last.
I sat and watched
  By the old plum-tree . . .
She squawked through the hedge
  And she came to me.

The Little Black Hen
  Said "Oh, it's you!"
I said "Thank you,
  How do you do?
And please will you tell me,
  Little Black Hen,
What did they want,
  Those five big men?"

The Little Black Hen
　　She said to me:
"They want me to lay them
　　An egg for tea.
If they were Emperors,
　　If they were Kings.
I'm much too busy
　　To lay them things."

"I'm not a King
　　And I haven't a crown;
I climb up trees,
　　And I tumble down.
I can shut one eye,
　　I can count to ten,
So lay me an egg, please,
　　Little Black Hen."

The Little Black Hen said,
　　"What will you pay,
If I lay you an egg
　　For Easter Day?"

"I'll give you a Please
    And a How-do-you-do,
I'll show you the Bear
    Who lives in the Zoo,
I'll show you the nettle-place
    On my leg,
If you'll lay me a great big
    Eastery egg."

The Little Black Hen
    Said "I don't care
For a How-do-you-do
    Or a Big-brown-bear,
But I'll lay you a beautiful
    Eastery egg,
If you'll show me the nettle-place
    On your leg."

I showed her the place
    Where I had my sting.
She touched it gently
    With one black wing.
"Nettles don't hurt
    If you count to ten.
And now for the egg,"
    Said the Little Black Hen.

When I wake up
  On Easter Day,
I shall see my egg
  She's promised to lay.
If I were Emperors,
  If I were Kings,
It couldn't be fuller
  Of wonderful things.

Berryman and Baxter,
  Prettiboy and Penn,
And Old Farmer Middleton
  Are five big men.
All of them are wanting
  An egg for their tea,
But the Little Black Hen is much too busy,
The Little Black Hen is *much* too busy,
The Little Black Hen is MUCH too busy . . .
  She's laying my egg for me!

The Friend

There are lots and lots of people who are always
  asking things,
Like Dates and Pounds-and-ounces and the names
  of funny Kings,
And the answer's either Sixpence or A Hundred
  Inches Long,
And I know they'll think me silly if I get the
  answer wrong.

So Pooh and I go whispering, and Pooh looks
  very bright,
And says, "Well, *I* say sixpence, but I don't suppose
  I'm right."
And then it doesn't matter what the answer ought
  to be,
'Cos if he's right, I'm Right, and if he's wrong,
  it isn't Me.

The Good Little Girl

It's funny how often they say to me, "Jane?
   "Have you been a *good* girl?"
   "Have you been a *good* girl?"
And when they have said it, they say it again,
   "Have you been a *good* girl?"
   "Have you been a *good* girl?"

I go to a party, I go out to tea,
I go to an aunt for a week at the sea,
I come back from school or from playing a game;
Wherever I come from, it's always the same:
   "Well?
   "Have you been a *good* girl, Jane?"

It's always the end of the loveliest day:
  "Have you been a *good* girl?"
  "Have you been a *good* girl?"
I went to the Zoo, and they waited to say:
  "Have you been a *good* girl?"
  "Have you been a *good* girl?"

Well, what did they think that I went there to do?
And why should I want to be bad at the Zoo?
And should I be likely to say if I had?
So that's why it's funny of Mummy and Dad,
This asking and asking, in case I was bad,
  "Well?
  "Have you been a *good* girl, Jane?"

A Thought

If I were John and John were Me,
Then he'd be six and I'd be three.
If John were Me and I were John,
I shouldn't have these trousers on.

King Hilary and the Beggarman

Of Hilary the Great and Good
      They tell a tale at Christmas time
I've often thought the story would
Be prettier but just as good
If almost anybody should
      Translate it into rime.
So I have done the best I can
For lack of some more learned man.

Good King Hilary
Said to his Chancellor
(Proud Lord Willoughby,
Lord High Chancellor):
"Run to the wicket-gate
Quickly, quickly,
Run to the wicket-gate
      And see who is knocking.
It may be a rich man,
Sea-borne from Araby,
Bringing me peacocks,
Emeralds and ivory;
It may be a poor man,
Travel-worn and weary,
Bringing me oranges
      To put in my stocking."

Proud Lord Willoughby,
Lord High Chancellor,
    Laughed both loud and free:*
"I've served Your Majesty, man to man,
Since first Your Majesty's reign began,
And I've often walked, but I never, never ran,
    Never, never, never," quoth he.

Good King Hilary
Said to his Chancellor
(Proud Lord Willoughby,
Lord High Chancellor):
"Walk to the wicket-gate
Quickly, quickly,
Walk to the wicket-gate
    And see who is knocking.

*Haw! Haw! Haw!

525

It may be a captain,
Hawk-nosed, bearded,
Bringing me gold-dust,
Spices, and sandalwood:

It may be a scullion,
Care-free, whistling,
Bringing me sugar-plums
    To put in my stocking."

Proud Lord Willoughby,
Lord High Chancellor,
    Laughed both loud and free:
"I've served in the Palace since I was
      four,
And I'll serve in the Palace a-many years
      more,
And I've opened a window, but never a
      door,
    Never, never, never," quoth he.

Good King Hilary
Said to his Chancellor
(Proud Lord Willoughby,
Lord High Chancellor):
"Open the window
Quickly, quickly,
Open the window
    And see who is knocking.

It may be a waiting-maid,
Apple-cheeked, dimpled,
Sent by her mistress
To bring me greeting;

It may be children,
Anxious, whispering,
Bringing me cobnuts,
    To put in my stocking."

Proud Lord Willoughby,
Lord High Chancellor,
        Laughed both loud and free;
"I'll serve Your Majesty till I die—
As Lord Chancellor, not as spy
To peep from lattices; no, not I,
        Never, never, never," quoth he.

Good King Hilary
Looked at his Chancellor
(Proud Lord Willoughby,
Lord High Chancellor):
He said no word
To his stiff-set Chancellor,
But ran to the wicket-gate
        To see who was knocking.
He found no rich man
Trading from Araby;
He found no captain,
Blue-eyed, weather-tanned;
He found no waiting-maid
Sent by her mistress;
But only a beggarman
        With one red stocking.

Good King Hilary
Looked at the beggarman,
        And laughed him three times three;
And he turned that beggarman round
                about:

"Your thews are strong, and your arm is
      stout;
Come, throw me a Lord High Chancellor
      out,
    And take his place," quoth he.

Of Hilary the Good and Great
Old wives at Christmas time relate
This tale, which points, at any rate,
    Two morals on the way.
The first: *"Whatever Fortune brings,*
Don't be afraid of doing things."
(Especially, of course, for Kings.)
    It also seems to say
(But not so wisely): *"He who begs*
With one red stocking on his legs
Will be, as sure as eggs are eggs,
    A Chancellor some day."

THE COMPLETE POEMS OF POOH

Swing Song

Here I go up in my swing
    Ever so high.
I am the King of the fields, and the King
    Of the town.
I am the King of the earth, and the King
    Of the sky.
Here I go up in my swing . . .
    Now I go down.

Explained

Elizabeth Ann
Said to her Nan:
"Please will you tell me how God began?
Somebody must have made Him. So
Who could it be, 'cos I want to know?"
And Nurse said, *"Well!"*
And Ann said, "Well?
I know you know, and I wish you'd tell."
And Nurse took pins from her mouth, and said,
"Now then, darling, it's time for bed."

Elizabeth Ann
Had a wonderful plan:
She would run round the world till she found
    a man
Who knew *exactly* how God began.

She got up early, she dressed, and ran
Trying to find an Important Man.
She ran to London and knocked at the door
Of the Lord High Doodelum's coach-and-four.
"Please, sir (if there's anyone in),
However-and-ever did God begin?"

533

The Lord High Doodelum lay in bed,
But out of the window, large and red,
Came the Lord High Coachman's face instead.
And the Lord High Coachman laughed and
    said:
"Well, what put *that* in your quaint little
    head?"

Elizabeth Ann went home again
And took from the ottoman Jennifer Jane.
"Jenniferjane," said Elizabeth Ann,
"Tell me *at once* how God began."
And Jane, who didn't much care for speaking,
Replied in her usual way by squeaking.

What did it mean? Well, to be quite candid,
I don't know, but Elizabeth Ann did.
Elizabeth Ann said softly, "Oh!
Thank you, Jennifer. Now I know."

Twice Times

There were Two little Bears who lived in a Wood,
And one of them was Bad and the other was Good.
Good Bear learnt his Twice Times One—
But Bad Bear left all his buttons undone.

They lived in a Tree when the weather was hot,
And one of them was Good, and the other was Not.
Good Bear learnt his Twice Times Two—
But Bad Bear's thingummies were worn right
    through.

They lived in a Cave when the weather was cold,
And they Did, and they Didn't Do, what they were
    told.
Good Bear learnt his Twice Times Three—
But Bad Bear *never* had his hand-ker-chee.

They lived in the Wood with a Kind Old Aunt,
And one said *"Yes'm,"* and the other said
    "Shan't!"
Good Bear learnt his Twice Times Four—
But Bad Bear's knicketies were terrible tore.

And then quite suddenly (just like Us)
One got Better and the other got Wuss.
Good Bear muddled his Twice Times Three—
But Bad Bear coughed *in his hand-ker-chee!*

Good Bear muddled his Twice Times Two—
But Bad Bear's thingummies looked like new.
Good Bear muddled his Twice Times One—
But Bad Bear *never* left his buttons undone.

There may be a Moral, though some say not;
I think there's a moral, though I don't know what.
But if one gets better, as the other gets wuss,
These Two Little Bears are just like Us.
For Christopher remembers up to Twice Times
        Ten . . .
But I keep forgetting where I've put my pen.*

*So I have had to write this one in pencil.

THE COMPLETE POEMS OF POOH

The Morning Walk

When Anne and I go out a walk,
We hold each other's hand and talk
Of all the things we mean to do
When Anne and I are forty-two.

And when we've thought about a thing,
Like bowling hoops or bicycling,
Or falling down on Anne's balloon,
We do it in the afternoon.

Cradle Song

O Timothy Tim
   Has ten pink toes,
   And ten pink toes
Has Timothy Tim.
They go with him
   Wherever he goes,
   And wherever he goes
They go with him.

O Timothy Tim
   Has two blue eyes,
   And two blue eyes
Has Timothy Tim.
They cry with him
   Whenever he cries,
   And whenever he cries,
They cry with him.

O Timothy Tim
   Has one red head,
   And one red head
Has Timothy Tim.
It sleeps with him
   In Timothy's bed.
   Sleep well, red head
Of Timothy Tim.

THE COMPLETE POEMS OF POOH

Waiting
at the Window

These are my two drops of rain
Waiting on the window-pane.

I am waiting here to see
Which the winning one will be.

Both of them have different names.
One is John and one is James.

All the best and all the worst
Comes from which of them is first.

James has just begun to ooze.
He's the one I want to lose.

John is waiting to begin.
He's the one I want to win.

James is going slowly on.
Something sort of sticks to John.

John is moving off at last.
James is going pretty fast.

John is rushing down the pane.
James is going slow again.

James has met a sort of smear.
John is getting very near.

Is he going fast enough?
(James has found a piece of fluff.)

John has hurried quickly by.
(James was talking to a fly.)

John is there, and John has won!
Look! I told you! Here's the sun!

Pinkle Purr

Tattoo was the mother of Pinkle Purr,
A little black nothing of feet and fur;
And by-and-by, when his eyes came through,
He saw his mother, the big Tattoo.
And all that he learned he learned from her.
"I'll ask my mother," says Pinkle Purr.

Tattoo was the mother of Pinkle Purr,
A ridiculous kitten with silky fur.
And little black Pinkle grew and grew
Till he got as big as the big Tattoo.
And all that he did he did with her.
"Two friends together," says Pinkle Purr.

Tattoo was the mother of Pinkle Purr,
An adventurous cat in a coat of fur.
And whenever he thought of a thing to do,
He didn't much bother about Tattoo,
For he knows it's nothing to do with her,
So "See you later," says Pinkle Purr.

Tattoo is the mother of Pinkle Purr,
An enormous leopard with coal-black fur.
A little brown kitten that's nearly new
Is now playing games with its big Tattoo . . .
And Pink looks lazily down at her:
"Dear little Tat," says Pinkle Purr.

Wind on the Hill

No one can tell me,
  Nobody knows,
Where the wind comes from,
  Where the wind goes.

It's flying from somewhere
    As fast as it can,
I couldn't keep up with it,
    Not if I ran.

But if I stopped holding
    The string of my kite,
It would blow with the wind
    For a day and a night.

And then when I found it,
    Wherever it blew,
I should know that the wind
    Had been going there too.

So then I could tell them
    Where the wind goes . . .
But where the wind comes from
    Nobody knows.

Forgotten

Lords of the Nursery
    Wait in a row,
Five on the high wall,
    And four on the low;
Big Kings and Little Kings,
    Brown Bears and Black,
All of them waiting
    Till John comes back.

Some think that John boy
 Is lost in the wood,
Some say he couldn't be,
 Some say he could.
Some think that John boy
 Hides on the hill;
Some say he won't come back,
 Some say he will.

High was the sun, when
 John went away . . .
Here they've been waiting
 All through the day;
Big Bears and Little Bears,
 White Kings and Black,
All of them waiting
 Till John comes back.

Lords of the Nursery
 Looked down the hill,
Some saw the sheep-fold,
 Some saw the mill;
Some saw the roofs
 Of the little grey town . . .
And their shadows grew long
 As the sun slipt down.

Gold between the poplars
 An old moon shows;
Silver up the star-way
 The full moon rose;
Silver down the star-way
 The old moon crept . . .
And, one by another,
 The grey fields slept.

Lords of the Nursery
   Their still watch keep . . .
They hear from the sheep-fold
   The rustle of sheep.
A young bird twitters
   And hides its head;
A little wind suddenly
   Breathes, and is dead.

Slowly and slowly
   Dawns the new day . . .
What's become of John boy?
   No one can say.
Some think that John boy
   Is lost on the hill;
Some say he won't come back,
   Some say he will.

What's become of John boy?
  Nothing at all,
He played with his skipping rope,
  He played with his ball.
He ran after butterflies,
  Blue ones and red;
He did a hundred happy things—
  And then went to bed.

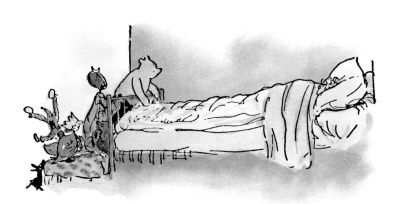

In the Dark

I've had my supper,
   And *had* my supper,
      And *HAD* my supper and all;
I've heard the story
   Of Cinderella,
      And how she went to the ball;
I've cleaned my teeth,
   And I've said my prayers,
      And I've cleaned and said them right;
And they've all of them been
   And kissed me lots,
      They've all of them said "Good-night."

So—here I am in the dark alone,
   There's nobody here to see;
       I think to myself,
       I play to myself,
     And nobody knows what I say to myself;
Here I am in the dark alone,
    What is it going to be?
I can think whatever I like to think,
I can play whatever I like to play,
I can laugh whatever I like to laugh,
    There's nobody here but me.

I'm talking to a rabbit . . .
    I'm talking to the sun . . .

I think I am a hundred—
    I'm one.
I'm lying in a forest . . .
    I'm lying in a cave . . .
I'm talking to a Dragon . . .
    I'm BRAVE.
I'm lying on my left side . . .
    I'm lying on my right . . .
I'll play a lot tomorrow . . .

    . . . .

I'll think a lot tomorrow . . .

    . . . .

I'll laugh . . .

        a lot . . .

          tomorrow . . .
      (Heigh-ho!)
        Good-night.

The End

When I was One,
I had just begun.

When I was Two,
I was nearly new.

When I was Three,
I was hardly Me.

When I was Four,
I was not much more.

When I was Five,
I was just alive.

But now I am Six, I'm as clever as clever.
So I think I'll be six now for ever and ever.